LAST SHOT

EVE GADDY

SxNW PUBLISHING

Cover Design: SxNW Publishing

ISBN: 978-1-946331-26-7

For Bob; I couldn't do this without your love and support. I love you.

CHAPTER ONE

CRAP, HE WAS BACK.

Della Rose scowled at the dark-haired man taking a seat at the corner table near the kitchen. The same guy who'd been in every night for the past week. Each night, when he first came in, he'd asked her to have a drink with him after work. Each night, she'd turned him down, but damn, she'd been tempted to take him up on it. A temptation that both annoyed and confused her.

Della had to admit he was hot. Brown hair, so dark it was almost black, fathoms-deep blue eyes, a strong jaw stubbled with beard, and shoulders broad enough to take on the woes of the world guaranteed him a second glance. And a third, and a fourth.

He waved at her and she cursed silently, realizing he'd caught her staring. Hell, he was bound to be used to it.

She glanced over to the bar at her boss. Charlie Burke was a soft touch. Everyone in Freedom, a flea bite of a town on the Texas Gulf coast, knew it. Charlie's inability to turn away a person in need wasn't the only reason the Last Shot was a favored local hangout. The food was good, the drinks decent, and it was one of the few places in town that stayed open past ten p.m.

No one knew more about Charlie's generous heart than Della, since he'd given her a job and a chance for a new life eight years before. Which was why she wasn't worried when she marched over to her boss, squinted through the haze of cigarette smoke, pressed a hand to the small of her aching back, and glared at him. "I'm not waiting on him. Do it yourself." She didn't have to identify *him*. She and Charlie had gone around about it all week.

"Oh, for—just go take his order," Charlie said, his voice grating harsh from years of chronic abuse. Grinding the butt of his cigarette out in the orange plastic ashtray beside the cash register, he shook his head, shaggy gray hair falling over his forehead. "What'd he do, pinch your butt last time he was in?"

Della scowled. Charlie looked out for her, but he'd been known to say that any woman with a world class ass like hers ought to expect an occasional pinch. Della didn't buy it, as many a customer had found out. "No, he didn't grab my butt. Or any other part of me. But I don't want to wait on him."

"Last I looked, you were the waitress here." He shuffled across the floor to draw a draft, shoving the handle back as cold beer streamed down the outside of the mug. Setting it down on the counter with a bang, he stabbed a gnarled finger at her. "Get your sweet fanny over there, or I swear to Mike, I will fire you." He glared at her a moment. "What is your problem, woman?" he asked, sounding more exasperated than angry.

Glancing over at the subject under discussion, she saw him wave at her again and gritted her teeth. "He's a cop." She picked up the mug to take it to old Pete Tripper, the only other customer in the place. They didn't do a lot of business at eleven-thirty on a Wednesday night.

Rubbing his chin thoughtfully, Charlie looked at the man in question, then back to her. "How do you know? Did you ask him?"

"No." He'd told her his name was Nick, but he hadn't said much else, other than to ask her to have a drink. He'd been nice, pleasant, and if he hadn't been a cop, she might have broken down and accepted the offer. She shoved her fingers through her bangs, brushing them back from her forehead as she always did. She wore her brown hair in a messy pixie, which suited her just fine. She didn't have the time or inclination to fuss with it. Her jaw muscles twitched, tight with irritation. "I didn't have to ask. I can smell a cop from half a mile away."

Charlie laughed, a wheezy, asthmatic sound. "Someday, honey, you're gonna tell me that story."

Oh, no I won't. Not even for you, Charlie.

Wiping down the bar and grunting for emphasis, Charlie continued. "But for now, I don't care if he's the Queen of the Nile in drag, he's still a customer. And closing time's not for half an hour. So get your butt over there and take his order." He gave a bark of laughter and added, "It ain't like he's gonna arrest you for doing your job, even if he is a cop."

Della cussed him under her breath but she went. If Esther, the other waitress, had been there, she'd have been glad to take it for Della. In fact, Esther would have been on the guy like cocktail sauce on shrimp. But she'd been out all week with a nasty virus, which left Della working double shifts.

Reaching his table, Della held her tray in front of her like a shield and looked down her nose at him. "What'll you have?"

She knew she sounded cranky. Hell, she had reason. Her

feet hurt, her back ached, her head pounded, and she had a bill due that was going to take a big chunk of change. Her daughter had called earlier to tell her she'd ripped a hole the size of the Gulf of Mexico in her best pair of jeans—the non-holey variety—and Della's budget wouldn't stretch another millimeter, much less spring for replacing them. To top it off, hunk of the year here had to pick her to fixate on.

He didn't push when she turned him down. No, the sneaky bastard just looked at her and smiled. And damn, what a smile. Every time he came in, he gave her that smile. The one that made her wonder just what she was missing.

Maybe her internal radar was wrong, for once. Nah, it didn't matter either way. She had no time for men. Especially not a tourist passing through town looking for an easy lay. Which is what she figured he wanted, even though he'd only asked her to have a drink with him. Men, in her experience, were one hundred percent predictable.

"Hi, sweet thing, I'm back," he said, his deep, husky voice sending ripples of awareness zinging up her spine. "Did you miss me?"

She had to clamp down on her lips to keep them from twitching. He took rejection well, she gave him that, not getting obnoxious when she shot him down, and not making free with his hands, like so many men. She'd thought he wasn't coming tonight, and had told herself it was a good thing. So why had she felt that ridiculous flash of pleasure when he'd shown up an hour before closing time?

"Desperately," she drawled. "Last call. What do you want?"

His gaze ran over her, lingered on her legs for a moment, raised to her face. Dressed in denim shorts and a loose maroon T-shirt, Della couldn't think why he seemed so appreciative of her. Or why the way he looked at her didn't piss her off more.

"I want a lot of things," he said, and smiled at her. "Doesn't look like I'll be getting any of them anytime soon, though."

Della tapped her foot. "To drink. What do you want to drink?"

He shrugged. "A draft." Before she could leave, his fingers wrapped around her wrist, but gently. "Have a drink with me. Come on, Della, what can one lousy drink hurt?"

"What makes you think I've changed my mind from the last time you were in here?" she asked, her voice huskier than she liked. She didn't mind his fingers touching her, and she should have.

His smile widened, an easy, sexy smile. Her pulse picked up and she cursed silently. "Hope springs eternal," he said with a laugh. "Why are you such a hard sell, Della?" he said when she didn't respond.

There was a question she could answer. "Not hard. Impossible."

"Why?" His thumb circled her wrist as he held her gaze.

Because you're dangerous, she started to say, staring down at him. The sincerity in his eyes sucked her in, asked her to believe he was on the level. That all he wanted was a little time with her. Della didn't like the way that made her feel, didn't like the way she found it hard to catch her breath, and she especially didn't like the fact she enjoyed feeling the soothing rasp of his fingers over her skin.

Before she could sink any deeper into those eyes, raised voices broke the spell. Della turned toward the bar to see two new customers—lowlifes, both of them—had come in and were having what looked like a deep discussion with Charlie. She didn't like the vibes she sensed. She liked what they were saying even less. Tripper, the only other customer, must not have liked it either. He was nowhere to be seen.

"Where is it, old man?" the one with a face like a bucket shouted, banging a fist on the counter. "We know Leon's been here. So just hand it over and make it easy on yourself."

"Hand what over? I got no clue what you're talking about," Charlie said, annoyance stamped on his face. "Or who you're talking about, either."

"Leon Rivers," said the other dirtbag, the one who had a face like a shark. "Don't act like you don't know him. You and him go way back."

Charlie hesitated briefly before he shrugged and spoke. "Yeah, I knew him. Twenty years ago. And that's the last time I saw him, too." He threw his towel down on the bar and jerked his head toward the door. "Beat it. I don't need your kind in here."

Della started toward Charlie, but the fingers locked around her wrist tightened. Impatiently, she yanked her arm, but he didn't loosen his hold. She looked down at him to demand he let her go but her words failed at the sight of his face. Intent, implacable, he was staring at the scene at the bar, and he looked like a man she didn't want to cross.

"Be still," he said, so softly she almost didn't hear him.

"But—"

"Shut up." Again, he said it quietly, but his tone meant business.

Bucketface reached across the bar and grabbed Charlie by the shirtfront. "Goddamn it, you tell me where it is! Don't fuck with me, old man."

Charlie reached beneath the bar. Della's stomach tightened with fear, and though she'd never been a big believer, she started praying. Bucketface released Charlie, who brought up his hand, holding the 9mm he kept close to the cash register for just this kind of occasion.

Della stood frozen, unable to move even without the steely fingers restraining her. A gun appeared in the second man's hand. His arm jerked just as Charlie's gun spit fire, and one loud crack of an explosion followed another and another. Then there was nothing but blood, blood everywhere.

A freight train hit her, and she slammed into the ground, rolling over and over the hard tile floor until she crashed into something and came to a stop. A man lay on top of her and she fought to catch her breath, struggling and beating her hands on his arms.

"Get off, get off, get off!" she shouted, thrashing beneath him as hot terror flooded her mind. She couldn't think, could only feel. Fear, pain, helplessness.

The heavy weight lifted. She sat up, gasping for air. A woman screamed, high-pitched and terrified. Screamed and screamed and screamed. Della wished she'd shut up and then realized it was her. Somebody—the freight train—clipped her across the mouth.

She stopped making noise abruptly and gulped, staring at the man now gripping her arms.

Disoriented, she looked around, realizing that instead of being in the bar, she and Nick had somehow rolled into the kitchen, through the swinging doors. In the kitchen, away from the danger. He hadn't been attacking her, he'd been protecting her.

He shook her, hard. "Is there a gun in here?"

Mouth agape, Della stared at him. "Charlie?" she croaked in a shaky whisper. "Where's Charlie?"

His eyes were so blue, and so empty. "Dead. Or if he isn't,

he will be soon. Now, where the hell is something I can use as a weapon?"

She shook her head, unable to think, or grasp what he said. *Charlie was . . . dead? How could that be?*

Nick cursed viciously and left her. She watched him stalk around the kitchen. His hand settled on a long, wickedly gleaming steel knife, Charlie's knife. The one he used to filet fish. But Charlie wouldn't be using it anymore. Her eyes closed, her breath caught on a sob, but she didn't cry. She hadn't cried since she was fifteen years old.

He came back over to her. "Get away from the door. We don't have more than a couple of minutes until they figure out where we are. I'd tell you to go out the back, but they probably have someone watching it." He must have seen something in her face that caused that inhuman mask to slip for a moment. "Find someplace to hide, Della. Don't worry, I'll take care of it."

She crawled to the corner, pulled her legs up to her chest and curled into a tight ball of fear. *Charlie's dead, Charlie's dead, Charlie's dead.* The words chanted in her mind but they didn't make sense.

Della heard someone shouting, though she couldn't make out the words. *Oh, God, what if he comes in here?* she thought, smothering a scream. She knew this feeling, though it had been years since she'd felt it so strongly. Helplessness. She hated it, couldn't tolerate it. Desperately grasping for calm, for control, she drew in a deep breath, then another. At last, her mind functioned, the crippling terror and despair receding as anger took hold.

What was she doing hiding in the corner, a victim waiting for something to happen to her? She'd sworn long ago she'd never be a victim again. Never again.

Della was a survivor. She had learned it the hard way. She would fight, or by God, die trying. Anything would be better than that paralyzing terror and loss of control.

She grabbed the only weapon she could find, a large cast-iron skillet, and crept back to the swinging doors, halting as she reached Nick.

"Goddamn it, I told you to hide," he snarled in a harsh whisper when she touched his back to let him know she was behind him.

"No," she whispered back. "I can help."

"More likely get us both killed," he said.

"How do you know he—they'll come in here?" she asked. "Maybe they left. Ran away."

He shot her a get real look. "We just witnessed a murder. At least one of them is alive. What do you think they'll do?"

The gunman came in fast, through the swinging doors with his gun drawn. He got a shot off as Nick hit him low, rolling with him over the floor, crashing into the stove and the grill. Skillet raised, Della ran over to them but couldn't tell who was winning. All she could see was a tangle of arms and legs as they struggled for possession of the gun. It was a silent fight, both men too intent on gaining control to waste time on breath or talking.

Sharkface came up with the gun.

Della shouted, hoping to distract him so Nick could do something. Instead, Sharkface swung around and aimed the gun at her.

Great idea, Della, she thought. Her gaze locked with his for a split second.

He pulled the trigger just as Nick lunged in front of her.

She dove to the side, hearing the crack of the gun as she went down. Her head hit the tile floor and she lay for a moment, dazed. She shook her head to clear her vision, wincing at the pain, and struggled to sit up.

Nick and Sharkface were on their knees, their hands straining together, again grappling for the gun between them as blood streamed down Nick's right arm.

Still grasping the heavy skillet, Della scrambled to her feet and ran to them. Fighting a wave of dizziness, she brought her hands up, fingers gripped tight around the handle, and swung down as hard as she could. It connected with the gunman's head with a dull thud. For a horrified instant, she thought she'd hit Nick, but then Sharkface slumped and pitched forward.

Nick rose, gasping for breath and holding the gun. "If he moves, hit him again."

"You're welcome," she said, as he headed for the swinging doors.

Nick didn't respond, but pushed the doors open just enough to peer into the other room, then went in. When he returned only minutes later, she knew what had happened to Charlie. The answer was plain on his face.

"Call nine-one-one," he said grimly. "But first, I need some rope so I can tie up this one."

Knowing the answer, she asked anyway. "What about Charlie? Maybe I can help—"

"No." Staring down at Sharkface, Nick shook his head. "No one can help him now."

Charlie's dead. He's really dead. She didn't want to believe it . . . but she did. She wanted to cry. Wanted to scream. But she did neither. No one knew better than Della how useless tears were.

Instead, she sucked it up. She pulled some twine out of the pantry and gave it to Nick. Then she called the cops, watching

Nick efficiently tie up Sharkface. Nick's expression had settled into harsh, determined lines. Business as usual.

"Is Bucketface dead?" she asked when he'd finished.

"Bucketface?"

Della shrugged. "The other guy. He has a face like a bucket."

Nick snorted. "Yeah, he does. And yes, he's dead. Why didn't you call nine-one-one?"

"Since they're in town, the cops are quicker, though that's not saying much. Emergency comes from twenty miles away, in Bay City. Once the cops get here and see what's going on, they'll call for EMS."

Nick started through the double doors once again. Della followed, but Nick blocked her way. "I don't think you want to—"

"Charlie was my boss and my friend. I'm going to see him. Don't get in my way."

Nick shrugged and let her through.

Della didn't spare a glance for the gunman lying on the floor in front of her. She crossed to the bar, braced herself, and walked behind it. Charlie lay crumpled on the planked floor; gun still in hand, his eyes glassy. There was a small hole in his forehead from the bullet that had killed him. Blood trickled down his cheek. After one glance, she didn't look at the back of his head. God knew his face would haunt her dreams as it was.

The blood she'd seen earlier must have come from the other man. Della knew a moment's savage satisfaction that at least one of the bastards had already paid for killing Charlie.

Her throat hurt, her heart felt numb. Della touched Charlie, leaned down close to him, laying her cheek against his, wishing she'd thought to tell him how much his friendship had meant to her. He'd known, but knowing it wasn't the same as hearing it. Neither of them ever had been great with words, so her feelings had gone unvoiced.

"Don't move him," Nick said from behind her. "In fact, you really shouldn't touch him. The crime scene should be preserved."

Della didn't respond. For the first time in a long time, she wanted to cry, but she couldn't. Tears wouldn't come, only a fuzzy unreality that this couldn't have happened. She drew back and looked at Charlie again, at the gun in his hand. "Oh, Charlie, why did you have to reach for the gun?"

"I doubt that mattered. They'd have killed him anyway. They wanted an answer he apparently didn't have. Or didn't want to give."

What could the gunmen have wanted? Wanted enough to kill for?

Della couldn't force herself to stand. She heard the scraping of a chair on the wood floor and realized Nick had left her, giving her a chance to grieve in private. She didn't know how long she sat there, dry-eyed with her heart aching. Finally, she got to her feet and walked around the bar. Eyes closed, Nick sat in a chair, blood welling through the fingers of his left hand where it covered his right arm. The arm that had been shot when he jumped in front of her and taken the bullet intended for her.

He didn't move. The lines had deepened in his face and he looked weary, hurt. Just what she needed, to be indebted to a stranger. And not just any old debt. Indebted for her life.

She couldn't help Charlie anymore, but she could help Nick. She owed him that much. "Let me see to your arm. You should have said something."

His eyes opened and his gaze caught hers. "It's nothing. I'll get the EMTs to check it out when they get here."

"Don't hold your breath. They're slow as molasses at the best of times. Meanwhile, you're bleeding to death." She grabbed a couple of towels from the bar and wet one before she advanced on him. "Come on, macho man, let me see it."

She pulled a chair up beside his and shoved his hand aside, giving him the clean, wet towel to wipe his hand with. The bullet had gone through the fleshy part of his arm, just below the short sleeve of his white Dallas Mavericks T-shirt. Blood dripped down and puddled on the floor. Unwilling to risk throwing up, she didn't look closely at the wound. Instead, she wrapped the towel around his wound as quickly as she could.

A corner of his mouth lifted. "Know anything about gunshot wounds?" His voice was husky, and surprisingly, held a note of amusement.

Her gaze dropped back to her handiwork. "No, but I've got a kid. I know enough to hold pressure on things that bleed. Here, put your hand on this and hold it while I tie this other one around it. That should work until EMS gets here."

He did what she told him, then said, "You're awfully calm to have just seen your boss blown away. Things like this happen often around here?"

She raised her eyes to meet his ironic gaze. "Sorry, I don't do hysterical. Not once I've figured out what's going on," she added, remembering screaming like a maniac when it first happened.

"Besides, freaking out won't do Charlie any good." Later. She'd think about Charlie later. Because it dawned on her that any minute now, the cops were going to come through that door. *Oh, God, cops.* And she was going to have to talk to them, deal with them. Fear skittered along her spine. Nausea bubbled in her stomach.

"You're tough."

Yeah, right, she thought. "I've had to be." But was she tough enough to face the cops without flipping out? She almost wished she'd been hurt, preferring the hospital a thousand times over to the cops.

Using his uninjured arm, Nick reached out and touched her swollen lip, very gently. His hand fell away. "I'm sorry I had to hit you."

She shrugged, wishing he weren't so close. Wishing he'd take that piercing blue-eyed gaze of his someplace else. "Why? Don't get your jollies from hitting women?"

"No. You're the first." His fingers brushed her mouth again. "Is that why you hate men?"

The wail of a siren split the air. For once in his worthless life, Police Chief Brumford Hayes from the Freedom PD had shown up at the right time. "I don't hate men." Her gaze fastened on his blue eyes, so calm, so knowledgeable. "Just cops."

CHAPTER TWO

C HIEF HAYES surveyed the scene from the doorway of the bar. With his oval-shaped head, burred haircut, and plump pink cheeks, he reminded Della of a watermelon, except he was anything but sweet. His belly lapped over his belt, his khaki pants cinched up so tightly she wondered he didn't bust a gut right there.

Holding the mangled remains of an unlit cigar clamped between his teeth, he glanced around. Della could almost hear him mentally cataloging what he saw. Two dead, two alive, and another—Sharkface must have come to—screaming bloody murder in the kitchen.

"Robbery," he pronounced, taking the cigar between two stubby nicotine-stained fingers.

"No," Nick muttered, his voice considerably weaker than the last time he'd spoken.

"This man needs help," Della said, afraid by his sudden pallor that he was going to pass out.

"EMT is on its way." Hayes advanced to their table, then

turned to the patrol officer, Kingston Knight. "Kingston, go see what that hollering's about."

"It's the other—the other gunman," Della said. "He's tied up in the kitchen."

Officer Knight looked at her with concern. "Are you hurt?"

Della shook her head, and with a last look at her, he left. Knight had hit on her when he first came to town a few months ago. He was tall, dark-haired, good-looking. Like Nick, though they looked nothing alike other than coloring. But Knight was a cop, in uniform yet, and Della could never see a cop in uniform without her stomach turning over. He was okay, she had to admit, but something about him didn't ring true.

At least he wasn't as disgusting as Hayes.

Hayes snorted and pulled up a chair. Ignoring Della, he stared at Nick. "I'm going to need to take a statement."

Nick sucked in his breath as Della's hand tightened on the pad she held over his wound. "Can't you see he's hurt? Ask him your stupid questions later."

"No, that's okay," Nick said, shooting her a glance.

She swore she saw a flash of amusement in his eyes before they flicked back to the chief.

"I can give you a statement now, while we're waiting."

"Appreciate it. You can wait over there," he said to Della, motioning to the opposite corner of the room. "I want to hear your accounts separately. I'll take your statement after Mister —" he paused, with an inquiring look at Nick.

"Nick Sheridan." He paused and added, "Detective Nick Sheridan, Dallas PD."

"Detective? Got any credentials to prove that?" Hayes sounded skeptical, but Nick had just confirmed Della's suspicions.

Nick's answer was to pull a wallet out of his back pocket and flip it open. Then he pulled what looked like a badge out of the same pocket and laid it beside the wallet.

After studying the IDs, Hayes grunted, then looked at her. "What are you waiting for? Go on over there," he said, jerking his head toward the corner. "I'll get to you in a bit." He paused and said sarcastically, "After I take *Detective* Sheridan's statement."

Making sure Nick could hold pressure on his wound, Della left them to it, choosing a seat with her back to the bar. She didn't want to look at the grim scene. She didn't want to think about the shooting, about Charlie's death, at all. But of course, she did. Charlie's face just before gunfire broke out. Charlie lying on the floor, crumpled, glassy-eyed. Dead.

To distract herself, she watched Hayes and Nick. Judging by the scowl on the chief's face, he didn't like what Nick was telling him. Probably because he'd made up his mind about what had happened within seconds of getting here. It wouldn't matter what they told him. The fact Nick was a cop wouldn't affect the chief, and he could even more easily ignore what Della said. Della doubted that even direct word from God himself would change Hayes's mind.

A few minutes later, he called her over. She went, resenting with every reluctant footstep that he had the authority to order her around. She knew he enjoyed it. Ever since she'd rejected his clumsy overtures when she first came to town, he'd given her a hard time every chance he got. And he hadn't let that or any rejection since stop him from looking her over like a piece of meat. She shuddered, thinking about it. Even if Hayes hadn't been a cop, he would have made her skin crawl. His profession just strengthened her aversion.

Turning her attention back to Nick, she realized he was

fading fast. His eyes were closed, his skin had taken on a grayish cast. At the rate EMT was going, he'd be lucky not to bleed to death.

"Somebody tied him up good," Knight said, emerging from the kitchen with the second gunman in tow. "He claims he's injured."

"Put him in the patrol car until we can transport him to the jail," Hayes said.

"Jail, my ass," Sharkface said. "I got the right to go to the hospital. That bastard must've slammed my head into something. I think I got a concussion."

"There was a skillet beside him," Knight interjected, his gaze darting to Della.

"A skillet?" Hayes looked at Della and Nick. "Did one of you hit him with a skillet?"

"I did," Della said.

"Bitch!" He lunged for her, but Knight jerked him back before he reached her.

"Sue me," she said. She thought she heard Knight laugh but couldn't be sure.

"Here's EMT now," the chief said at the sound of a siren. "They can decide if the suspect needs to go to the hospital. If he does, you'll have to go with him, Kingston. Otherwise, take him in and book him."

As they passed by Della, Knight smiled at her. He was always nice to her, even though she'd turned him down as surely as she had his boss. Maybe he thought if he was nice he still had a shot. *Oh, get over yourself, Della. All he did was smile at you.*

Knight leaned down and said something to Hayes that Della couldn't hear. Hayes frowned, but got up. "I'll want to talk to you again, Detective, so don't be leaving the area." To

Della he added, "I'll get to you in a minute," before following Knight outside.

A few minutes later, Hayes returned, along with the EMT team. They loaded up Nick and headed out, leaving Della alone—completely alone, since Officer Knight had gone with the prisoner—in the bar with two dead men and Freedom's Chief of Police. Not that she liked Knight much more than the chief, and she had reason to know that safety in numbers was a joke.

Her throat started to close up, and her heart began pounding in her chest. Hayes said nothing for some time, letting the silence breed and grow until Della wanted to scream at the tension. Sweat stained his uniform, and she caught a whiff of him, so strong the odor made her stomach churn with nausea. Or was it simple fear that had her stomach jumping through hoops?

She should have left with Nick, should have smeared blood on herself and claimed to be hurt. She couldn't take this, couldn't do it, couldn't be questioned by a cop and not run screaming into the night. Not a cop in uniform, not like this. Not for Charlie, not for anyone.

Della rose and began to babble. "I'd better go. I, uh, I told Nick I'd meet him at the hospital," she added, inspired. Oh, God, yes. Why hadn't she thought of that sooner?

Hayes stared at her, his squinty eyes bright. "You know that guy? Thought he was a tourist?"

"N—no. He's—" She twisted her hands together and bit her lips, too flipped out to care what Hayes thought of her behavior. "He's an old friend. Look, I have to go see him."

"He won't be goin' anywhere anytime soon. You know how hospitals are. Besides, it didn't look like a life-threatening injury." He glanced down at his notebook, then back to her. "Tell me what happened here."

Out of options, Della told him, including the fact the men had seemed to think Charlie was hiding something from them and they hadn't made a move toward the cash register.

"So these two dudes just came in and started shooting?" He sounded skeptical.

"Not exactly. I told you, they were arguing with Charlie, and when he came up with his gun, the shooting started." Her voice sounded shrill, even to her ears.

"Now I wonder what they were arguing about if it wasn't cash?" Rubbing his chin with a beefy hand, he pinned her with a sharp-eyed gaze. "Could be something to do with a drug deal. Maybe they wanted their drugs, and your boss was hiding them. You wouldn't happen to know anything about that, now would you, Miz Rose?"

Della clamped down tight on the nerves that were bouncing like Mexican jumping beans. Deep breath, she told herself. She was the injured one here, not the criminal. No two-bit police chief was going to pin a crime on her—especially one she hadn't committed. Anger helped soothe her nerves. "Charlie wasn't into that scene and you know it. Neither was anyone who worked here. He didn't tolerate drugs, much less deal them."

Hayes nodded, smirking a little. "So you say." He glanced around, then jerked his head toward a table with a half-empty beer mug sitting on it. "Was there another witness?"

Pete. Ashamed, Della realized she'd totally forgotten about the old man. "Pete Tripper was here just before it happened. But he was gone by the time the shooting started." She thought, but she wasn't sure. "Maybe he went home."

"Tripper," Hayes said and snorted. "That old drunk can't

see two feet in front of him anyway. I don't doubt he beat it before the action started. We'll have to check it out, though. In the meantime, don't leave the area. Not until after I've talked to you again."

Hayes knew good and well that Della wouldn't be going anywhere, not with her daughter in school and a house she owned free and clear in Freedom. She held her tongue though, unwilling to give him the satisfaction of knowing he'd gotten to her.

When he realized she wouldn't respond, he turned his back and stepped toward the bar.

Della didn't give him a chance to change his mind. She took one last look at the wood bar, knowing Charlie's body lay behind it. And left.

FORTY MINUTES later, Della pulled into the lot at the hospital in Bay City. She'd texted Mary Lou that she'd be very late, but hadn't told her about Charlie. Her friend was used to Della's hours, but tonight went beyond late. Mary Lou had moved in with Della and Allie shortly after Della returned to town, and she'd been taking care of Allie ever since. Della felt she had to tell Mary Lou about Charlie's murder in person. She wasn't about to put news like that in a text.

Charlie had befriended Mary Lou shortly before Della met him. In fact, Mary Lou had slept on his couch for a month. Then, when Della came to town, desperately in need of child care, and with Mary Lou needing a job and place to stay, Charlie put the two of them together. The arrangement had worked out great for both of them.

Tonight, Della had been so tempted to go home, curl up in

bed, and try to forget the past few hours, forget the sight of Charlie's lifeless eyes, forget Hayes's interrogation. Her conscience wouldn't let her. Nick Sheridan had saved her life, and the least she owed him was to see if he was all right and offer a ride from the hospital back to Freedom. *If* they let him go home.

It wasn't hard to find him, since she took the easy way and claimed to be his fiancée. The nurse gave her one of those looks that said, *yeah, right*, but she led Della to him. He'd fallen asleep on the gurney. Drug-induced, Della figured. People were shouting, screaming, and barking out orders, a voice came over the overhead speaker every other second, phones were ringing. Anybody who could sleep through that racket had to be drugged.

She dragged up a chair and prepared to wait. Since Nick was conked, and far and away the most interesting thing in the tiny cubicle, she took the opportunity to study him. He didn't, as some men did, look boyish in sleep. No, he was definitely all grown up.

It was a gorgeous face. A shock of dark, wavy hair fell over his forehead. With a mouth designed to give a woman pleasure, a strong jaw, high cheekbones, and a no-nonsense nose, his was a face more often seen in a glossy magazine or on the screen than in real life. Not in *her* real life, anyway.

The floral-patterned hospital gown covered his chest, but judging from the breadth of his shoulders, she imagined it was one worth looking at bare. His arm was in a sling, but she could see the bandage peeking out from the sleeve above it, standing out starkly against his tanned skin.

Della had a feeling he didn't get too many rejections from women. Not with those looks. She wondered if he'd pursued her out of irritation that she wasn't interested or if it had simply been boredom.

He mumbled something, turned his head toward her, and opened his eyes. They were blue enough to drown in. They stared at each other in silence before he broke it with a single word. "Shit."

Della choked back a laugh. "Gee, thanks."

"What the hell did they give me? It was just a flesh wound." His words were slightly slurred, which strengthened her impression that he'd been given something for the pain.

She grinned. "You think I'm a hallucination?"

He started to sit up, swore, and sank back down when the movement jarred his arm. "You wouldn't even have a drink with me. Why else would you be sitting here like some ministering angel?"

Della had never heard herself described quite like that. She kind of liked it, but his next words burst her bubble.

"Except you don't look like any angel I ever heard of." He mumbled something that sounded like "sexy" and shut his eyes again.

She scowled. "I thought you'd need a ride home. The nurse said they weren't keeping you."

"I'll call an Uber."

Perversely, his attitude irritated her. "Look, I said I'd give you a ride. What difference does it make to you?"

He opened his eyes and glared at her. "Who are you, Florence Flippin' Nightingale?"

"Just call me Flo." The more he balked, the more determined it made her to drive him home. She owed him, and by God, Della Rose paid her debts. Besides, she couldn't imagine why he didn't want to go with her, and it piqued her interest.

"Have you been discharged?"

"Would I still be here if I had? The doc patched me up and disappeared. Guess they're busy tonight."

"I'll see what I can do to speed things up," she said and rose to find help. At the doorway, she hesitated and looked back at him. "Can I ask you something?"

"No."

She ignored that and asked anyway. "Why did you do it? Why did you get between me and that bullet?"

Wearily, he scrubbed a hand over his face. "Reflex."

"You did it without thinking about it."

"Yeah. Look, sweet cheeks, I'm tired. Go away."

Her fingers tightened on the doorjamb. She asked, even though she'd heard the answer earlier. "You're a cop, aren't you?"

For an instant, his eyes were bleak, hopeless as they gazed into hers. "I was."

"And now?"

He didn't speak for a long moment. "I don't know," he finally said. Then he closed his eyes, ending the conversation.

Great, she'd been right. He was a cop. And she owed him her life.

Bummer, she thought, and left to find the doctor.

NOTHING EVER *happens in Freedom,* Nick mimicked silently, shifting uncomfortably on the hard hospital gurney. He could hear his buddy assuring him that the little town south of Houston would be the perfect place for what Nick had in mind. Drinking. Thinking. Fishing. If he was lucky, a warm, willing woman. And what had he gotten? Involved in some kind of pseudo-robbery shoot-out, that's what.

At first, he'd regretted leaving his weapons locked up at the apartment, but he didn't like to carry when he'd been drinking too much. Maybe that had been a good thing, though. At least he hadn't shot or killed one of them. That's all he needed, another shooting investigation. Especially since he was on a leave of absence from the Dallas PD.

Instead of a willing woman, he'd found Della Rose. A waitress with an attitude who had a grudge against cops. Too bad that lush, curvy body and husky drawl had been invading his dreams lately. Still, she was better than his other dream. Anything was better than his other dream.

His head swam as he sat up, and he cursed again. While he didn't mind being minus the pain, he didn't like the woozy feeling the drugs gave him. By the time he'd reached the hospital, his arm had been throbbing like a bitch. He thought he must have passed out when they started working on him, because he was real hazy on the details. That must have been when they loaded him up with painkillers. He'd been too light-headed to refuse.

He stood, then had to clutch at the bed to keep from falling over. His legs felt like gelatin, his head spun like a top. "What the hell did they give me?" he asked aloud.

"Hydrocodone," the doctor said, entering the room with Della hot on his heels. "The EMTs gave you a little Fentanyl before that."

"Yeah, well, I didn't ask for it. I don't like drugs."

The doctor took a look at his chart. "You said you weren't allergic and you were in a lot of pain." The doc glanced at him with a half-smile. "I'd say you still are."

"Yeah, yeah, whatever," Nick interrupted, keeping his uninjured hand on the bed to steady himself. "It's done now. Just find my shirt and let me out of here."

It wasn't the first time he'd landed in emergency with some kind of trauma done to his body. He had the scars from a knife fight and another shoot-out to remind him why he hated hospitals.

The doc gave him an instruction sheet, a few pain pills to tide him over until he could get the prescription filled, the remnants of his bloody T-shirt, and a bunch of advice. "Yeah, I know the drill," he interrupted, having heard it all before. "You can leave. And take little Miss Do-Gooder with you."

"I thought she was your fiancée?" the doctor said. They both turned to look at Della, who'd entered the room behind the doc.

"Must be the drugs," Della said blandly. "He doesn't know what he's saying."

The doctor shrugged and left them to it.

Nick glared at Della. "My fiancée? You wouldn't even have a drink with me and suddenly you're claiming to be engaged to me? What gives?"

She didn't look the least bit uncomfortable. "They wouldn't have let me in to see you if I hadn't told them that. Here." She held out a scrub shirt. "Your shirt was ruined. Unless you want to wear that gown out of here, put this on and let's go."

"No way."

"Why not?"

"No buttons. I'm not trying to wrestle my way into that thing."

She dug in a huge shoulder bag full of God only knew what and pulled out a small pair of scissors. She slit the shirt from collar to hem and handed it to him again. "Here. I'd like to get home sometime in this century." She turned away and paced to the door, waiting with her back toward him.

He tilted his head and considered her as he slipped his

good arm into the sleeve and arranged the other over the sling. "If we're engaged, that means we're sleeping together."

She shot him a dirty look over her shoulder. "Not necessarily. Besides, it was a lie."

"I'd never marry someone I hadn't slept with." Not that he ever planned on getting married.

"Try to keep your mind out of the bedroom for ten seconds, Romeo. You need a ride and I can give it to you. Why are you making such a big deal about it?"

Because he was the one who did the caretaking, not the other way around. Because he didn't need some bleeding-heart female fussing over him. Because, damn it, he just wanted to be left alone. "I don't need a woman at my bedside. Now, if you want to talk about being in my bed . . ." he let his voice trail off expectantly.

"Sorry." She shoved her hair out of her face and smiled. "Macho cops aren't my thing. Let's go."

He was tired. So tired. She wanted to play taxi, why not let her? A few minutes later, he followed Della out of the hospital. Her hips swung in a decisive rhythm that had nothing to do with seduction. He found it sexy as sin anyway. She was a contradiction, and the cop in him liked trying to figure her out. For instance, she had the kind of body that was made for love, and yet everything about her, from body language to spoken language, shouted hands-off.

Remembering the crack she'd made earlier about hating cops, he wondered how she'd tagged him, so perfectly and so quickly. "How did you know I was a cop? You knew before I told the Chief, didn't you?"

She shrugged, without turning around. "If it quacks . . ."

And how would you know that? "Seen a little trouble with the law, Della?"

"None of your business," she said, halting in front of—

He blinked and stared at the thing in front of him. How much pain med had they given him? "What is that?"

"It's a car. What does it look like?"

"A piece of crap," he said truthfully. Rust spots so big you could drive a tank through them, the rear windshield cracked, another window opened, he suspected permanently, vinyl seats faded, cracked, torn, held together with duct tape. The only thing lacking was a bunch of trash piled in the back seat, but she obviously kept it cleaned out.

"Yeah, well, right now it's your chariot, macho man. Get in. No, not there," she said when he tried to open the passenger side door.

He realized the door was wired shut. He walked around to her side and attempted a grin. "Are you sure it will make it back to Freedom?"

Deadpan, she answered. "No, but beggars can't be choosers."

"I don't recall asking for a ride, much less begging."

"A technicality," she said, sliding in beside him and cranking the engine.

To his amazement, the car started. Before long, they were tooling down the highway at what he estimated was a roaring forty mph. The dash lights didn't work, and he couldn't read the speedometer. He wondered how it passed inspection. *Probably has a hole in the muffler, too,* he thought, hearing the blaring roar and occasional backfires. Oddly enough, he found the noise soothing. He closed his eyes, leaned his head back, and the next thing he knew, she was poking him in the side to wake him.

"We're almost there. Where are you staying?"

Husky, inviting, he heard the feminine voice as he swam

back to consciousness. Then the pain rolled through him and he remembered.

She lifted an eyebrow when he gave her the address. "Ritzy digs for a cop."

He might have been flying on painkillers, but he could still tell when he was being insulted. She thought he was on the take. Man, she sure had a poor opinion of cops. "Belongs to a buddy of mine."

"Lucky you."

Nick didn't waste his breath arguing when she walked him to his door. By this time, he was so tired, all he wanted to do was crawl in bed and sleep for about fourteen hours.

"There's just one thing," she said, hesitating before she left. "If Chief Hayes talks to you again—"

"He will," Nick interrupted. "Sometime tomorrow, I'm sure."

"I told him—" she hesitated, bit her lip, turned away. "I told him we were old friends."

"Why?"

"I just did. So could you go along with me on this?"

He couldn't figure her out. Maybe tomorrow, when he was thinking more clearly. "Okay. On one condition."

"What?" she asked suspiciously.

He smiled and opened his door. "I'll tell you tomorrow."

CHAPTER THREE

A BOUT TIME HE *got here*, Kingston Knight thought as Chief Hayes walked into the police station.

The chief seemed awfully nonchalant to have had three dead bodies in town—two of them murders, and in the same day. Earlier that evening, Hayes and Knight had responded to a call about a disturbance in an abandoned warehouse along the waterfront. When they arrived, they'd found a dead man who had clearly been tortured. A man King had recognized from his days with the Houston PD.

Leon Rivers was a well-known suspect in a number of jewel heists in the Houston area, but after he made parole for his first conviction, he'd managed to avoid getting caught again. Someone had caught up with him, though, and King doubted it was the police. That was reason enough to wonder what in the hell a semi-notorious jewel thief had been doing in a town like Freedom. And what he'd been doing to get himself killed. But the real kicker had been finding two of Rivers's pals at the Last Shot. One dead, and one very much alive.

He'd told all this to the chief before he left the Last Shot with the surviving gunman. After a long moment, Hayes had told him to take Frampton, the gunman, to jail but "Don't let him talk to anyone but you. And for God's sake, don't let him call his lawyer."

King had argued that while the EMTs didn't think Frampton was badly injured, he should probably go to the hospital to be safe. The chief had nixed that. But now King wasn't supposed to let the man call his lawyer? What the hell was Hayes thinking?

Hayes had taken his sweet time getting there. "Where are Jenkins and Picket?" the chief asked, referring to the police officers he'd left in charge of the first crime scene.

"Louisa talked to them," King said, referring to the dispatcher. "They should be home by now. Jenkins called and said the Bay City Crime Scene Investigators showed up right after you and I left. Once the CSIs were finished and the ME took the body, they secured the scene and left." King glanced at his watch. "Do you want me to tell Louisa to call them back in?"

"Leave them be," Hayes said. "We don't need them here."

King had seen that look on his boss's face before. Usually when the man was thinking about doing something that skirted the law. "What are you planning, Chief?"

"I mean to find out why three jewel thieves from Houston were in our little town. And why one of them was lying dead in a waterfront warehouse. And most of all, I intend to find out what in the hell they wanted with Charlie Burke."

"Frampton won't talk," Knight said. "He's already been yammering about his lawyer. We're going to catch hell for not giving him a phone call. This could compromise our case against him."

As far as King could tell, Hayes wasn't a bit worried. "Bring him to interrogation," he told King.

"Interrogation" referred to a small room with a steel table, a couple of chairs, and nothing else. The Freedom PD couldn't afford a one-way mirror, nor did they need one in most cases.

They hadn't needed one in any of the cases since King joined the force six months ago. Murder wasn't only rare in Freedom, it was nonexistent. So three dead bodies in one night, in a town that had never seen a murder, was sure as shit something to think about.

Hayes knew how to make a suspect nervous, King would give him that. The Chief had several methods. The one he'd decided on for this perp was silence.

After leaving Frampton completely alone for half an hour, Knight and Hayes both entered. Hayes took the seat across from the suspect while King stood beside him. Neither said anything. Hayes simply fixed Frampton with his most penetrating gaze, then sat back and waited.

King had never seen the method fail, and this time was no exception. In about ten minutes, Frampton broke, demanding his lawyer again.

"No lawyer," Hayes finally said. Frampton stared at him with his mouth open. "You won't need one where you're going."

"What are you talking about? Everyone gets a lawyer."

"Well, now, you might rethink that." Hayes leaned back in his chair and steepled his hands over his ample belly. "Once I tell the Blasters where you are and what you're looking for, you won't need anything but a coffin."

Frampton's face drained of all color. King's would have too if he'd been threatened with a gang associated with the Death Tangos, one of the largest, most violent gangs in the state. The

Blasters were the clique that operated in Houston and surrounding areas.

"I see you know who I'm talking about."

Frampton found his voice. "Everyone knows the Blasters. They got nothing to do with me."

"Then why'd you go sheet white when I mentioned them?" Hayes laughed, straightened, and leaned forward. "I have a contact in that gang. What do you say I call him and tell him who I've got here?"

"You're lying. You don't know anyone."

"Are you willing to risk it?" Hayes pulled out his cell phone and started punching buttons. "Make a decision," he said with his finger poised over the last button.

"Damn you! Stop! I'll talk. Just don't call them."

Hayes smiled. "King, take off those cuffs. We want Mr. Frampton to be comfortable."

"I don't think that's a good idea, Chief."

"I don't recall asking for your opinion, Officer Knight. Do it."

Damn, Hayes meant to let the bastard go? What the hell? King did as his boss instructed, though. King had argued with the chief a few times, but he'd soon learned it wasn't worth it. Hayes could make things damned unpleasant when he wanted.

Once started, Frampton couldn't talk fast enough. He mentioned a heist, but his account was disjointed and it was clear he was keeping a lot back. He talked, but basically said nothing.

After listening a bit, Hayes snorted in disgust and picked up his cell phone. "This is bullshit. Unless you've got something better to tell me, I got a phone call to make."

"No, don't," Frampton almost shrieked. "I'll tell you every-thing, but I want a deal."

"What kind of a deal?" the chief asked.

"I want a cut of the money. And I want you to let me go. No charges."

"What money?"

Frampton drew in a breath. "There's a fortune in stolen jewels, somewhere in this town."

"Keep talking," Hayes said.

Leon Rivers, Frampton, and their partner, Mario Woods, had schemed to abscond with a large part of the loot from a recent heist. Planned by the Blasters, the heist was executed at one of Houston's fanciest balls. The three conspirators meant to leave the country with their plunder immediately, before the gang realized a large portion of the stolen goods had disap-peared. But instead, Leon had double-crossed his co-conspira-tors and vanished with the loot.

Loot which included a million dollar diamond and emerald bracelet.

"The Blasters don't know where you are?" Hayes asked.

"No. If they did, I'd be dead too. Mario and I just found Rivers tonight."

Hayes didn't respond but seemed to be considering his next move.

"What do you say?" Frampton asked impatiently. "I've told you everything I know."

Hayes looked him over. "You realize I don't have to cut you in for anything." Frampton started to protest, but Hayes held up a hand. "However, I'm a fair-minded man. You'll get what's coming to you."

"Chief, can I talk to you a moment?" King might not know what was going on in the chief's mind, but he knew damn well it shouldn't include letting a murderer and jewel thief walk free.

They stepped out of the room into the hallway. "You can't mean to let this bastard go? We've got him cold for homicide," King said.

"A deal's a deal." Hayes opened the door to the room. "Come on, Frampton. King here will let you out the back way."

Hayes was crazy. That's all there was to it. "No. I'm not having any part in letting this piece of shit go. What in the hell is wrong with you? He's a fucking felon, and you mean to let him walk out of here without even a wrist slap?"

"I can think of a million reasons why we should," Hayes said.

"You mean . . . You mean go along with Frampton? Keep the stolen goods for ourselves?" Of course, they had to find them first.

"Sharp as a tack, that's you," his boss said. "Go on, take him out the back."

Even on the black market, a million dollar bracelet would bring a lot of money. Plus there was other loot with it. All that money . . . easy money.

What choice did he have? King asked himself. He could report Hayes to the Houston cops, but what would that accomplish—other than bringing down the chief? And even that wasn't a certainty.

But the money—damn, that was tempting. So he caved. King walked Frampton down the hall to the back door of the building.

Frampton halted and turned around. "I need my cell phone. You won't be able to get in touch with me otherwise."

"Can't have that," Hayes said, and shot him in the chest, three times.

Frampton crumpled with a surprised look on his face.

"Jesus Christ!" King said. "Why did you shoot him?" He knelt down beside the man, feeling for a pulse. "He's dead. What the fuck are you doing?"

Hayes stood over them. "Saving your ass." The chief plucked King's weapon from his holster. Handling it with a handkerchief, he fitted it into Frampton's hand.

"Are you crazy?"

"Nope," the chief stated. "Now we can play it two ways. Either you made a deal with the suspect and allowed him access to your weapon, at which point I shot him. Or—" he smiled briefly, "the suspect got hold of your gun and threatened you with it, and I shot him to save you."

"That's not what happened."

"The two of us are the only ones who know what really went down." He shrugged. "Either way, I'm in the clear, but if you made a deal with him, you're really screwed," Hayes continued as he stuffed the handkerchief back in his pocket.

King stared at the dead man. The chief had set him up perfectly. King would take the fall for anything from corruption to accessory to murder if he turned Hayes in.

"Louisa's going to be in here any minute now," Hayes said. "Are you willing to give up that much money—not to mention, risk losing your job and facing criminal charges yourself—because a scumbag like him is dead?" He gestured to the dead man with distaste.

King hadn't signed up for murder. Even though Frampton had been a piece of shit, murder was murder. But Chief Brumford Hayes had made damn sure he had King's balls in a vise.

Anything King said would be his word against the chief's. He was fucked.

THE LAST PERSON Della expected to find on her doorstep the next day was Phillip Simms, Freedom's resident, and only, lawyer. Mystified, Della let him in and waved a hand at the ratty, faded rust couch in her living room. She didn't know Simms well, but he ate at the Last Shot from time to time, usually with his wife and kid in tow, and he'd always seemed like a decent enough guy.

He sat and adjusted his glasses, shoving them upward on the bridge of his aquiline nose. Clearing his throat, he looked at her closely. "How are you, Della?"

"Crappy. I guess you heard about Charlie."

"Yes. On the news this morning. Chief Hayes confirmed it. He'll be missed."

"Yeah." Della tried unsuccessfully to block out her last image of him, lying on the floor. Dead. "What can I do for you, Mr. Simms?"

"Well, I'll get right to the point." He opened his briefcase, shuffling papers. "Charlie Burke left his estate to you."

Uncomprehending, Della stared at him. "What?"

Simms handed her a sheaf of papers. "Charlie left you everything he had. Around fifteen thousand in cash and the Last Shot Bar and Grill, free and clear. And his personal belongings, of course. I believe he kept a safe in his apartment?"

Della nodded, still in shock.

"Since he'd already given you his legal power of attorney, you shouldn't have any problems continuing to run the business." His lips thinned as he grimaced. "As soon as the police are finished there, that is."

Della stared at the papers in her hand, at what she realized was a copy of a will. "I can't believe he did this. He never said a word. He told me he wanted me to have the power of attorney so I could pay bills and handle his business if something happened to him. If he was incapacitated." Raising her gaze to meet the lawyer's, she asked, "Why me? Why did he leave it to me?"

Simms wiped his glasses with a handkerchief he'd pulled from his pocket, then put them back on. "He said something once that makes me think you reminded him of his daughter."

"His daughter? I didn't know he had one. Where is she?"

"Dead. Drug overdose. Years ago. I don't imagine he told many people about it. He only told me to assure me there would be no heirs popping out of the woodwork. His wife has been dead for years and he has no other relations."

Della shook her head. She still couldn't take it in. Charlie had had a wife and child. He'd never mentioned either. And this inheritance—that Charlie had even had that much money surprised her. But leaving it and the bar to her—that blew her mind.

"Mom?" Allie stood in the doorway. "There's no peanut butter." Her eyes were red from crying, but Della thought she looked pretty good considering she'd just lost the closest thing she'd ever had to a grandfather. An image of Allie, seated on the dark wood bar, peeling boiled shrimp and laughing at one of Charlie's improbable fishing stories made Della's throat close up again. The memories would come more often, she thought, now that the reality of his death was truly sinking in.

Hunger was a good sign, though. Her daughter would be

all right. Della would make sure of it. "Eat something else. I'll go to the store later."

Allie nodded and withdrew.

"Pretty girl," Simms said after Allie left the room.

"Thanks." Blond-haired, blue-eyed Allie looked like an angel. Of course, she wasn't. She was a good kid, a normal twelve-year-old girl, sweet, moody, unpredictable, talkative. And just now, heartbroken.

Della put a hand to her head and rubbed her throbbing temples. "It doesn't feel right, taking Charlie's money. I feel like a ghoul, benefitting from his death. Isn't there someone else, someone who . . ." her voice trailed off. *Someone who deserves it.*

"There's no one. You can't bring him back, Della," Simms said quietly. "Whether you take the inheritance or not, you can't bring him back. He wanted you to have it. He was very fond of you."

Fifteen thousand dollars. And the Last Shot. She could pay off her credit cards. Buy Allie all the jeans she needed. Fix up the Last Shot. She might even look for a decent used car.

All she had to do was say yes. And all Charlie had had to do was . . . die.

CHAPTER FOUR

F IRST THING THE next morning, Della went by the bar. A CSI team was there from Bay City. The bar and kitchen were still taped off. To her surprise, they allowed her to go up to Charlie's apartment above the bar. It was undisturbed, and Della retrieved the contents of the safe. She and the lawyer had talked about it, and he'd urged her to take what was in there and make use of it. There wasn't much. Some papers, a few silver dollars, the money from the night before, up to the time of the robbery. There were also a couple of lockets, one with a baby picture and what she supposed was baby hair, and another with pictures of a much younger Charlie and a woman who had to be his wife. The whole thing depressed the hell out of her, so she stuffed everything in her purse and resolved to look through it all later.

She went home to drop off the safe's contents, then she re-read the will, trying to make sense of it. She still couldn't quite grasp what Charlie had done. Or why. But when she considered it, she knew Charlie hadn't been all that close to anyone else. And he'd loved Allie like a grandfather.

Around three, Della drove to the condo where she'd dropped off Nick early that morning. A black Harley-Davidson sat in the parking lot, the only vehicle other than Della's. It would be just her luck if it was Nick's. No way could he drive a motorcycle with his arm injured and in a sling. Which meant he'd need even more help than she'd thought.

She grabbed the paper sack off the seat, filled with a batch of Mary Lou's brownies. Mary Lou had insisted that Della take them to him after hearing Nick's part in what had happened the night before. Rather than fighting a losing battle, she'd agreed. She banged on the door.

He's bound to be here, she thought, and pounded on it again. Any normal person who'd been shot the night before would be spending time in bed.

She should be home with her daughter, but instead, she'd felt duty bound to check on Nick. Frustrated, she gave the door a savage kick and nearly fell over as it swung open. Obviously, it hadn't been securely fastened if it opened that easily.

"Nick?" She stepped inside, glancing around. "Anybody ho—" the words died in her throat as her gaze seized on the man standing three feet away from her. The sight of him flashed in her mind like the neon lights on the Las Vegas strip.

He was there all right. Every stark naked inch of him, standing in his kitchen doorway, drinking straight from a milk jug. Rational thought took its sweet time flowing back into her brain. And no wonder. His body—oh, God, what a body. A chest beyond belief, with sleek, beautifully rippling muscles. Perfect, flat abs. A sprinkling of dark hair arrowed down the center of his chest, drawing her gaze lower to arrest on what lay between thighs of steel. No problems there, either. She gulped and ripped her gaze upward to his face, totally shaken to be able to put a name to the feelings dive-bombing her.

Lust. Pure lust.

No, tell me this isn't happening. She'd seen naked men before. Plenty of them. And lust had been the last thing they'd inspired in her. But there was naked, and then there was Nick Sheridan, naked. And Della wasn't blind or gay, even if she didn't much like men.

He wasn't quite naked, if you counted the sling his arm rested in. "I knocked," she finally managed to spit out.

Unshaven, bleary-eyed, he looked surly and dangerous, even doing something as prosaic as drinking milk. Lowering the plastic jug, he narrowed those incredible baby blues at her. "What the hell do you want?" When she didn't answer he said, "Are you going to stand there all day staring at me?"

Irritated by her reaction as much as his, she frowned. "You're naked."

He looked down, then back up at her. "Very observant. That's what you get for barging in uninvited." He finished the milk, then turned his back and tossed the empty jug left-handed at the trash. "Damn," he said when it bounced off the rim and landed in the floor. "Never could shoot left-handed."

Great, the rear view was as good as the front. "You could have locked the door."

He turned around and leaned his uninjured shoulder against the door frame. "And you could have minded your own business. Still playing Nurse Nancy?"

"Sheridan!" A gruff voice came from the open doorway. "Are you—" Chief Hayes stomped inside and halted in mid-sentence. "Sorry. Door was open." His gaze flicked from Della to Nick and back to Della. He didn't say a word but a smarmy smile came over his face.

She wanted to punch him smack dab in the middle of that smirk.

"That's right," Hayes said. "I forgot, you're old friends."

"What is this, Grand fucking Central?" Nick asked.

Hayes chuckled. "Sorry," he repeated. "I had a couple of questions and thought I'd just run by here instead of bringing you down to the station."

"Ever hear of a telephone? I gave you my numbers."

"It won't take long."

Nick stalked past them, disappearing through a doorway.

Please, God, let him put on some clothes, Della thought. Naked, he was way too distracting.

"Glad you're here, *Miz* Rose. Saves me a trip. I've got some more questions for you too." He rested his hand on the butt of his gun.

Della suppressed a shiver of revulsion. Attack first, she thought and launched into speech. "Have you found out any more about who was behind Charlie's murder?"

Hayes's brow furrowed. "What do you mean? We know who killed him. You're an eyewitness. You told me yourself who shot him."

"Not who pulled the trigger," she said impatiently. "Who was behind it? I told you what they said. What they did. And I'm sure Nick told you—"

The chief interrupted. "No need to look further. Robbery, plain and simple. The CSI team hasn't found anything to contradict that, either."

Della stared at him, amazed he could be so bull-headed. Two eyewitness accounts—one of them a fellow cop's—and he hadn't heard a word they'd said. What would it take to get him to consider that he just might be wrong?

NICK WALKED into the bedroom and snagged a pair of cutoffs. Being naked put him at a definite disadvantage. But then, he hadn't expected or wanted company. He took off the sling, carefully pulled on a button-down shirt. When he'd finished fastening it, he put the sling back on, resolving to get rid of it at the earliest possible moment. While dressing wasn't fun, it wasn't nearly as bad as when he'd broken his collarbone in a raid a few years before.

Between the drug-induced more-lurid-than-usual dreams and his arm throbbing as the painkillers wore off, he'd spent a miserable night. He didn't feel much better now. Still, as long as he didn't do anything with the bad arm, it had quit throbbing like a son of a bitch. The sooner he talked to the chief, the sooner he could throw Della out and go back to bed.

He looked at the lockbox where he kept his weapons but didn't open it. He'd given the chief his credentials last night. Hayes would have checked out Nick by now. His Sig and his back-up gun lay inside. What if he'd been carrying last night? Charlie might not be dead. He should have been carrying. He shook his head. No, he wasn't going there. He'd just be happy he didn't have to go to the shrink again. The shrink who'd recommended he take some time off so he could wrap his head around what had happened on the last case. And his captain, who had all but commanded him to take time off.

Yeah, right. What a joke.

The investigation had cleared him of wrongdoing. Only he and his partner knew what had really happened that night.

As Nick walked back in he heard Della say, "How can you just ignore what we've told you?"

Hayes looked annoyed and strangely smug. "It was a robbery. Plain and simple, armed robbery."

"No, it wasn't," Nick said.

The chief turned to stare at him. His dark eyes hardened and narrowed. "Why do you say that? It's clear to me that robbery was the object."

"I don't know how you came to that conclusion, Chief. Considering what both Della and I told you."

"Folks don't always remember exactly," he muttered. "They get excited when something like this happens."

Nick laughed. "Come on, Chief. I'm homicide from Dallas."

Hayes snorted. "I'm aware, Detective. But Miz Rose here isn't."

A weak argument, Nick thought and continued, "As I told you last night, no attempt was made to get any money from the cash register. They weren't looking for money. There wasn't even a mention of cash. They wanted something else—information—from the old man."

"I talked to your Captain this morning," Hayes said, disregarding Nick's statement. "Said you'd told him you were coming down here. On a leave of absence."

Hayes's tone implied there was more to it. Or maybe that was just Nick's knee-jerk reaction. "I told you that last night."

"Not that I recall," Hayes said.

Bullshit, Nick thought. He was positive he'd told him.

"What would you be doing here, Sheridan? You aren't working on a case. Least, not one your Captain knows about."

An image flashed in his mind of his last case. Steel glinting in the candlelight. Blood, rivers of it, dripping steadily. Laughter. Madness.

Clenching his jaw, he fought back the surge of despair. "I'm taking a vacation," he finally said. "But just because I'm on leave of absence doesn't mean my brain is on leave. I'm telling you, what happened last night was no robbery attempt."

Judging from his expression, Hayes wasn't buying it. Nick wondered again why the chief was so anxious to label the crime robbery. Simple laziness? Or was there more to it?

"Did the suspect cop to robbery?" Nick asked.

Hayes drew himself up to his full height, puffing out his chest. "Now listen here, Sheridan, you can be whatever you want in Dallas, but this is my jurisdiction. That suspect's none of your affair."

"No? I've got a hole in my arm that says otherwise." Hayes looked ripe for explosion, so to placate him, Nick added, "I'm not looking to get involved in your business, Chief. I'm sure that now that you know the facts, you'll act accordingly."

Not much mollified, Hayes snorted. "I don't need some smart-ass city cop telling me how to do my job."

"Wouldn't dream of it," Nick said, though someone needed to. Sloppy police work irritated him, whether it was in his own department or someone else's. "You said you had more questions?"

Lips thinned in anger, Hayes seated himself at the dining room table, shoving the glasses that littered it to the center. Nick took a chair, noticing Della chose a seat as far from Hayes as possible. He thought she'd have been out the door if she could have managed it.

The chief drew out his notebook and consulted it, then leveled a hard stare at Nick. "I want you to tell me what the two men said, as closely as you can remember."

Though he'd told him last night, Nick repeated, nearly verbatim, what he'd heard the night before. It wasn't much to go on, and he felt a reluctant sympathy for the police chief. If Hayes hadn't been such a jerk, Nick might have felt more.

Hayes frowned as he looked over his notes. "Neither one ever said what it was they were looking for?"

"No. And there was no demand for cash."

Hayes continued for a while, twisting a question and repeating it, then finally turned to Della.

Her hands were clenched, white-knuckled, in front of her on the table. She looked nervous as a long-tailed cat in a roomful of rocking chairs. Not unusual for someone dealing with the cops, but since she wasn't a suspect, Nick had to wonder why she was so uptight.

"How much money did Burke keep in the till?"

"Not much. After the dinner crowd left, about fifty."

"What did he do with the rest?"

"He had a safe upstairs in his living quarters."

Of course, Nick mused, as the questions continued, the chief's interrogation technique didn't help. Any fool could see Hayes's manner was making her even more skittish. Nick suspected the man enjoyed upsetting her, and a few minutes later, he was sure of it.

"Now, to get back to the actual shooting," Hayes began.

"Why drag her through that again?" Nick interrupted after a glance at Della's pale, drawn face. Whether Hayes had a grudge against her or he was simply a sadistic jerk, Nick didn't know or care. "We've both repeated our statements several times. Go rag on the suspect. You might even get something useful out of him."

"Well, now, Detective Sheridan, I don't believe I asked for your input here."

"Can't you see you're accomplishing nothing?" Except possibly driving Della Rose to the breaking point. The glare she leveled at Hayes held both hatred and vulnerability.

"That's a matter of opinion," Hayes said as he rose. "But as it happens, I can't question the suspect."

Della made a choked sound of outrage.

"Why not?" Nick asked.

Pausing in the doorway, Hayes gazed at Della and continued. "The suspect was shot and killed last night during an escape attempt." With that, he walked out.

CHAPTER FIVE

THE DOOR CLOSED behind the police chief. Seconds later, a glass smashed into it, shattering.

"Hey!" Nick jumped to his feet, grabbing Della's arm before she could let fly with another one. "Take it easy. This isn't my place."

She jerked her arm out of his grasp, then slammed her hand down on the table so hard the glasses rattled. "That sorry son of a bitch! He's already filed this as over and done with. He's not going to do anything to find out the truth."

"Probably not," Nick agreed, moving the other glasses out of her reach. . . . Just in case. "What did you expect? The men who shot your boss are both dead. To investigate further, to find out who was behind it, Hayes would have to believe it was something more than a robbery. And he doesn't."

She sliced him with a scathing look. "I should have expected you to take his side. Cops have to stick together, don't they?"

Irritated at being lumped in the same category as Hayes, Nick frowned. He started to shrug it off, but his arm hurt and he changed his mind. A wave of weariness hit him. He took a chair, straddled it and propped his good arm across the back. "I'm not taking his side, I'm merely making a reasonable observation. Besides, I don't imagine Hayes has enough manpower to launch a full scale investigation, even if he wanted to continue."

"Someone could. He could call in someone else to help him. If he wanted to. But Charlie wasn't important enough to warrant it, right?"

He frowned again. "That's not what I said."

"You can bet your ass that's how Hayes sees it." She paused and added, "He's not getting away with this."

Nick eyed her skeptically. "Yeah? How do you figure that?"

She jammed her hands on her hips and glared at the closed door. "If I can't force Hayes to investigate further, I'll just have to find out the truth myself."

Nick snorted. "Right. You have any experience in investigation?"

"No." Her gaze met his. Her eyes were a rich, dark caramel brown and huge with emotion. "But you do."

He'd walked right into that one. "No."

She turned to face him, looking like she wanted to shake him. "What do you mean, no? I haven't even asked you anything yet."

"I'm saving you the trouble. I'm not getting involved in this case."

"You already are."

"Since when does being a witness to a crime constitute being involved?"

"You were shot. You were there. You're a cop. Of course you're involved." Taking the chair beside him, she stretched a hand out, but stopped just short of touching him. She gnawed her lip uncertainly a moment before she started in again. "You said you were a homicide detective. Investigating this case would be right up your alley. And I don't expect you to do it for free. I'll pay you the going rate."

Nick's instincts told him to stay out of it. He gazed at her impassively. "Read my lips. No."

"Why not? Give me one good reason why you won't do it."

Because he was still a fucking mess from his last case. "Because I don't want to. I'm a cop, not a private investigator." Was a cop. Was he still? He didn't know.

This time, she did touch him. Her fingers felt warm and strong on his arm. Her expression held frustration and even more, determination. "You know how to investigate a murder. You do it all the time."

No more, he thought, flinching as the memories flooded his mind. Might never again, either.

He forced himself to look at her, to face the entreaty in her eyes. Della didn't strike him as a woman who begged easily. Even so, he couldn't let any pull or sympathy he felt toward her affect his decision. "Forget it, Della. I'm on a leave of absence. Vacation, remember?"

"Nothing I can say or do will change your mind?"

He let his silence speak for itself. This wasn't his concern. So why did he feel even the slightest twinge of guilt? He saw the anger flash in her eyes before her lashes lowered. Yet when she raised her gaze to his once again, her face was empty of emotion. He admired that about her. She thought quickly, reacted quickly. Didn't spend time on a lot of useless emotion or bewailing her fate. He'd seen it the night of the murder, when she'd pulled herself together and conquered her fear— and ended up saving his sorry ass.

She didn't speak, she simply stood and walked to the door.

"Della," he said, irritated that he felt forced to expand. This wasn't his problem. He'd come to Freedom to get away from murder, not be sucked into a case that was none of his business. He'd come here looking for peace. Which he sure as hell wouldn't find if he did what she asked him to do. "Can't you just let it go? The men who shot your boss are dead. Why can't that be enough?"

For a long moment, she stared at him without answering. "Don't deny that there's more to it than a random shooting. I told you Charlie was my friend. Is that how you treat your friends? Just forget them because they've become inconvenient?"

"We're not talking inconvenience, we're talking danger. You stick your untrained nose into this and you could get hurt. Do you want to wind up dead? Like your boss?"

Her voice was flat and final when she spoke. "I don't have a choice. I owe Charlie. And I pay my debts."

The door slammed behind her, which brought a rueful smile to his lips. He doubted she'd be back. And even though he had no intention of getting involved in the case, he wouldn't have minded getting to know Della. Well, getting to know her body, anyway.

Not much chance of that now.

He wondered just what, exactly, Della Rose owed her boss. His gaze caught on the paper sack she'd left on his table. Curious, he opened it up and looked inside.

She'd brought him brownies. He reached in and took one, tasted it, closed his eyes when the rich chocolate flavor hit his tongue and filled his mouth with pleasure. Melt-in-your-mouth, sweeter-than-sin delicious, homemade brownies.

He'd have bet his shield that Della Rose and homemade brownies were as far apart as you could get.

He'd always been drawn to a mystery. Not that it mattered. The last thing he needed was another case—even one that wouldn't haunt his dreams. Even one that came with a dark-haired, brown-eyed, sexy-as-sin, prickly waitress with the body of a goddess.

He ate another brownie, lay down on the bed and went back to sleep.

AN IMAGE FORMED in his mind, shimmering, flickering as it slowly solidified. A moonless night. Inky black, quiet. The prosaic suburban house, sheltering the sickest son of a bitch it had ever been his job to find.

"The bastard's in there," he told his partner, his gut tightening at the thought of what they might see when they went in. What they'd seen at every other one of Crazy Larry's crime scenes.

"Maybe," Brad Renfro said. "But it could be another dead-end tip."

"Not this time. He's in there." Nick stared at the darkened house and planned his approach, savage pleasure filling him at the thought of finally getting his hands on the sadistic psycho who'd eluded him for so long.

"How can you be so sure?"

"I can feel him," Nick said. "I know he's in there. I know. And by God, this time I'm bringing the perverted bastard in." They had spent the last two years trying to find him, and no one, not the cops or the FBI, had even come close.

"I hope you're right," Renfro said. "Backup should be here any minute. I wish they'd move it."

"Any minute? Are you kidding? You heard what they said.

With a traffic jam the size of Oklahoma, we have no clue how long it will be before backup gets here. I'm not losing the son of a bitch again. I'm going in."

"Are you nuts? We can't take this guy without help." Brad said.

They shouldn't. Nick knew that. But he also knew if he waited and the killer got away again . . . No, he couldn't live with that.

Even his ten years as a Dallas Police Department homicide detective hadn't prepared him for what Crazy Larry did to his victims. Nothing could have. Nick's gorge rose at the stark, bloody images screaming in his mind.

"You can't go in, Nick," his partner repeated, more strongly this time. "Not alone."

"Watch me," he said. He pulled out his Sig. "He won't get away this time. I'm going around to the back door. You can either take the front or sit here on your ass."

Just as Nick figured, Renfro agreed to take the front. He wanted the pervert as much as Nick did.

Making sure his movements coincided with his partner's arrival at the front door, he made his way silently to the back.

"Police! Open up!" he shouted, and kicked in the door. Swinging his gun right, left, straight ahead, he scanned the room, his gaze halting on a set of stairs leading to a basement. As he advanced, he saw a dim light emanating from the bottom of them.

Music. He heard the sweet whine of violins in a classical arrangement he didn't recognize. Loud enough to mask the sound of his break-in? Nick crept silently down the stairs, moving toward the sound, his nerves wound to bowstring tautness.

The unmistakable smell of blood hit his nostrils before he

reached the partially open door. Goddamn it, he swore silently, was he too late?

AS SOON AS THE crime scene tape was removed, Della went in, determined to clean up the place and reopen as soon as possible. She started in the kitchen because there wasn't as much to do, and besides, she didn't figure it would bother her as much as the main bar area. Tackling the cordoned-off space where the two men had died was harder in more ways than one. She cleaned up the shooter's blood first. She saved Charlie's until last. She'd have given anything not to have to do it at all.

It wasn't hard. It was hell. With every rub of the cloth, every time she dunked the rag in the water and squeezed it out, she felt like she was washing Charlie away. Every time she squeezed and the water ran red, she had to struggle not to cry. God, when had she become such a wuss? All the tears in the world wouldn't bring him back, so she needed to suck it up. It took all that day and part of the night, but by the time she locked up and headed home, she had hopes that she could reopen fairly quickly. She fell into bed, so exhausted she actually slept through the night.

When she got to the Last Shot the next morning, she was certain that it had to be a better day than the one before. At least she wouldn't be facing blood.

Della started to put the key in the lock when she realized there was no need. The door had been kicked in and then pulled closed. Or as close as you could come to closed with a broken lock. Della sucked in a breath and stepped inside.

Goddamn it. Her stomach rolled. Destruction. Everywhere.

A wrecking crew had been in the place. She closed her eyes, hoping it was a bad dream, then opened them. It was all too real. At first glance, it looked like every liquor bottle and glass in the bar had been shattered. The vinyl booth seats had been ripped open, the stuffing pulled out. Even the salt and pepper shakers had been smashed, the contents spread everywhere.

The glass on the old jukebox, which had stood by the wall for as long as anyone could remember, was shattered, and there was a big dent in one side, but it was so heavy she doubted much more had been done to it. Looking over the bar, there was only a gaping hole in the sheetrock where Charlie's prized sailfish had hung. She found it behind the bar, the bill broken clean off and the sail damaged nearly as badly.

Her eyes stung. *Damn it.* Charlie had been so proud of that stupid fish. Maybe it could be fixed.

Oh, hell, she had a lot more to worry about than the jukebox and sailfish. Like the kitchen. If the bar looked this bad, what had they done to the kitchen? And who was responsible for this wreckage?

Who do you think, dumbass? she asked herself. The same people who were involved in Charlie's murder. They'd sent someone else to find whatever the hell the two gunmen had been looking for.

Oh, shit, what if they were still there? She should have thought about that before barging in. She stood and listened for some time, but she didn't hear a thing. No doubt Mary Lou would tell her to call the cops immediately, but she couldn't bring herself to do it.

Whoever had been there was long gone. She could feel it. Della braced herself and pushed open the swinging doors to the kitchen. If anything, it was worse than the bar. She fought more nausea as she stood there looking. Dishes were shattered, glasses broken. Food spread everywhere.

The walk-in refrigerator had suffered some damage to the outside where the vandals had tried to break open the lock, but they hadn't managed to do it. She remembered laughing at Charlie when he'd bought new locks for the refrigerator. A disgruntled waitress had walked off with all of the refrigerated food she could carry when she quit, so he'd decided to lock the fridge as well as the storeroom. They only locked the fridge upon leaving, but it had cut down on food going missing.

The pantry hadn't been spared either. Sacks of flour, sugar, salt, and cornmeal had been sliced open and spread over the floor and other surfaces. A huge jar of oil had been broken open and coated the sink and drainboards. Heart sinking, she walked farther inside to see if the room where they kept the liquor locked up had suffered the same fate.

The door to the storeroom had been kicked in, the lock hanging forlornly on the broken door. As she moved closer, the smell of liquor grew overpowering, until she almost gagged. She took a quick glance inside, enough to know it looked as if every bottle had been broken, and then she backed out and left.

Della told herself she'd look closer later. She needed the big picture now.

The big picture was a total disaster. That was just the downstairs. Oh, God, she thought, had they hit Charlie's apartment as well? She climbed the stairs and opened the door, holding her breath as she did so. It wasn't as bad as the downstairs, but someone had definitely been there. They'd blown the safe, which had been cleverly disguised behind a painting in the living area. Not that it would have mattered if it had been well hidden. At least they'd used the explosives on the safe and not the walk-in refrigerator.

Another miracle. She'd taken the contents of the safe home yesterday. Not that there'd been a lot in there. She hadn't really had a chance to look at the contents closely, but had put them away to worry about later.

Charlie had insurance. He'd bitched about paying the premiums often enough. For her to get anything from the insurance company, she had to have a police report. She would have to call the cops. Again. Deal with Hayes again.

Could it get any worse? Sure it could, she thought sourly. And it usually did. But Allie and Mary Lou—her family—were safe. And Della herself was still kicking. At least there was something to be grateful for. Looking at the near total devastation made it hard to be grateful, though.

She went back downstairs, took out her cell phone, the cheapest she could find with the cheapest plan, and opened it. She had the police station's number in her memory, since she'd been calling daily to see if she could convince Hayes to look into Charlie's murder more carefully.

He wouldn't, of course. She wondered what he'd say about the break-in. If there was anything worse than having to deal with this crap, it was dealing with Freedom's police chief.

OFFICER KNIGHT walked into the Last Shot just as Della ended her call with the insurance company. They'd assured her they would send someone as soon as possible, but Della knew she'd be lucky if she saw a claims adjustor before a month had passed.

Considering Hayes' habits, she'd thought she was in for a

long wait. She had to look twice to believe the cops had actually shown up in a reasonable amount of time. Better yet, Hayes was nowhere to be seen.

Not that she liked Knight. He was a cop, after all. But she *knew* Hayes was an asshole. She wasn't certain about Knight.

What about Nick? Are you sure about him?

Oh, hell no. The only thing she was sure of about Nick was that she thought about him way more than she should. Irritably, she shoved all thoughts of Nick Sheridan out of her mind.

"Where's Chief Hayes?" If he was coming, she wanted to be prepared.

"He's on another call," Knight said. "Don't worry. I'll take care of you."

She didn't need to be "taken care of," but she kept her mouth shut.

"Somebody sure did a number on your place," Knight said, looking around. "What about the upstairs? Charlie's apartment is above the bar, isn't it?"

"Yes. They hit it too. Not nearly as bad. Do you want to see upstairs or downstairs first?"

"Upstairs. If it's not bad it won't take as long."

She led him upstairs and watched as he took pictures and made notes in a small notebook. "The safe's blown," he observed. "Do you know what was in it?"

Della wasn't sure why, but she didn't tell him she knew exactly what had been in it and had the contents at her house. "Money from the till. Probably not a lot else."

"But you don't know?"

When in doubt, lie, she thought. "No. Not a clue."

Knight finished up, and they both went back downstairs. He took out his notebook and pencil again and asked, "Is there anything in particular you can tell me about the break-in, Ms. Rose?"

At least he didn't drawl out her name sarcastically like Hayes always did. But she didn't much care to be addressed as Ms. Rose. "Not much. As soon as CSI took off the crime scene tape, I cleaned up the blood. Last night when I left, I locked up." She gestured at the mess. "When I came in this morning, this is what I found."

He frowned. "You came in before you knew the intruders were gone? You really should have called us first."

Maybe not her smartest move. "No one was here. Just the mess was left."

"But you didn't know that before you went in, did you?"

Della shrugged in answer.

Knight changed the subject. "Can you think of a reason anyone would have done this?" He glanced around, then walked over to the swinging doors to the kitchen and pushed them open.

Della followed. "I figure they were looking for the same thing the men who killed Charlie were looking for."

"The chief says that was a robbery."

"Your chief is full of shit."

Knight laughed. "Even so, when he hears the safe was blown, he'll be even more certain that robbery is the motive."

"Yes, and it's not a bit suspicious that just days after Charlie was murdered, the bar and Charlie's apartment are vandalized." The two events were connected. They had to be.

Knight appeared thoughtful, taking his time checking things out, making notes in his notebook. "It's a possibility," he admitted. A little later he looked up from the notebook. "Assuming you're right, you could have more trouble still to come. If the intruders *were* looking for something, I don't think they found it."

"Oh, joy." Great. Stupidly, she hadn't gotten around to that possibility. What would she do if they came back? She was already going to have a hard time cleaning up this disaster. Worse, what if the bad guys came back and she was still there?

Officer Knight made another note and changed the subject. "Who inherits the bar? Do you know?"

"Yes, me."

"When did you know you would inherit? Are you family?"

"Not by blood." She sighed and added, "It was a total surprise. The lawyer told me the day after Charlie was murdered."

"Maybe a member of his family is angry you inherited."

"Mr. Simms told me Charlie didn't have any family. That's why he left the bar to me. We were . . . tight," she said, choking up.

"How tight?"

Della glared at him. "Very. But not in the way you're implying."

He looked up and said, "I'm not implying anything, and even if I was, I wouldn't judge you. I'm just trying to get the facts."

"The fact is, Charlie was old enough to be my father. And I don't have a thing for older men. So I repeat, we were friends."

"Okay," was all he said as he wrote something in his notebook. "Don't worry, Ms. Rose. We'll get to the bottom of this."

Oh, right. That's gonna happen. "Stop calling me Ms. Rose. It reminds me of your boss."

Knight smiled. "No problem, Della."

He pulled out his phone again and began taking pictures. Della went out to the back porch and sat at one of the tables.

She wouldn't leave, but she didn't want to watch the process either. Watching him work upstairs had been bad enough, but she hadn't felt right leaving him alone in Charlie's apartment. There was nothing personal in the bar or restaurant. Just a hell of a lot of destruction.

A good while later, Knight came out holding a black briefcase and sat down at the rickety table next to her. "Do you mind giving me your fingerprints, Della?"

"Why?" she asked suspiciously. The last thing she wanted to do was give the cops her fingerprints.

He looked a little surprised. "The more prints I have that I can identify, the easier it will be to find any that belong to the vandals."

"There were a zillion cops in here day before yesterday. Are you going to rule them out too?"

"Yes, ma'am, I am. We might get lucky and get a few good ones."

He set out the equipment and held out his hand. Reluctantly, Della let him take hold of her fingers to press each one to the ink and then onto the paper. He was gentle. Not rough. Not like before.

Cold. Hungry. Thankful to be in a warm car. At first. She closed her eyes, willing that fifteen-year-old girl's memories to disappear. *You don't have to go there. Never again.*

"Della, are you all right?" Though he'd finished, he was still holding her hand.

Quickly, she jerked it away and grabbed the cloth to wipe the ink off her fingers. "I'm fine." Just fine. She would not have a panic attack over something that happened years ago. That part of her life was over and done with.

She stood and so did he. "Do you need anything else from me?"

"No, this should do it for now." He followed her inside and added, "As soon as we learn anything, I'll contact you."

In the time she'd been sitting outside, she had forgotten how bad the place actually looked. A wave of weariness hit her. How in the hell was she going to get this cleaned up?

"Is there someone to help you with cleanup?" Knight asked, sounding concerned.

"Yes," she replied automatically. She would call Mary Lou and have her bring Allie, but there was a limit to what three women, one of them a young girl, could do.

He didn't look convinced. "I could help you out after my shift."

"You could help me more by getting Hayes to look at Charlie's murder instead of just filing it away. That first time wasn't a robbery attempt. Anyone with half a brain can see that, especially now that the place has been trashed."

He nodded. "It certainly looks that way. I'll try to talk to the chief, but I can't promise anything. Once Chief Hayes makes up his mind, he's pretty stubborn about changing it." Knight looked around again. "Are you sure you don't want help cleaning up this mess?"

Not from you, she thought. "I can handle it." It occurred to her that since she and the Chief were hardly friends, maybe she shouldn't alienate Knight as well. So she added grudgingly, "But thanks."

"Any time." He paused a moment and added, "I'm not just saying that, Della. I mean it."

Was he hitting on her? Maybe, weird as it seemed, he was just being nice. But if he was hitting on her . . . She repressed a shudder. *God, no.*

So why doesn't Nick Sheridan set off your creep alarm? You've known he was a cop from day one, yet you asked him for help. What is it about Nick that makes you want to trust him?

Because of Charlie, she thought. She wanted his help to find the truth about Charlie's murder. No other reason.

The door to the back deck banged open. Nick Sheridan stood in the doorway, looking around in disbelief. "What the hell happened here?"

CHAPTER SIX

"WHAT IN THE hell happened?" Nick repeated.

Knight answered him. "Vandals."

"Vandals? Are you kidding me? Vandals hit the place just two days after Charlie was shot by those men obviously looking for something here? Try again."

"We'll look into all the possibilities," Knight said repressively.

"Somebody damn sure better." Turning to Della, he asked, "Are you all right?"

It looked like a tornado had hit the place. Crap was spread everywhere. Salt, pepper, condiments, you name it. Chairs and tables were overturned, broken glassware littered the bar. It looked and smelled like every liquor bottle in the joint was busted open and had spewed everywhere. The bar hadn't been a showplace, but at least it had been functional. It sure as hell wasn't now.

Della shrugged. "What are you doing here?"

He ignored the question, since he really didn't have a good answer. He'd been walking on the beach, and when he'd seen

Della's car and a cop car in the parking lot, he decided to see what was going on. And yeah, he admitted he'd been thinking about Della since she walked out of his apartment. So what?

He hadn't expected this. He should have at least thought of the possibility that whoever had been behind the murder would try again. Damn, he really was screwed up.

Knight took Della's hand and said sincerely, "I'll be in touch soon. Anything I can do, just let me know."

"Thanks." Della looked uncomfortable, pulling her hand away quickly. No wonder, since she claimed to hate cops. For at least the twentieth time since the night of the murder, he wondered why.

Knight left.

Della didn't say another word, ignoring him completely as if he weren't even there. She left the room and went to the kitchen, returning a few moments later with a large trashcan, an equally large broom, and a dustpan. Then she set to work.

"Did Officer Knight take pictures for your insurance claim?" Nick asked. "You should make sure you have plenty of pictures before you clean up."

Della paused in her clean up long enough to give him a dirty look. "I took some. My camera is shit, but I took them. Knight took a bunch, so that will have to do." She went back to sweeping.

"Was the upstairs hit as well?"

"Yes. Not as bad, but it's still a mess."

"Shouldn't you leave the cleanup to the new owner?"

She shot him an annoyed glance. "That would be me. I want to reopen as quickly as possible since this place is my livelihood now. I'd barely gotten the blood cleaned up when I came in and found this," she said, gesturing at the mess.

He began picking up large chunks of glass. "Looks like you could use some help."

"I have help coming."

He paused, looked around again and sighed. Damn, he was going to regret this. "What do you plan to do about tonight?"

She frowned. "Nothing."

"You're just going to go home when you finish for the day. With the front door busted wide open." He made it a statement, not a question.

She looked at him a moment and grimaced. "What else am I supposed to do? Stay here all night?"

"Did Knight say they would put a patrol on your place? If there's some police protection—"

She interrupted him with a sharp laugh. "That's an oxymoron. Police protection. Besides, Freedom has a very small police force, and they're sure not going to waste time watching out for me. You saw how long it took Hayes to get here the night Charlie was killed."

God, she really didn't like cops. "Does the place have an alarm?" he asked, but he'd bet his last buck it didn't.

"In Freedom?" She laughed again. "Get real."

Don't do it. Don't get involved in another murder.

Good idea, except he already was involved, even if he wouldn't admit it to Della. "The first thing to do is fix the front door. No sense making it any easier for a return visit." When she didn't answer he continued. "You need someone to watch the place for you. Day and night."

"Even if I had the money for that, who would I hire?"

"I'm available." And he needed something to occupy his time. Right? It had nothing to do with wanting to take Della to bed. Not a thing.

She stopped sweeping and stared at him. "You want to stay

here." Leaning on the broom, she gave him a skeptical look. "Here, instead of your cushy digs. Out of the goodness of your heart."

He forgot and shrugged. Damn, that hurt. "I only have the condo for a few more days. It's rented out after that. I was going to have to find another place to stay anyway. Or go back to Dallas."

"So go back to Dallas."

He wasn't ready to face Dallas yet. He didn't know if he ever would be. "I remember you saying something to me about beggars not being choosers."

She bit her lip and turned aside, hiding a smile, he suspected. "I couldn't pay you. Or not much."

"I could stay in Charlie's apartment. Room and board is fine. We can renegotiate later, once you're up and running again."

She stared at him for a long moment. "You've got a gun?"

"I'm a cop," he said. "What do you think?"

"I think, if you had a gun, why the hell didn't you shoot the bastards who killed Charlie?"

"I wasn't carrying that night." He didn't explain why. She didn't need to know. Besides, Freedom hadn't seemed like a hot spot of crime. He sure as hell hadn't expected a murder. But he should have known better than to take anything at face value. Even a sleepy little fishing town like Freedom. Blame it on the fact that his head was still completely screwed up.

"Typical." She gave him another long flinty gaze, then shrugged. "You're hired. Knock yourself out. But bring your gun this time."

"Deal." He held out his hand.

She stared at it without taking it, then looked at him. "Why are you really helping me?"

"I'm not talking about doing this forever. Just for a while." Which didn't answer her question. Because he wasn't quite sure of his motives even if he had wanted to answer her.

"So you're helping me because you're such a swell guy."

He grinned. "Yeah."

"Why?" she asked again.

He stepped close, laid his fingers on her wrist. She didn't pull away but she stiffened. "You need help, and I've got nothing else I need to do." He shot her another smile. "Besides, I like you. I haven't totally given up on convincing you that you like me too."

"You can dream," she said.

Oh, yeah. And he would. "I'll see what I can do to make the upstairs habitable."

"Nick," she called as he headed out the door and for the stairs to the living quarters above the bar. "I'm not going to sleep with you."

Which would be a damn shame. "Not very trusting, are you? Is it totally unbelievable that I might want to help with no ulterior motive?"

Della looked at him a moment, then smiled. "Yes."

MAYBE NOT TOTALLY unbelievable, Della thought, watching Nick leave. But he was a man, after all. And a cop. Which made it all the weirder that she was trusting him enough to let him work for her and stay in Charlie's apartment. As she saw it, she had a choice. Let him work for her and be a night watchman, or don't and have the place wrecked again. Or worse. She looked around and groaned at the amount of work still to be done. Some choice.

He'd offered and she'd accepted. That was that. Her reasons had nothing to do with wondering what it would be like to kiss him. *Jesus! Where did that come from?*

Della heard a clattering at the screen door of the front door and looked up to see Mary Lou and Allie coming in. She did not want to think about Nick. Especially not kissing him, for Chrissake.

"Oh my God, Della," Mary Lou said, stopping at the threshold with her hand over her heart. "You told us it was bad but I never expected something like this."

Allie came in behind Mary Lou, silent for a change. Usually she was a chatterbox, but if the destruction was overwhelming for Della, it must be doubly so for a child. Della put her arm around her daughter and hugged her.

Allie hugged her back, then let go and slowly took in the mess. "Mom, where's Charlie's fish?"

Damn, of course Allie would notice the missing fish. "It's behind the bar but don't go—"

Allie ignored her and ran over to look behind the bar. "They broke it. Why? Why would anyone do that, Mom?"

Della followed to see her daughter kneel beside the fish and burst into tears. For Allie, that sailfish represented Charlie, just as it did for Della. The broken fish really brought home that Charlie was gone. Della put her arm around Allie, helped her up and walked her away from the sad reminder.

"I don't know, honey. Just being mean, I guess." Mean, but was there a point to it? Was all the wanton destruction meant to scare the shit out of her so she would . . . what? Find whatever the hell they were looking for? How could she when she didn't even know what it was?

"The jukebox is broken too. At least, the glass is." Mary

Lou spoke from the other side of the room. "Oh, Della, this is awful."

"I know. That's why I need your help. Both of you," she added.

Allie sniffled, then stood up straight. "Charlie would be so pissed if he could see this."

"Language," Della said automatically. One of Charlie's biggest faults was his mouth. Della had been trying since Allie met him to curb his tendency to cuss and say other things she'd prefer her daughter didn't repeat.

"Well, he would," Allie muttered.

"Yes, but you can say it another way." Della sighed and let it go. "We can worry about fixing things later. For now, we just need to clean up." And pray the insurance came through.

AFTER MAKING some headway with the broken glass in the dining and bar area, Della decided she needed a change of scene. She left Allie cleaning up the salt and pepper spilled all over each table, with instructions to leave the remainder of the broken glass for Della or Mary Lou. The last thing Della needed was for Allie to cut herself, and there was an impressive amount of broken glass still littering the floor.

"Mary Lou and I will be in the kitchen if you need us," she told Allie.

"Okay. I'm gonna go down to the beach in a minute."

"Be careful and don't get in the water."

"Mom, you act like I can't swim. I'm not a baby. I'm almost a teenager."

Della sucked in a breath. How was it possible her baby had

grown up so much? A teenager. Lord save them. "That's the rule," Della said. "Live with it."

Maybe she was overprotective. But she didn't think it was unreasonable to not want Allie in the ocean without an adult—one who could swim—with her.

"This is as bad as the main room," Mary Lou said upon entering the kitchen. "Why would anyone do this?" she asked. "What could they hope to gain? Or was it just pure meanness?"

"No, I think there was a purpose. It's bound to be connected to Charlie's murder. Too coincidental not to be. They want something. Question is, what the hell is it?"

Mary Lou laid her hand on Della's arm, tears shining in her eyes. She'd loved Charlie too. Charlie had saved both of them. "I'm so sorry, Della. What can I do to help?"

"Other than helping me clean this mess, nothing. You do it by keeping Allie." She debated taking the easy way out and hustling Mary Lou out before Nick returned, but she decided she might as well suck it up. Mary Lou would find out at some point. "I, um, hired some extra help."

"To help you clean up?"

"Sort of. For now, he's the night watchman. We'll see how well he can do the rest of it."

Mary Lou looked puzzled. "He? I can't think of who—"

Della heard Nick coming down the stairs. "You're about to meet him."

"It's not too bad," Nick said as he entered the kitchen. "The safe is a lost cause, but the rest just needs a little cleanup."

"Small favors," Della said.

"Hi, I'm Mary Lou. I live with Della and take care of Allie."

"And I'm Nick Sheridan." He stuck out a hand and gave Mary Lou that lethal smile. "I bet you're the brownie lady. Any chance you'll make another batch? I ate the last one the same day Della brought them."

Mary Lou laughed. "I could probably be convinced."

"How do you know I didn't make them?" Della asked, irritated.

"Can you cook?"

"Not exactly." She could heat things up. But she was no homemaker, like Mary Lou.

"I didn't think so," he said, with a smug smile that made her want to smack him.

Observing their interaction, Mary Lou arched a brow at Della, then turned back to Nick. "Thank you for what you did for Della."

"No problem," he said, blowing off his gunshot wound as if it were nothing. Maybe he was used to it. "I'm sorry I couldn't do anything for Della's boss. Was he a friend of yours too?"

"Charlie was a friend to everybody in this town," Mary Lou said simply. "Or most of them, anyway."

"Coffee break's over," Della said before they could continue. "Think you can push a broom one-armed?"

"Yes, ma'am," he said with a cheerful salute. He smiled at both of them, that damn smile she couldn't get out of her head, and left the kitchen through the swinging doors leading to the dining area.

CHAPTER SEVEN

A S SOON AS NICK walked out, Mary Lou turned to Della. "OMG. Be still my beating heart. That's him? That's the guy who saved you?

Della grimaced. "He didn't save me. Exactly."

Mary Lou waved a hand. "He took a bullet for you. What's the difference?"

Della didn't respond because she couldn't think of what to say.

"You didn't tell me what he looked like," Mary Lou continued. "Oh, my God, he's gorgeous."

"He's okay," Della said, hunching a shoulder—uncomfortably aware that she was lying through her teeth. "Gorgeous is an exaggeration."

"Oh, please," Mary Lou said. "You know he's—"

Della interrupted before her friend got on a roll. "Fine. You're right, he's hot. But that's not why I hired him."

"Why *did* you hire him? You never wanted Charlie to hire a man. You always talked him out of it."

"That's because the only men who wanted a job here were

worthless bums." Or worse. "I need a night watchman if I don't want a repeat performance of this." She motioned to the destruction in the kitchen. "Nick's a cop. It seemed logical." She didn't add that she also wanted Nick to help her find the man who was behind Charlie's death. Time enough to tell Mary Lou if Nick actually agreed to do it.

"A cop?" Her voice rose in disbelief. "You hired a cop?" She rapped a hand against her ear. "You hate cops. Did I hear you right?"

"Ha ha," Della said. "I don't have to love him to hire him."

Mary Lou looked at her penetratingly. "There's more to it. What are you up to?"

"Nothing." Della turned away, pulled the trashcan up next to the stainless shelving and proceeded to throw broken crockery into it. "I hired a man to help. Big damn deal."

"Do you have the hots for him?" Mary Lou asked from directly behind her.

"Damn, Mary Lou, I barely know the guy." Her face felt warm, making her glad her back was to her friend. She tossed more broken glass into the can. "He needed a job and a place to stay. I needed a night watchman. He's working for room and board. I couldn't pass up a deal like that."

Mary Lou gave her a knowing smile. "Whatever you say, honey. If it makes you feel better to tell yourself you're just being practical, go right ahead."

Della gritted her teeth but didn't answer. Arguing would only make Mary Lou more convinced she was right and Della had the hots for Nick Sheridan. Which she absolutely did not.

NICK TOOK THREE steps into the bar's dining room and stopped cold.

The smell of blood hit, so strong he almost gagged. Goddamn it, was he too late?

Silently, he edged the door open with his foot.

The knife gleamed silver and red in the muted glow of light thrown by a ring of candles. Blood ran, rivers of it, crimson shades of death.

"Mister, are you okay?"

Nick sucked in a breath, expelled it. Blond hair. Blue eyes. Just like Angelina.

"Mister?" the girl said again, concern coloring a sweet, melodic voice.

Her eyes, though clear blue as the sky, were shaped exactly like Della's. He cleared his throat, found his voice. Hoping it didn't shake. "You must be Della's daughter."

She nodded. "Allie. Are you the one who helped my mom?"

"Yeah," he said, feeling steadier as time passed. So she was blond. So her eyes were blue. Jesus, if he reacted like this to every blue-eyed blonde, he'd be in the nut house in no time.

"Are you a policeman?" she demanded.

His knee-jerk reaction was yes. After all, he'd said it easily enough when Della had asked if he had a gun. He wondered how much longer he could say that. "Yes. I'm with the Dallas police department."

Allie smiled blindingly. "Are you gonna arrest the bad guy?"

"I can't arrest him. Them. The men who shot Charlie are dead."

"I know," she said impatiently. "But somebody made them do it. That's what Mom said."

"Your mother told you that?" It didn't seem like something you'd share with a kid.

"Well, um, no." She ducked her head and looked sheepish. "Not exactly. I heard her and Mary Lou talking."

"Maybe you heard wrong."

Allie shook her head. "Nuh-uh. Mom said Chief Hayes wouldn't do anything, but she was. And you were gonna help her."

"You misunderstood," he said deliberately. "Your mom hired me to watch over the bar and to help with the cleanup. Not to catch bad guys."

Allie looked doubtful and started to respond.

Damn, the kid was as persistent as her mother. He spoke before she could. "In fact, I'm supposed to be cleaning up right now." He grabbed the broom, thankful to have something to do rather than think about . . . her.

She has a name, his mind whispered. *Angelina.*

"Can I help?"

"Yeah, sure. You can hold the dustpan when I need it."

She retrieved the dustpan and waited until he had a pile growing. "I hate them," she said fiercely, squatting down to hold the pan for him to sweep the refuse into.

He didn't need to ask who.

"I miss Charlie."

"I'm sorry."

Allie hunched a shoulder. "Charlie was the best." She got up and continued talking, making the man sound like a paragon Nick doubted he'd been. But he'd obviously meant a lot to the kid.

She helped him for a bit, but he could see she was restless. Dropping the dustpan, she asked, "Want to hear some music?"

"Sure."

She skipped over to the old jukebox standing against a wall. Nick was a little surprised it still worked, judging from its obvious age. Come to think of it, though, he remembered hearing music the times he was in here before. The perps hadn't helped it, breaking the glass top and putting a big dent in the side, but obviously it still worked.

"Cream?" he asked, as *I'm So Glad* blasted from the jukebox. "That's before my time, much less yours."

"Charlie liked it," she said simply. "Charlie said classic rock was the only thing worth listening to, and he wasn't gonna have all that other sh—I mean, stuff, taking up room when he didn't want to hear it anyway."

Come to think of it, Nick didn't remember hearing anything new the nights he'd come in. Charlie had a point. Why have music you didn't like in your own bar?

"What else did Charlie say?"

Allie perched on a barstool, happily abandoning her job. "No shirt, no shoes, get the h-e-double L out of here. 'Cept he didn't spell it."

Nick laughed.

Encouraged, Allie continued. "Sometimes you get the bear. Sometimes the bear gets you."

"What does that mean?"

"I don't know exactly. But he sure said it a lot." Her expression clouded. "But he won't be sayin' it anymore."

Crap. She was going to cry. Sure enough, tears began to spill from those pretty blue eyes. Nick set the broom aside and walked over to her, placing a hand on her shoulder. "It's rough when someone you love dies."

Allie turned into him, burying her head against him and starting to cry in earnest. "I don't want him to be dead."

"I know, kid. I know. Go ahead and cry." He patted her

back, made soothing noises, just as he had so many times with so many other people grieving loved ones. And he felt useless, just as he had so many other times. But the difference was, in the past, he went after the bad guys. This time, he was letting them get away with it.

Which didn't sit right, no matter how much he wanted to avoid another murder.

"ALLIE MUST HAVE run out of quarters," Mary Lou said. "She only played two songs."

"I can't believe Charlie's not in there feeding her quarters," Della said. "It doesn't seem right."

"No, it doesn't," Mary Lou agreed.

Then it hit her. Della hadn't thought anything of the music coming from the other room because it was such a common thing for Allie to play the jukebox.

Music. The jukebox. Oh, shit. Allie's in there with Nick. Alone. She gripped a piece of broken glass so hard, it drew blood.

"Della, you're bleeding. What are you doing?"

Not bothering to staunch it, she rushed into the other room, ignoring Mary Lou's startled comment.

Allie was sitting on a barstool with Nick standing beside her. His hand was on Allie's shoulder and her tear-drenched face was turned up toward him. Nick and her little girl. Alone. A wave of nausea swept over Della as she remembered . . .

"All alone here? Where's your mom?" He lounged against the doorjamb, giving her the full body scan that made her so uncomfortable.

"She'll be back any minute." She wouldn't, but he didn't need to know that.

"Good. I'll wait for her."

Della's skin crawled. "You can't. I'm about to leave."

He pushed the door open against her resistance and came inside. "No rush. Keep me company until your mom gets back," he said and locked the door behind him.

Della put her fingers to her temple, willing the vision away. Though she'd never forget, she didn't have to allow it to take up space in her head. She needed to worry about the present, not the past.

"Take your hands off her," Della said, advancing on the two of them.

Allie and Nick both looked at her. "Mom, what's wrong?"

"You're crying. What did he do to you?" If he'd hurt her baby, she'd kill him with her bare hands.

"Nothing, Mom. We were talking about Charlie and Nick tried to make me feel better."

Nick still hadn't said anything, but he'd dropped his hand at her initial demand.

"What happened to your hand?" Allie asked. "You're bleeding."

"It's nothing," she said, but she picked up a napkin to staunch the flow of blood. Della shot Nick a furious glance before talking to Allie. "Why aren't you at the beach?"

"I was helping Nick clean up." Allie's eyes were round with surprise. "What's wrong, Mom? You're acting weird."

You're overreacting, Della. Nothing's going on. Slowly the vise around her heart loosened.

"Nick doesn't need any help. Go on out to the beach. And don't go far. Stay in sight. We'll call you when Mary Lou is ready to go."

"But Mom, I want to stay here," Allie protested. "Nick said—"

"Allie, go." She pointed at the door. Reluctantly, Allie walked to the screen door to the back deck, dragging her shoes on the wood floor.

" 'Bye, Nick. See you later."

" 'Bye, Allie." He waited until the door banged behind Allie, then turned to Della. "Are you okay?"

No, she wasn't okay. She took a deep breath to steady herself. Nick was still looking at her quizzically. Nick, who had been all alone with her innocent little girl. Della felt her temper rising like the tide. So what if she was being irrational? Her daughter had been alone with a man Della barely knew.

Nick hadn't done anything to earn her distrust. Except he's a cop, she thought sourly. And a man. "I don't like my daughter being alone with strange men."

"Reasonable. Except I'm not a strange man. You know me. I'm your night watchman. And hired help."

She'd known Bart too. Sometimes that only made it worse. "I don't need to explain myself to you. I don't want Allie alone with you. Period." She didn't like the way he looked at her. As if he understood far too much. But he didn't. He couldn't.

"Your call," was all he said.

"Yes, it is." She turned away to go into the kitchen and try to pull herself together.

"Della."

She turned to look at him.

He gazed at her with those fathoms-deep blue eyes, oh so knowing. Seeing far more than she wanted him to. More than she wanted anyone to see. "I would never hurt your daughter. Or any child. I put the people who do that in jail."

"I—" She wanted to say she knew. She wanted to trust him. But she couldn't afford to. Charlie was the only man she'd ever let close to her and Allie. It hadn't been quick, it hadn't been easy. Charlie had broken down her defenses by being himself. Often cranky, sometimes short-tempered. But straight as an arrow. And always, always her friend. The man who'd loaned her the money to pay the taxes on the house when she and Allie first came to town. Who'd given her a job when she was desperate. The man who'd given her and her daughter a decent family with him and Mary Lou. The man who expected nothing more from her than honesty, and hard work. The man whose crankiness hid the proverbial heart of gold.

But Charlie was dead, and Nick was sure as hell not him.

"I don't care. I know what can happen to little girls who aren't—" she hesitated, then finished harshly. "Girls who aren't protected. I don't want Allie being alone with you or any other man."

He looked at her a moment, compassion in his gaze. She didn't want it. She didn't need it. "I'm sorry, Della."

"For what?" she asked reluctantly.

"I'm sorry no one protected you."

This conversation was getting way too personal. Damn him, he saw too much. "So am I," she said and walked out.

CHAPTER EIGHT

EVERAL DAYS LATER, Della found Nick out on the back deck, nailing down loose boards. He was handy, she'd give him that. His arm didn't seem to bother him much anymore, judging by how much he'd been using it.

She didn't know how Nick had accomplished it so quickly, but in a little over a week, he'd managed to make himself damn near irreplaceable. Not only had he been a huge help cleaning up, but he'd also been doing all sorts of handyman jobs that Charlie had never had time for or interest in.

Della was still suspicious of him. Hell, she was suspicious of everyone. But she admitted he was useful. He seemed willing to do anything she asked of him. Except look for the man responsible for Charlie's death. Still, she hadn't brought it up again. She was waiting for the right moment.

Nick and Allie had seen each other a few times, but always with Della or Mary Lou around. Allie liked him. That was obvious. And Nick liked Allie, but not in a weird, scary way. If he'd been a pervert, she felt sure either she, Mary Lou, or Allie —if not all three of them—would have picked up on it. She still didn't want Allie alone with him, but Della was no longer worried he'd hurt her daughter.

There hadn't been any more break-ins. Once Ethel, the blabbermouth waitress who worked at the Last Shot part-time, knew Nick was staying in Charlie's rooms, everyone in town knew. And they knew he was a cop, as well. And that was obviously a deterrent to anyone who planned to break in.

All that was good. As for the business of the Last Shot, though, even if the insurance claim came through, it wouldn't cover everything that needed fixing or replacing. And it wouldn't make up for the business lost while the Last Shot was closed down.

She could survive for a while on the money Charlie had left her. But she didn't want to spend any more of it than she had to on mere survival. The place needed a facelift, badly. There were things she'd been wanting to do to the Last Shot for a long time, but Charlie never would go for it. Now that she could actually do something, she found herself reluctant to change anything. It seemed disrespectful to Charlie, though he would have laughed at her sentimentality. She could hear his response. "Get real, girlie. Just go on and do what you want. I sure ain't gonna stop you."

She was torn. Part of her wanted to reopen as soon as humanly possible. Everyone who had worked there, from Ethel to the cooks, wanted that too. A couple of them had already been forced to look for other work. Still, reopening would take time, given the condition of the place and the cost of replacing food, liquor, and barware before the insurance money came in. So, it might be reasonable to update a bar that hadn't changed in at least twenty years.

Unless she had to close it down for good. There were several scenarios in which that might happen. First, the insurance might not come through. It *should*, but Della would believe it when she had the money in her hand. Besides that, she needed to have a long talk with Mary Lou about the state of the Last Shot's finances. Although she had a good idea what Charlie had grossed, she didn't know exactly what the cost of running the bar and restaurant involved. Mary Lou would have a much better idea. And knowing Mary Lou, there would be things she'd been urging Charlie to do to save money that he never would consider. But the bottom line was, could she depend on the Last Shot to support her family?

First things first. "Can you help me with the storeroom?"

Nick looked up. "The storeroom? Sure." He stood, set the hammer on one of the tables, and then wiped his hands on his jeans. "But didn't you tell me you'd cleaned that room out last week, when I offered to do it for you?"

"I did clean it, but not very carefully. I just picked up the glass on the floor and mopped up the liquor as best I could." The state of the storeroom had been far too depressing at the time. The rest of the place was such a shambles, she'd decided she'd leave it until last. "But now I need to see if there's anything salvageable in there."

"Didn't you have to give the insurance company an estimate of your losses?"

"I did. But it was just a ballpark estimate. I'm going to need to be more detailed before they'll cover anything. Assuming they will, of course."

He followed her to the back of the kitchen. "They should. Your insurance covers vandalism, doesn't it?"

"Yes." She hesitated at the broken door. She'd been so upset when she'd been in here before, she didn't remember much about its condition. Della pushed open the door. *Oh, God*, she thought. *No wonder I didn't want to deal with it.* Shambles didn't touch it. There was still broken glass all over the shelves, empty cases that had held liquor bottles, and the place still stunk to high heaven. She should have at least cleaned up the liquor and aired it out.

Della couldn't make herself move forward. Her feet felt glued to the floor.

Nick put his hand on her shoulder. Firm, and somehow comforting. "Steady."

Tears pricked at her eyes. Damn, she knew tears were worthless. What was wrong with her? Life slapped you down over and over again. But when you had a kid, you just picked yourself up and pushed back, no matter how much you wanted to give up. She didn't have that choice. Not if she was going to support herself and her daughter.

Turning to look at Nick, she finally managed to speak. "I don't even know where to start."

His expression remained neutral, not giving away what he thought. "Open it up and bring in a fan to dissipate some of the fumes. Does that window open?" he asked, pointing to a small window on the outside wall.

"Maybe," she said doubtfully. "It's as bad as I think it is, isn't it?"

Nick nodded. "Yeah."

She appreciated that he didn't sugarcoat the situation. He kept his hand on her shoulder and, instead of pulling away, she wanted to lean into him—just for a moment to let someone else be the strong one, someone else be the person to depend on. That would be a mistake on so many levels. She made herself move away from him. She was on her own, just as she'd always been.

NICK WONDERED if Della would give in to despair, but he should have known better. Though she was obviously upset, he could see her gathering herself together.

"I—give me a minute," Della said, and left the storeroom to go sit on one of the kitchen stools by the cook's island.

Nick walked over and pulled up another seat. "It's okay to be upset, Della."

"It doesn't do any good. This is just one more thing that makes me wonder if I shouldn't cut my losses. Try to sell the place and take what I can get out of it."

"Is that what you want?"

"No." She closed her eyes and rubbed her temples before looking at him again. "But it may be what I'm forced to do. Charlie left me some money too, but it's not enough to cover everything that needs to be done. The liquor alone was worth thousands."

"You said you had insurance and that it should cover the damage."

"It should, but I don't trust it until I have it. Besides, who knows when I'll get that money? The claims adjustor hasn't even given me a date yet for his inspection. And I'm not sure what the insurance will cover."

"You could get a loan. This is one of the few places in town where you can have a real sit-down meal and a drink. There isn't another bar and grill that I've seen." There was a diner "downtown" and a few sandwich shops and several shrimp stands. But the Last Shot was as close as Freedom came to an honest-to-God restaurant.

She laughed without pleasure. "Yeah, a loan's not an option."

"Why not? You should be able to get a small business loan from your local bank."

"You don't understand."

"What don't I understand?"

He didn't think she was going to talk. She seemed to wrestle with herself, then shrugged. "Some people in town have long memories. Especially the bank owner. He wouldn't spit on me if I was on fire."

"Why?"

"He and my mother had an affair years ago. A couple of years before I left home. There was a big scandal and blowup when his wife found out." She didn't look at him while she spoke, but her delivery of the story was so detached, she might have been talking about someone she didn't even know.

"That was your mother, not you."

She looked at him then, anger in her gaze. "Ever hear of guilt by association? My mother didn't go away quietly. She claimed she was pregnant and managed to extort a good bit of money from him before she 'miscarried.'" She made air quotes when she said the last word.

"I take it she wasn't pregnant?"

"Hell, no. But he could never prove it. He still hates me because I remind him of her, I guess. He was not happy when Allie and I came back to town."

Her mother sounded like a real winner. "I'm sorry he's taking it out on you. Maybe you could get a loan from another bank."

"Yeah, right. I'm sure there are lots of bankers just dying to loan me money. The son of a bitch would blackball me at any bank within two hundred miles."

Nick seriously doubted the man was that powerful. But he could look into that later. "Take it one day at a time. You can't decide before you find out about the insurance, so you might as well try to get the place in shape to reopen."

"I wanted to change some things. Bring the Last Shot into this century. Clean it up, paint it, get new tables and chairs. Maybe even expand the restaurant. But there's no way I can do that now."

"Sure you could. At least the paint. I can help you there."

"Why are you willing to help me with everything except finding the men responsible for Charlie's murder?"

He'd known she wouldn't give up on that. "The chief wouldn't appreciate my interference." Which was true, but not the whole reason.

"So? Don't tell me you're afraid of Hayes?"

He laughed. "No." He felt like he had to give her something. "My last case, the reason I took a leave of absence, was bad. Really bad. I'm not even sure I'm going back to the department."

"Is this the same kind of case?"

"No," he had to admit. It was a murder, but other than that, there was no similarity between the two cases.

"Then what does it have to do with Charlie's case?"

Not a lot. Would working on a different case help him put the one that haunted him to rest? He felt himself wavering. "I'm not sure how much I could find out. Especially with Hayes being obstructive."

"Officer Knight might help."

"Knight? Why do you say that?"

"When he was here right after the break-in, he said he'd try to change the chief's mind. He was nice," she said, as if surprised.

"How nice? Did he hit on you?" *Hello*? Where did that come from? He wasn't the jealous type. Even if he was, he had no claim on Della. But the very fact that she would admit another cop—when she supposedly hated them—was nice, while still giving Nick a hard time pissed him off.

"No. You're the one who's been hitting on me."

"I didn't hit on you. I asked you to have a drink with me."

"Same thing. And when you were in the hospital, you said a lot more than 'have a drink with me.'"

"That was before I started working for you. Besides, I was on painkillers then." He let that hang for a moment and added, "Do you want me to?"

She stared at him. "Do I want you to hit on me?"

"Yeah. Do you?"

"I—this is a stupid conversation. Don't try to distract me. Will you help me or not?"

She hadn't said yes, but she hadn't said no, either. But whatever her response, it had nothing to do with her boss's murder and Nick's involvement in the case. He had a feeling he would regret this. "All right. I'll do what I can, but that may not be much."

She eyed him suspiciously. "You changed your mind awfully quickly. I can't pay you. I know I offered to before, but that was before someone wrecked the Last Shot."

"Money's not an issue." Being single and never taking a vacation had resulted in Nick having a nice nest egg. He could live on his savings for quite a while before he needed a paying job again.

"Must be nice. In my world, money's always an issue." She crossed her arms over her chest. "I won't sleep with you just because you agreed to help me."

He stared at her. She was serious. "Jesus, Della, I don't blackmail women into sleeping with me." Good God, is that what she really thought about him? And if she did, was it just him—or any man—or cop?

She shrugged in response.

"What kind of men have you been dealing with?"

"Other than Charlie, nobody decent."

"You seem to think Knight is decent." *What's with the jealousy, Nick? You don't do jealousy.*

"Not necessarily. I said he was nice. I didn't say I trusted him."

"You're trusting me."

Della simply shrugged.

It meant something that she trusted him, even if only a little. He took her hand, keeping hold of it as she tried to tug it away. "I promise you that if we do sleep together, you'll want to as much as I do."

"Don't hold your breath."

He smiled and let go of her hand. "Now that that's settled, I'll open that window and get a fan. Let's give it an hour or so and then we can tackle it."

AN HOUR LATER, Della and Nick stood looking at the shelves in the storeroom.

"Which shelf do you want to start with?" Nick asked.

"Right in the middle. Where it's the worst. We can leave the top two shelves for last. I never looked closely, but I think what's up there is mostly old cookware. Cast-iron pots and pans aren't breakable."

"No, but they didn't leave them alone, either. They were searching for something," Nick said. "See how some of the pots are on their sides? There are some empty spaces too. I'll bet they threw at least a couple of them down on the floor."

"They did," Della remembered. "I moved them when I cleaned up shortly after the break-in."

"When they didn't find what they wanted—which they clearly haven't yet—they got pissed and broke everything they could."

"What were they looking for?" Della asked. "They kept saying 'where is it?' the night Charlie died. But I never heard what 'it' was. Did you?" Della asked.

"No, they never said."

"The search looks pretty thorough. Even all the wreckage doesn't cover up the fact it was a search job. Why haven't they found it? What could it be?"

"My best guess would be drugs, cash, or stolen goods."

"Why would they think Charlie had anything to do with something like that? I'm telling you, he was a straight arrow."

"Maybe you didn't know him as well as you thought. Did he always live in Freedom?"

Her immediate response was anger that anyone would imply Charlie could have been involved in something as unsavory as drug dealing or anything else Nick had mentioned. Could she be wrong? Could all this have to do with Charlie's past? He had rarely mentioned his life prior to moving to Freedom. Maybe he had good reasons. Still, she couldn't bring herself to believe her boss had ever been anything but honest.

"No," she finally answered. She felt disloyal to even speculate that Charlie was dishonest. "He moved here from Houston and opened the Last Shot. About twenty years ago, I think."

"Did you know him then? Before you left town and came back?"

"No. I was pretty young."

"You never ate here?"

She laughed, but not with amusement. Hell, she'd been lucky to eat, period. Much less at a restaurant. Even a tiny one like the Last Shot had almost certainly been back then. As always, she pushed away thoughts that brought to mind. Thoughts of her mother and Della's miserable childhood. "No."

She could feel him looking at her and turned away. Damn the man, he saw too much. She changed the subject. "So far, I haven't found much to salvage, either in the storeroom or the rest of the place." God, talk about depressing.

"They were thorough. Someone didn't want you to reopen —at least, not anytime soon."

It took them a couple of hours, but eventually they had cleared all but the top two shelves. "Do you want to leave those for tomorrow?" Nick asked. "You look like you could use a break."

"We should go on and finish." She glanced up at the top shelves. "But I don't want to. They're not going anywhere."

"Good. I've got a great idea. Come on," Nick said as he left the kitchen.

Della shrugged and followed.

CHAPTER NINE

"ALLIE WAS RIGHT," Nick said after he dragged her into the bar with him.

"Right about what?"

He looked up from the song list he'd been studying. "There's nothing newer here than the early seventies."

"Charlie's era. He thought classic rock was the answer to everything."

"Maybe it is." He grinned at her, selected a few songs and walked over to sit beside her at the bar.

"Good song," Nick said when the Allman Brothers' *Blue Sky* started playing. "Even if it is old."

Apparently, Della couldn't sit still. Instead of relaxing, she had gotten up to get a cloth and wipe down the bar. "I like it, but it's totally unrealistic."

"It's a song. It doesn't have to be realistic."

"Yeah, well it isn't. A song about being carefree." She snorted.

"What's wrong with being carefree?"

"Nothing. But it's bullshit. Are any of us ever carefree?"

Nick thought about that. Had there been a time he wasn't weighed down by shadows of the past? Before he became a homicide detective? He remembered those times, when he'd been a fresh young cop. But he couldn't feel them. Too much had happened. Too many dead. Too much evil. *A knife gleamed, blood red in the candlelight. . . .* God, no. He pushed the memory from his mind.

"Sure. I was carefree. But it was a long time ago. When I was a kid. Didn't you have some times when you didn't worry about anything? Like when you were a kid?"

She shook her head. "Especially not when I was a kid."

"Why?"

"What do you mean, why? I had a crappy childhood. It was anything but carefree."

He wondered just how bad her childhood had been. He'd seen so many messed-up people. Messed-up families. He hated to think of Della being one of them.

To his surprise, she continued. "I had a crappy childhood because I had a crappy mother. The earliest memory I have is of her and one of her boyfriends fighting. I remember hiding under the bed in my room. Falling asleep. And my mother yanking me out from beneath the bed, slapping the shit out of me, and screaming at me that it was my fault he'd left."

"I'm sorry." It was a story he'd heard before, but made worse because he knew her. Because he liked her. A little more than he wanted to.

She eyed him skeptically. "You're not going to tell me it couldn't have been that bad all the time? That there must have been times when she was decent? Even though I can't remember one single solitary instance?"

Nick shook his head. "I'm a cop, Della. I've seen a lot of shitty homes."

"I don't know why we're talking about this."

"Me neither." He took the rag she was using on the bar and tossed it into the sink. "I have an idea." Maybe he could show her what carefree felt like. Just for a little while.

"It's late. I should get home."

"You said Allie and Mary Lou weren't there. What's your rush?"

"I'm not in a rush," she snapped.

"Good. Stay right there."

DELLA WATCHED him select more songs, then smiled when *This Magic Moment* came on. She would not have pegged him for a romantic. "Really?" she asked.

Nick pulled her into his arms and held her close, swaying to the music. "Really. I always liked this song. My mom and dad used to play it. A lot."

"What are you doing?" She felt stupid, clumsy and tried to pull away.

"Dancing. What's wrong, don't you like to dance?" He drew back to look down at her, smiling that damn smile that got to her every time.

"I don't know how."

"Sure you do. You're doing it right now," he pointed out.

"I call this swaying, not dancing."

"That's the point," he said with a chuckle. "Slow dances are just an excuse to hold a pretty girl."

God, how long had it been since anyone called her a girl? Bitch, trash . . . slut, she'd been called all of those and more even less complimentary. Still, it felt nice, she decided. She could afford to relax for a few minutes. She didn't have to leave anytime soon.

But being in Nick's arms was not exactly relaxing. She was all too aware of the feel of his muscles beneath her hands. Of the strength, yet gentleness of his hands on her waist. Good Lord. Maybe there was a reason to dance. She'd always assumed she just didn't have it in her.

"Della?"

"Hmm."

"You haven't danced a lot, have you?"

Insulted, she looked up at him. "I haven't danced any, smart ass."

"Never?" He sounded surprised.

"Never," she said firmly. The minute the words had left her mouth, she knew she shouldn't have said them. She knew it would lead to questions she didn't intend to answer.

But he didn't push. Instead, he said, "We'll have to change that, then."

Which made her think about telling him . . . something. What would happen if she shared something personal with him? Something beyond having a shitty mother, which anyone in town could tell him. Could she do it? Did she even want to?

"You're thinking too hard," he said. "Relax. Enjoy yourself."

Another song came on. This one was about temptation. *Well, damn, that's appropriate*, she thought. Tempted. She hadn't thought she could be. But that was before she'd met Nick. What was it about him that drew her to him? Why him? He was a cop, after all.

A cop who had saved her life.

Gratitude. That's all it was. She was confusing whatever it

was she felt for Nick with being grateful to him. *You know that's a big fat lie.* Damn it, she could lie to others, but she'd never been one to lie to herself. It wasn't gratitude she felt. It was lust. She'd felt it from the first, and it had only intensified the longer she knew him. These feelings baffled her. In the past—since adulthood—there had been times when she had *wanted* to want a man. When she'd tried her best to give a man a chance, yet she couldn't feel anything. Not disgust, not pleasure, nothing.

She'd been so caught up in her thoughts it took her a moment to realize the music had stopped. When she would have pulled away, Nick simply drew her close and swayed, just as though the music still played.

"Relax," he said again.

Relax? For Chrissake, she'd just admitted to herself that she wanted him. For the first time in—maybe ever—she, Della, the eternally frozen, wanted a man.

"What's going through your mind?" he asked, amused. "I can hear the gears turning."

"The music stopped," she blurted. "You're still holding me."

He looked down at her and smiled. "Yeah. I am."

He was still close, too close. God, his eyes were ocean blue. How could anyone have eyes so deep a blue? "Do you wear contacts?"

He blinked. "Where did that come from?"

"Your eyes are so blue. I wondered if they had help."

"Nope. I've got twenty-twenty and no contacts."

"They're so pretty," she said, inanely. He was still smiling at her. His dimples—God, no grown man should have dimples like that—deepened.

"Thanks," he said, and then he kissed her.

Her eyes drifted closed. At first, she could barely feel his lips on hers. He drew her out slowly, a nibble, a taste, slow, deliciously slow. When his tongue sought entrance, her lips opened without conscious thought. And then she was sinking. Sinking into the kiss, into him, into the touch, the taste, the pleasure.

She wanted him, she wanted more.

She made a sound. To her despair, it was a moan. Oh, God, she was in trouble now.

NICK BROKE THE kiss before he devoured her. She was skittish enough without him swallowing her whole. God, who would have thought a simple kiss would have him so churned up? It had been a while since he'd been with a woman. Months, in fact. But kissing Della shouldn't have shot him into instant overload. Except that it had.

Maybe it had been a fluke. Her mouth was right there, ripe, rosy, begging to be kissed again. So he did.

Oh, man, this was no fluke. He was drowning. Drowning in the taste, the smell of her. He kept his hands on her waist, because if he didn't, he would fill them with those luscious curves that had driven him crazy since he'd met her. His tongue played with hers and she met him thrust for thrust.

Without breaking the kiss, he boosted her onto one of the barstools. Giving up the battle, he filled his hands with the perfect breasts he'd known lay beneath the loose T-shirts she favored. Groaning, all thought of taking it slow vanished. He was ready, willing, and able right now, and judging by the way she melted against him, she was too.

Her hands came up and pushed against his chest and she wrenched her mouth away. "Stop. Don't—I can't do this."

"Can't do what?" he asked, his lips against her neck and dropping his hands reluctantly away from her breasts.

"This. You and me. Sex."

He made himself step away from her. Obviously, he wasn't going to think well with those soft curves so temptingly close. And her mouth—God, what he wanted to do to her mouth. What he wanted her mouth to do to him.

"Why not?"

She shook her head. She looked upset, very upset. It dawned on him that he was an idiot. "I'm rushing you, aren't I?"

"That's not it. Exactly."

"What is it, then?"

She bit her lip, making him wish he was the one biting it. *Down, you fool*, he told himself.

"I don't do sex."

He didn't point out that she obviously had at one point, or she wouldn't have a child. Before he could think of a response —other than why not—she added, "I think I'm asexual."

Nick started to laugh, but realizing she was serious, he turned it into a cough. "I'm pretty sure you're not."

"You don't know me," she said. "I'm no good with men, or relationships, or any of that."

"That's okay. I'm no good at relationships either." *Not since Lucianna*, he thought. She'd cured him of ever wanting anything serious. He stepped toward Della and stroked a finger down her cheek before cupping it. "It was a kiss, Della, not a commitment."

"It was a little more than that. Besides, we both know kissing leads to other things. Don't try to tell me you don't expect more."

"Expect? No." He shook his head. "Want? Definitely."

"God, you're stubborn. You have an answer to everything."

Nick laughed. "Yes, Ms. Pot." He took her hand and smiled at her. "I have an idea. Let's just take it easy and see what happens."

She still looked doubtful.

What could he say to get her to relax? To stop looking at him like he was going to turn into a monster any minute? "Tell you what. Next time, you kiss me."

"You want me to kiss you? You won't kiss me unless I kiss you first?"

"Right. You get to initiate it."

"What if I don't?"

If she didn't, he'd kick his own ass into next week. "Then you don't. Your call, Della."

"And if I do?"

"We'll see where it goes."

Her eyes narrowed. "You think there's no way I won't kiss you, don't you? Haven't you ever struck out before?"

"Sure. Many times." He smiled and added, "But you have to admit you're curious now." *He* wasn't curious. He knew it would be great between them. He just had to wait until she quit fighting herself long enough to realize it too.

CHAPTER TEN

"WHATCHA DOIN'?" Allie asked Nick on a bright, sunny Saturday.

"Hey, Allie. I'm wondering if this dog belongs to anyone." He'd gone for a run on the beach and when he'd returned, he'd found a shaggy little mutt waiting for him in the sand below the back deck.

Allie crouched down beside them and stretched out a hand to pet the dog. "It's pretty dirty. Does it have a collar?"

"No collar, no tag. It's a girl. I think she must be a stray."

"She's not very pretty."

No, she really wasn't. "She'll look better once she's cleaned up," he said firmly. But not much better, he thought. Her hair, an indiscriminate shade of grayish black, was matted and tangled. She had stubby little legs and what would have been a round body if she hadn't been starving. Her face could only be described as homely. But her tail was wagging madly as they petted her, and when Allie leaned down, the dog licked her face.

"Look, she likes me."

"I think you're right. Why don't you stay with her, and I'll go get her some food and water."

"Okay."

As he climbed the stairs, he looked back and saw that Allie had already pulled the little dog into her lap and was crooning to her. He wondered if Della liked dogs, because he had a feeling Allie wouldn't give up this one easily.

Della was in the bar area and on the phone when he came in. First, he went upstairs and got his shampoo. He had a comb, but it was his only one and he wasn't enthusiastic about sharing it with the mutt. Once they got some of the grunge off of her she'd look better—he hoped. Her fur was going to require scissors for sure and he didn't know where to find any.

A short while later, he took the supplies he'd gathered and went back down. He heard Allie say, "You're gonna live with me now, Sophia. I'm gonna take real good care of you. I promise."

Uh-oh. Della sure better like dogs, he thought again. "So you've already named her?"

Allie looked up and smiled as he set everything down. "Yes. I don't think she belongs to anyone, because if she did, why would she be so skinny?" She thought about that a minute and added, "If they made her that skinny on purpose, they don't deserve her."

"Nope. They don't." He filled the water bowl with water from the hose. Sophia immediately began lapping at it. Then he set the other bowl down and unwrapped a piece of chicken he'd cooked the night before, handing it to Allie. "We don't want to give her too much at first. I'll go buy her some dog food in a little while. In the meantime, why don't you tear this into small pieces and give it to her a little at a time. Put it in the bowl, because she might bite you, she's so hungry."

Allie did as he suggested, but her expression grew more worried.

"What's wrong?" Nick asked. "Are you afraid your mom won't let you keep her?"

"Maybe. We've never had a dog. Every time I asked Mom, she said we couldn't afford to take care of it," she said glumly.

Which was undoubtedly true since Della had been supporting herself and her daughter, and for all he knew, Mary Lou as well. On a waitress's pay. But damn, the kid had already fallen in love with the mutt. He didn't think Della was nearly hard-hearted enough to turn Allie down.

Well, hell. Della couldn't afford it, but he could. "I can help," he said.

"Really?" She turned a ridiculously hopeful face up to his.

"Sure."

"Allie," Della called from the deck. "Where are you, Allie?"

Nick and Allie looked at each other. Nick shrugged and said, "Might as well tell her now as later." He'd wanted to bathe the dog before they showed her to Della, not that he believed it would make that much difference in her looks.

"I'm down here, Mom."

She looked over the railing and saw Nick. "What are you doing there?"

He heard the slight note of panic in her voice. Again, he wondered what had happened to Della to make her so overly-protective. At least she hadn't totally freaked out this time. Yet, anyway. "Come down here and you'll see."

She made it down the stairs in record time. "I've told you before—" she started to say. "What have you got there?"

"She's a dog. Nick found her. I'm gonna call her Sophia. I can keep her, can't I, Mom?"

"Keep her?"

"Well, yeah. Nick and me are pretty sure she's a stray. You won't make her go to the shelter, will you Mom? Look how sweet she is."

Nick had to bite his lip to keep from laughing. Della looked totally at a loss. Finally she said, "She's really ugly."

"I know," Allie said. "But she can't help it. And she already loves me." She leaned down and Sophia licked her cheek. "Besides, Nick says she'll look better once we get her cleaned up."

"Oh, he does, does he? What else did Nick say?" She turned the evil eye on him. "I'd like to hear how this went down."

Nick picked up the shampoo bottle and handed it to Allie. "Why don't you take her over to the hose and start washing her? I'll talk to your Mom."

"Okay." She looked at her mother. Nick knew where the expression "with her heart in her eyes" came from. A little girl like Allie. "I love her, Mom. Please say we can keep her." She didn't wait for an answer, but carried the little dog over to the water faucet.

"What in the hell do you think you're doing?" Della asked him. "That's the ugliest dog I ever saw."

"Like Allie said, she can't help that. She's a stray. She was here waiting for me after I went for a run on the beach."

"That doesn't explain Allie's involvement. You put her up to this, didn't you?"

"I didn't have to. Della, once she saw that dog, Ironman couldn't have stopped her. It was love at first sight for both of them."

"Oh, please." Crossing her arms over her chest, she tapped her foot and glared at him.

"What, you don't believe in love at first sight?"

"No. And that's beside the point. I can't afford a dog. Especially not with everything that's happened to the bar."

"I'll help you. I'll cover the vet and her food until you get back on your feet." Which might be a long time, he thought. He glanced at Allie. It was a good cause.

"You think I won't take you up on that, but I will." Della shoved her hands through her hair and watched Allie and the little dog spreading shampoo and water everywhere. "I've never seen her look so happy," she murmured. "What am I supposed to do?"

"That's easy. Adopt the dog."

"What if it—she belongs to someone?"

Nick hid a grin. She was definitely wavering. "Do you really think she does?"

Della looked over at the little dog. "No." Shrugging, she conceded his point. "But I guess we should post some flyers."

"Can't hurt." Unless someone did claim her, but in his opinion there wasn't a chance in hell that would happen.

"I've never had a pet," Della said. "I don't know anything about dogs."

"You never had a pet growing up?"

She gave a short, humorless laugh. "Are you kidding? No animal was stupid enough to come near our house. God knows what my mother would have done to one dumb enough to get in her way."

"You had a really lousy childhood, didn't you?"

"What childhood? I was never a child."

He waited, but she didn't elaborate. He wished she would. For the first time in years, he wanted to know more about a woman. It had nothing to do with the case. No, he wanted to know Della. The woman she kept so close, so guarded. So tightly in control. What would she be like if she let go of that control?

She made an impatient gesture. "That doesn't matter. This is about right now, and right now, that dog is the problem. I don't know anything about dogs," she repeated.

"It's not hard. Just love them, feed and water them, give them shots, and neuter them. Piece of cake."

"An expensive piece of cake."

"I told you I'd take care of her vet bills."

"Why would you do that?"

"Damn, Della, you are the most suspicious woman I've ever known. I know you can't afford it. I'm doing it for Allie. And for that little mutt. Look at them." He gestured to the two who were now playing with the hose. "They're happy." He'd seen so much darkness. He couldn't explain what seeing that innocent happiness meant to him.

"I don't like to owe people. I already owe you. This just adds one more thing, and like before, I can't repay the debt."

"You don't owe me a damn thing." The last thing he wanted from her was gratitude. "I'm doing it more for me than you."

Those big, brown, caramel-colored eyes were clouded as she looked at him for a long moment. He couldn't read her, which bothered him, because he usually could read women easily. Not this one.

She sighed. "All right. I'm not going to break my kid's heart, and if that's the only way we can keep the dog, then that's what we'll have to do."

"Good. I'm going to the store to get food and a few other things the dog will need."

"I hope I don't regret this." She started to walk over to the pair, but stopped and asked him, "What if it hates me?"

"*She*, not it. She's starving for love, among other things. That dog will like anyone who gives her a break."

"Don't forget to buy some scissors and a brush. I am not using my good kitchen scissors on a dog." Della turned away, but he heard her mutter, "Damn the man. I hope he's right."

He grinned. Maybe a dog was just what Della needed.

SEVERAL HOURS later, Della was in the kitchen trying to get a handle on exactly what food and glassware she needed in order to reopen. She still couldn't decide about the liquor. On the one hand, it was incredibly expensive to replace. On the other, liquor sales made up a lot of the Last Shot's business.

The dog, Sophia, as Allie insisted on calling her, was clean, fed, watered, and had been to the vet. They'd cut her fur as close as they could since it was the only way to get rid of the mats. It—she—should have looked better, Della thought, but she was still ugly as sin. Maybe if she filled out a little . . .

What did the damn dog's looks matter? Della asked herself. Allie was madly in love with the animal, so that was that. Della admitted she was a sweet little thing. So ugly she was cute. Allie had staked out one of the booths in the bar and the little dog was asleep with its—her—head in Allie's lap.

Della wondered how much Nick had to do with Allie falling for the dog. He, Mary Lou, and Allie had taken Sophia to the vet, where they had done everything Nick had talked about and more. Plus, they'd made another appointment on Monday to spay her. Nick refused to tell her what it cost.

Though Della now admitted she didn't believe Nick would do anything to hurt Allie, she still wasn't comfortable with her daughter being alone with any man. Other than Charlie, she thought with a pang. So Mary Lou had taken both of them.

Nick, the macho man, was a softie. Who would have thought it? She'd have thought a homicide detective would be a harder case. He wasn't, at least around women, children, and dogs.

Sighing, she went back to work, stopping gratefully when Mary Lou came through the swinging doors. "That dog is really, really ugly," she said in a low voice.

"You don't have to be quiet. Allie knows it. She loves it— damn it, her—anyway."

"We really lucked out that she didn't have heartworms," Mary Lou said.

"What are those? They sound gross."

"They're nasty, just like the name sounds. Treatment costs an arm and a leg." She took a seat on the bar stool and looked at Della innocently. "But your prince would have sprung for that, too."

"My what?"

"Prince. You know, as in Prince Charming."

"Oh, give me a break."

"He did take a bullet for you," Mary Lou reminded her. "And now he's come to the rescue of the little dog. And Allie, of course."

"Please, he felt sorry for the dog. Who wouldn't?"

"A lot of people, unfortunately." She considered Della with shrewd eyes. "Nick likes you."

"So? He likes you too. And Esther and Allie and almost everyone in town. Except Chief Hayes and Officer Knight. I don't think he likes them."

"Hayes I can understand, but what's not to like about

Officer Knight?" She put a hand over her heart and patted it. "He is one damn fine-looking man."

Della wondered if she should mention Knight hitting on her the day after the break-in. But she hadn't been positive he wasn't just being nice, so she didn't say anything. Still, the men Mary Lou usually went for had all been varying degrees of rotten. Her ex being the worst. "You don't have a thing for him, do you?"

"I might if he were to show any interest in me. But we were talking about you and Nick. You know, Nick, the cop you have the hots for."

Della started to deny it. She wanted to deny it.

Goddamn it, was Mary Lou right? So what if she did? *It's just a crush*, she thought. As a teenager, she'd never had a chance to have crushes, to talk to other girls and giggle about boys, or any of that. She hadn't had any friends. How could she when she couldn't bring anyone home? God knew what they'd have walked in on.

Anyway, her feelings for Nick—no, make that her reaction to Nick— was understandable. He was a great-looking guy, after all. Thinking about him bare-assed naked at his apartment had sparked erotic thoughts she'd never had before.

The man could kiss too. God could he kiss. Maybe—

No. It was no use. She'd tried sex before, she reminded herself. As an adult. Voluntarily. She was too . . . broken . . . to have a sexual relationship with anyone, never mind something deeper.

But that man had been nothing like Nick. He'd been nice. She'd liked him. But there'd been no spark, no reaction other than dissatisfaction. To be honest, she'd felt nothing. Nick elicited strong reactions from her. Some good, some bad. But never indifference.

"I'm waiting," Mary Lou said.

"I do not have the hots for Nick," she told Mary Lou.

"That's a shame," Nick said from the doorway. "I was hoping you did." He gave her a killer smile.

"Eavesdroppers never hear anything good," she said, annoyed and a little embarrassed. "Serves you right."

Mary Lou laughed and got up. "I'm going to take Allie and Sophia home. Stay as long as you want, Della," she told her and winked.

Ignoring her, Della went out of the kitchen to kiss Allie good-bye. "Have Mary Lou find an old blanket for the dog to sleep on. She can stay in the laundry room."

Allie hugged her mother and skipped out, the little dog stuck to her like glue. Della didn't think the dog would get lost anytime soon.

"Do you really expect that dog to sleep in the laundry room?" Nick asked her after the three left.

"Why wouldn't she?"

"I keep forgetting you never had a pet. That dog will be asleep in bed with Allie when you get home. I guarantee it."

"Isn't that kind of unsanitary?"

"She's clean and has no ticks or fleas. Best you can hope for."

Della must have looked appalled. "Stop laughing," she said irritably. Fleas and ticks? What in the world had she gotten herself into?

"Sophia's a sweet little dog. You'll get used to her, don't worry."

"Thanks to you and Allie, I don't have a lot of choice, do I?"

"None at all," Nick said cheerfully.

CHAPTER ELEVEN

A FEW DAYS LATER, Mary Lou dropped off Allie, and the dog, of course, at the Last Shot while she ran errands after school. Allie had been acting odd for the last few days, and after Della heard her sigh heavily for the fifth time, she decided she had to address the problem. Whatever it was. "Is something wrong, Allie?"

Allie had staked out her usual booth in the bar, with her homework spread out in front of her, but as far as Della could tell, she hadn't touched it. "Dunno."

"Sophia's okay, isn't she?" She certainly looked okay. The dog was lying on the seat beside Allie with her head in Allie's lap. Snoozing. She slept a lot. Maybe she was making up for lost time.

"She's fine."

"Then tell me what's going on. Did something happen at school?"

"Sorta."

Della slid into the seat across from her and waited.

"We have to make a chart about our family, way back to our great-grandparents."

Wonderful. Della had no idea who her mother's parents were, and of course, knew even less about Allie's father's family. What in the hell was that teacher thinking? Allie couldn't be the only one with this problem.

"Did you talk to your teacher? Not everyone can find out enough about their family to make a chart."

"No."

"Do you want me to—"

"I don't want you to talk to her! Promise me you won't. Promise!"

Good God. "Calm down. I won't if you don't want me to. But why won't you talk to her?"

"Because it's embarrassing."

"Surely you're not the only one who—"

"I don't even know who my father is," Allie said before Della could finish the sentence. "You never talk about him. You've never told me anything about him."

"That's not true. I've told you—"

Allie interrupted yet again. "All you said was that he was bad and you don't know where he is."

Which was absolutely true. Just not all of the truth. And though Della was sympathetic, it irritated the hell out of her to not be allowed to finish a sentence.

"We've talked about this before," Della reminded her. She had known this day was coming. Allie was far too curious to let something as important as her parentage be a mystery forever. But she had no intention of telling her daughter the true circumstances of her birth. If Allie were to find out the truth about Della's past . . . Her stomach flipped over at the thought.

"We're supposed to be making a chart. Only I can't, because I don't know who my father is. Or my grandparents. I don't know anything about his parents or yours. I don't know anything about anyone but you."

"I'm sorry, Allie."

"No, you're not. If you were, you'd tell me something. Maybe I don't even have a father," she shouted.

"Of course you have a father. He's just not in our lives. I can't believe there aren't other kids who don't know much about their families."

"My friends know. Everybody else knows who their father is. Everyone but me. Even if their fathers are gone, they know about them." She started ticking her friends off on her fingers. Della's heart sank more with every word. "Angela's parents are divorced and her dad moved to California. Trina's dad is dead. Selena's dad is in prison. She didn't want to say, but one of the others told us. She cried and left. Is that where my dad is?"

"I don't know," Della said truthfully. "But he should be."

"Why? What did he do?"

Della prayed that Allie never found out. She took one of Allie's hands and spoke carefully. "Your father was a bad man. Neither of us will ever see him again. And that's a good thing. I'm sorry, honey, but that's the truth."

"If he was so bad, then why did you have sex with him?"

Oh, baby, if only it were that simple, she thought. "I didn't know what he was like until it was too late." Which was true in a way. She'd been so stupid. So naive. She'd gotten in the patrol car thinking they would help her. That anything would be better than what she'd been doing for the past weeks. Even now, years later, thinking about that day made her ill. "If you want to tell your friends something, just say your father's not around and you don't know where he is."

"That doesn't help me with my chart. What about your mother? Was she bad too?"

Della answered truthfully. "Yes."

"So bad you won't even talk about her? She left you her house. That was nice."

Only because she hadn't expected to die. If her mother had realized how close she'd been to dying, Della was sure she'd have done anything to see the house didn't go to Della. "I left home at fifteen, Allie. You know that. I wouldn't have left home so young if I'd had a choice."

Allie looked skeptical, which coming from a twelve-year-old could look pretty scathing. So Della added, "I didn't just leave. My mother threw me out."

"Why?"

"It doesn't matter. That's what happened."

Allie seemed to weigh that, and to Della's surprise, she dropped the subject. Only to return to questions about her father. Which was worse.

"After you left home, you met my father. And got pregnant with me. Did you love him? Before you knew he was bad?"

Jesus, would this conversation never end? She couldn't tell Allie what she wanted to know. Even if she'd wanted to, Della didn't know herself who had fathered Allie. "All that matters is that you are the best thing that ever happened to me." Despite how she was conceived.

Della looked up and saw Nick standing in the kitchen doorway. She hadn't heard him come in. Wondering how much he'd heard, she ignored him and focused on Allie. Clearly, her daughter wasn't finished.

"What did my father look like?"

"He looked like you. Blond hair, blue eyes." One of them had, anyway.

"You hate him, don't you, Mom?"

How to answer her? Della decided on the truth. Maybe she couldn't tell Allie everything that had happened, but she would give her the truth when possible. "Yes. I told you, he was a very bad man."

"Why don't you hate me? I look like him and you hate him."

Della gathered Allie's hands together in hers. "I could never, ever hate you. You're the most precious thing in the world to me. I love you very much, Allie." Della would always remember the feelings of awe and pure love that swept over her the first time she held her baby.

"I know." Finally resigned, Allie said, "I love you too."

Della blinked away tears. She, who never cried, was about to lose it for the second time in a matter of weeks. "Are we okay now?"

Allie nodded. "But I still don't know what to do about the project."

"I'll help you. We'll think of something."

Della got up. "I think I hear Mary Lou honking. You'd better take Sophia out to go to the bathroom before she gets in the car." Mary Lou's car was almost as decrepit as Della's, except Mary Lou cleaned hers out more often. She'd brought the car, a fifteen-year-old Buick, with her when she'd come to Freedom. In fact, she'd lived in it for a while. It hadn't been new then, but it still ran, which was the most important thing.

Allie's face brightened as she and Sophia got out of the booth. She took her papers and stuffed them in her backpack. "Mary Lou said we were gonna have McBurgers tonight."

"Yummy. Have fun." Della ruffled her daughter's hair and watched her go.

"Hey, Nick," Allie said as she passed him. "S'up?"

"Hey, Allie. Not much." He smiled as she and Sophia went out the back door.

Della stared at him for a long moment. He didn't look in the least abashed that he'd been listening to a very private conversation. "How much did you hear?"

ENOUGH TO MAKE him realize Della's life had been even harder than she'd admitted to. "Your mother threw you out when you were fifteen. You wouldn't tell Allie why. Allie's father was no prize, and you didn't want to talk about him either."

"The operative words being, 'I don't want to talk about either of them.'"

He hesitated, unable to believe he was going to offer advice. Who the hell was he to give his opinion when he sure as shit couldn't talk about his last case? He'd tried. With his partner, with the shrink. Even with his sister. But what little he'd been able to verbalize hadn't helped a damn bit. "Maybe you should. Not to Allie, but to someone else. You haven't, have you?" He didn't know why he was so sure she hadn't talked about it, but he'd make book on it.

"My mother and Allie's father are two things I don't ever intend to talk about. I never have and never will."

So he'd been right. "You could use a friend, Della."

"I have one," she snapped.

"Just one?"

"So?"

"Damn, Della, don't you ever let anyone in? I want to be your friend."

"That sounds very noble, but that's not all you want."

He smiled. "No, but one doesn't have to rule out the other."

"Why do you want to be my *friend*?" she asked, emphasizing the last word.

"Damned if I know. You are the most suspicious, tight-assed woman I've ever known."

Her mouth fell open. "I am not a tight-ass."

"No? You work all the time. I haven't seen you take fifteen minutes to have fun. You're more close-mouthed than a clam. What would you call it?"

"I'm cautious. What's wrong with that? And I do have fun. Sometimes."

He stepped closer and touched her cheek with the backs of his fingers. Her skin was soft. Her lips were slightly parted and so damn tempting. As he started to kiss her, he remembered. He'd promised he'd let her make the first move the next time. Well, shit. Why had he said a stupid thing like that?

"You said you wouldn't," Della murmured but she didn't move away.

He lifted an eyebrow. "Reading my mind?"

"Hell, Nick, you practically hung out a sign."

He supposed he had. "Remind me not to make such a dumb-ass promise again." Regretfully, he dropped his hand and stepped back. Damned if she didn't follow him. "What are you doing?"

She laughed. "What does it look like? I'm going to see if the last time was a fluke."

"It wasn't," he said positively.

She put her hands on his arms. "Lean down."

He couldn't help grinning as he obeyed. "Do I get to react?"

Della appeared to think about that. "Just with your mouth. No touching otherwise."

"What's the fun of that?"

"The fun is, I get to touch you. Take it or leave it."

"Are you kidding? I'll take it." She rose on her tiptoes and laid her lips against his. Her lips and tongue explored his mouth, leisurely, but not tentatively. His instinct was to gather her against him and take the kiss deeper, but he remembered what she'd said, relaxed, and let her be in charge.

Della's hands crept up to link behind his neck and she pressed closer, went deeper. Her tongue made darting forays against his, her soft breasts pressed against his chest. He wouldn't have thought a kiss, just a kiss, would be so seductive. Or make him ache. How did she do that?

Slowly, she broke the kiss. Her arms still linked around his neck, she looked at him. Her whisky-colored eyes had darkened to a deep brown. She looked surprised.

"That was no fluke," he said, wondering if she'd contradict him.

"No, damn it. It wasn't a fluke." She let go of him and moved away.

"Why do you sound pissed?"

"I'm not pissed, exactly. I'm not used to—" she waved a hand. "This."

Now *he* was confused. "Not used to what?" She just looked at him. "You're not used to kissing?" He tried not to sound incredulous, but that's what her comment had sounded like to him.

"Don't be ridiculous," she said, but she hesitated before saying it. "I'm going home," she said abruptly.

The next thing Nick knew, she was out the door, and he was left wondering what the hell she'd really meant. Was he reading something into it that wasn't there? Or had Della's previous life been even worse than he'd thought?

If it had been, would she ever open up to him?

CHAPTER TWELVE

THE NEXT MORNING at the Last Shot, Della sighed and rubbed her back. "I am tired. Tired, tired, tired," she said aloud. It was Nick's fault. Instead of sleeping soundly, she'd tossed and turned and dreamed. Erotic dreams. She never had dreams like that before. She hadn't known she was capable of having dreams like that.

Why had she thought kissing Nick was such a good idea? She'd told herself kissing him again wouldn't be the same as the first time. That it hadn't been as good as she remembered. And it hadn't been. It had been better. Oh, for God's sake, she thought. *Get over yourself, Della. So you have the hots for him. Either do something about it or forget it. It just means you're a normal woman. With normal urges.*

Except that she wasn't.

"What's the plan for today?" Nick asked right by her ear.

She jumped. "Don't sneak up on me like that," she said crankily.

"I didn't. I said your name three times. You must have been thinking of something else," he said with a knowing smile.

Ignoring that comment she said, "I want to clean off the top two shelves in the storeroom. After that, I'm not sure."

"All right." He opened the door and she walked inside. "Have you thought any more about whether you're going to keep the place open?"

"I think about it all the time. Mary Lou and I looked over the books. She knows more about the bottom line than I do. She's kept the books for the Long Shot for six or seven years now."

"How do they look? Are you making a profit?"

"We were. Prior to the break-in. Just as I thought, we make more money off drinks than anything else," she said glumly.

"What's wrong with that? You still have a liquor license, don't you?"

"Yes, it transferred. I have a liquor license and no liquor to sell. The insurance adjustor hasn't been here yet. No telling when that money will come through. Or how much it will be."

"Are you positive you don't want to try for a loan?"

"There's no point. The only thing is . . ." She hesitated then decided to hell with it. "Charlie left me some cash."

"Enough to restock and reopen?"

"Yeah. I can probably squeeze out a little for remodeling too, but there won't be much left over if I do."

"If you don't reopen, what are you going to do?"

What would she do? Try to get some dead end job in town? The Last Shot was her only means of support. "It would be a miracle if someone bought it. And even if they did, we couldn't live off the money forever."

"Looks like you have your answer."

"It does, doesn't it?" She felt curiously light-hearted. Making a decision instead of dithering helped. She didn't like uncertainty. "Thanks. I don't know why it took me so long to figure that out."

"It's a big decision. Nothing wrong with looking at all the angles."

She looked up at the shelves and sighed. Going to the back of the room, she grabbed the ten-foot ladder and dragged it back with her.

Della opened the ladder next to the shelves, but, as she put her foot on the bottom rung, Nick stepped up and blocked her from going farther. "Let me do the climbing," he said.

"Why?"

"Everything up there looks heavy. It will be easier if I get it down and hand it to you."

Della never admitted to weakness if she could help it. "I'm perfectly capable of getting it down myself."

"I didn't say you weren't. I said it would be easier if I handed things to you."

Della opened her mouth, but Nick cut her off. "Damn, you just love to argue, don't you? What's the big deal?"

"I don't love to argue," she said, incensed.

"What do you call what you're doing right now?"

Della ground her teeth. "Fine. Climb the damn ladder. Don't blame me if you fall off because your arm's still gimpy."

He laughed and flicked his fingers beneath her chin. "You're worried about me. I told you you'd start to like me if you gave me a chance."

"Get over yourself," she told him, annoyingly aware of the tingle that shot through her whenever he touched her. And when he kissed her, oh, God it went from tingle to fire. What the hell was up with that? "I don't want any accidents here, that's all."

"Nope. That's not it. You like me." He started up the ladder while she stood there trying to deny it. And damn it, she couldn't. How did that happen? She'd have bet her last dollar that she could never be friendly with a cop. Much less like one. But she did, she *liked* Nick. And that was totally in addition to any other feelings she had for him.

"What are you going to do with all this?" Nick asked as he handed pieces down to her.

"I'll see if Mary Lou can sell it on eBay. I have no idea how to do that, but Mary Lou does."

Since they only moved one item at a time, it took forever to clear the two shelves. "Is that it?" she asked after setting aside at least the fifth fry pan. There was quite an assortment of cast-iron fry pans, pots, Dutch ovens of all sizes, as well as some other random pieces, some of which she couldn't even identify.

"One more thing." His voice sounded muffled as he was speaking into the back of the shelf. "I almost missed it. It's far back and dark as pitch back there." After several minutes, he managed to wrestle it to the front. "There's no way you can hold this. I'm not even sure I can get it down other than by pushing it off the shelf and letting it land on the floor. I think it's an old-fashioned kettle or cauldron that you hang over a campfire and cook crab or shrimp. Or maybe gumbo. I wonder how Charlie got it up here?"

"Maybe you should just leave it."

"It might bring some good money on eBay. Let me think about it. I'll figure out some way to get it down. Hand me that flashlight and let me make sure I've gotten everything else."

Della did as he asked, waiting impatiently for him to finish. "Well, is that it?"

"Not quite. There was something beneath the cauldron."

"You're not supposed to stand on that top step."

"I know. But I can't reach it if I don't."

"I'm not taking you to the hospital if you fall off," she warned him. But she held the ladder to steady it.

He emerged with a large, dirty old book in his hands. "What is that?" Della asked.

"It's a ledger," Nick said as he climbed down the ladder with it. "An old one by the looks of it."

"What was it doing up there?"

Nick opened it, and they stood side by side looking at it. It didn't make a lot of sense to her. "I don't understand. This is Charlie's handwriting, but—it isn't a ledger for the Last Shot. So what's it for?"

Nick flipped through a few more pages, then closed it. "You're not going to like this."

"Why? What do you think it is?"

"I think it's a ledger recording stolen goods and where they went. From about twenty years ago."

"Stolen goods? You can't mean—"

He nodded. "Afraid so. Charlie was a fence. At least, he was twenty years ago."

"ARE YOU SAYING Charlie was a criminal?" Della asked as she followed Nick from the room. "That he ran stolen goods?"

"Looks like. At least he did years ago." Could this ledger be the key to Charlie's murder? If so, why had it taken twenty years to track it down?

"I don't believe it. Couldn't this be a pawn shop ledger?"

Nick set the large, dusty volume on the kitchen table and opened it again. Leafing through it, the purpose became clearer. "He owned a pawn shop. But this ledger was for goods that didn't go through the shop. Mostly jewelry. High-end jewelry. And there's some kind of code beside each entry. That could indicate where he got the goods."

"You're asking me to believe Charlie was part of a ring that stole jewelry?" Her voice rose on the final word and she looked shell-shocked.

"More likely he fenced stolen jewels for anyone who brought them to him. You say he came from Houston?"

Dazed, Della simply nodded.

"Houston is one of the main fencing hubs in the U.S. Has been for decades."

She recovered a bit. "So?" she snapped. "That doesn't mean Charlie was a fence. That's like saying because Freedom's a fishing hub everyone here must fish."

"Not quite."

Della took it from him to look at more closely. Nick didn't say anything. This was something she'd clearly not expected and she needed time to process it. However unsure Della was, to Nick, this explained a lot.

After flipping through the book and muttering under her breath, she closed it. "Do you think this is what those men were looking for? Is this why they killed Charlie?"

"Could be. It's something to look into, anyway."

"You think someone could want it, even though it's from twenty years ago? Badly enough to kill someone?"

"Killing doesn't bother everyone, Della," he said, thinking of Crazy Larry. "Some of them get off on it." He shook off those thoughts. "The statute of limitations would have run out on these thefts, but if someone died during the commission of any of these robberies, then the case would remain open. If Charlie was a fence, and if this ledger incriminates suspects in a murder, then yes, someone would absolutely kill to keep it out of the police's hands."

"Are you going to tell Hayes about the ledger?"

Nick hesitated. He didn't trust Hayes to do anything different from what he'd been doing. Which was a big fat nothing. "Not until I have to. At this point, all we have is an old ledger and some suspicions. I have a friend who's a Houston detective. I'd like him to see this and tell me what he thinks. There could be something more current going on that's tied to Charlie's past."

"I'm having a hard time taking this in."

"This is our best lead to finding out who had Charlie murdered and why. In fact, it's the only substantial lead so far."

Della frowned, concentrating. "Before they shot him, they asked him about someone. I can't remember the name. But I remember Charlie said he knew him twenty years ago."

"Leon Rivers," Nick said.

"You remember that?"

Nick shrugged. "I'm a cop. I pay attention to details. I'll have Travis see what he can find out about this Leon Rivers when he's looking into the ledger."

"Travis?"

"Travis Taylor. My friend in the Houston PD."

"So you have to take it to him?"

"I'll ask him to come to me." It probably wouldn't be as quick, since he'd have to wait until Travis had time off, but Nick wasn't about to leave Della alone right now. Too many things had been happening. There was no guarantee that a situation that began with murder and included vandalism wouldn't include further violence. He wouldn't leave Della alone to test the theory.

"You think something else is going to happen. That's why you won't go to him."

"I think it's damn sure a possibility."

A FEW DAYS LATER, Nick's friend still hadn't showed up. Della had better things to do than wonder what the man would find out from the old ledger or any of his other investigations. Having decided not to close the Last Shot, she threw herself into planning how to update it. She wanted to make it more appealing to the transient fishing crowd as well as the full-time residents. And she needed to do it as economically as possible—which meant doing everything she possibly could herself.

It also meant she needed Nick's help as much for fixing the bar as she did to find out who killed Charlie. He still hadn't said anything about going back to Dallas, and she was afraid to bring it up.

Those are the only reasons you don't want him to leave, right, Della? Not because she kept thinking about what it was like to kiss him. Not because she was thinking more and more about what sex would be like with him. Would it be fun? Exciting? Or would she feel nothing?

As for the ledger, and the possibility that Charlie had been a criminal once, she had a hard time believing it. But if she thought about it logically, and not emotionally, what did she really know about Charlie's life before she met him? Even if he had been a fence in his younger years, Charlie had been straight as an arrow when she knew him. Besides, she had no room to judge, given her own past. She resolved to put it out of her mind until and unless Nick's friend had more to tell them.

Della went looking for Nick and found him out on the back porch, talking to someone on his cell phone. She heard him say Travis, so she knew his cop friend was on the line. Anxious to know what the other man had found out about Charlie, she stood behind the screen door and listened.

"Sounds like a bitch of a case," Nick said. "No. Just get to it when you can, Travis." He frowned and paced a few steps. "I've thought about it. But I think Houston is more likely to have the information I need. Besides that, Brad's caught up in another homicide. I haven't talked to him recently. Actually, since I left, I haven't talked to anyone in Dallas."

Damn, she thought. That didn't sound promising from her perspective. From Nick's comment, she couldn't be sure when his friend would come pick up Charlie's ledger.

Della could see Nick clearly through the screen door, but with the sun at an angle, he wouldn't know she was there. She started to open the door and say something when his body language changed. His whole demeanor went from relaxed to reverberating with tension in the space of a heartbeat.

Then, "Goddamn it, what happened? You wouldn't have brought it up if you didn't think I should know."

He paced the deck in long strides while he talked. "I haven't looked at the Internet or read a paper since I came down here," he said harshly. "What happened?" He listened intently for a few moments, then closed his eyes.

Della had heard the term "his face drained of color" but

she'd never actually seen it until just now. Nick went sheet white. It was spooky. Disturbing.

"She killed herself," he said flatly. "No, not surprised. Sick, but not surprised. She was fragile from the first. She wasn't dealing well last time I saw her." He laughed harshly, without humor. "Not that anyone could." Gripping the cell phone tightly, he said, "If the bastard wasn't already dead, I'd shoot him again."

He sat in one of the chairs—almost staggered into it. What in the hell had he heard? Whatever it was, it had nothing to do with Charlie. No, this was something connected to whatever haunted Nick. What she saw in his eyes sometimes. Desolation. Quickly masked, but there.

"Don't beat yourself up, Travis. I needed to know. I'd rather hear it from you than read it somewhere. It's not like I can get the fucking case out of my mind, anyway."

He listened again, then nodded. "Right. Good luck. Yeah, I'll talk with you later." He hung up and carefully set his phone on the table, then buried his head in his hands. She heard him mutter, "God damn it."

Della didn't think, she just reacted. She pushed open the door, walked over to Nick and put a hand on his shoulder, not saying anything but offering silent support.

Nick stiffened, then looked up at her, his eyes deep, brilliant blue and glistening with moisture. He was crying, she realized, shocked out of her mind. Tough cop Nick Sheridan was crying. Then he turned into her, his arms going around her and his head nestled just beneath her breasts.

A wave of tenderness swamped her, something she'd only experienced with her daughter. "What happened?" She looked down at the dark head resting against her and couldn't help but place a gentle hand on it. His hair was so soft, like silk against her fingers.

He was quiet for a long time, just holding her. It wasn't sexual at all. She felt like she was his lifeline and he was drawing strength from her. Not even Allie had ever made her feel that way.

Finally, he said, "My last case. The victim's mother killed herself. Yesterday." He let go of her and pushed himself away. "Sorry. I—" He rubbed his hands over his face, dropped them. "Shit."

"Who was the victim?" she asked quietly.

His eyes had gone bleak. So bleak, so empty. "Her name was Angelina."

"What happened?" she repeated.

"She died. She was murdered."

"I got that. But that's not all there is to it, is it?"

He collected himself, shook it off. Gone was the devastated, grieving man, back in place was the hard-nosed detective that nothing bothered. "You don't need to know the rest of it."

"I've seen bad, Nick." Bad and worse. "You can talk to me."

"No," he said, his tone daring her to argue. "No, you haven't seen this. I'm not going to put this picture in your head. I wish to God I could get it out of mine."

He was a homicide detective. How horrific had this case been that Nick couldn't deal with it? "This is why you left Dallas. Why you're taking a leave of absence."

"Yeah. This is why."

A thought occurred to her. "Is this case the reason you didn't want to get involved with Charlie's murder?" He shook his head, but she didn't believe him. "It is. They're similar. Charlie's case and that awful one you can't even talk about."

"God, no. They're nothing alike."

She didn't know why, but she believed him.

"Look, I don't want to talk about this anymore."

Della understood that. She understood it totally. "All right. But if you ever want to talk about it, you can."

"Thanks. I won't."

And that, so it seemed, was that. "What did your friend say about Charlie's ledger?"

"Nothing. He's in the middle of a bitch of a homicide case. He said he'd come get it as soon as he can. For now, when he has a minute, he'll check into Charlie's past and whether that has any bearing on his murder. He'll look into recent jewelry heists too, since Charlie fenced jewelry."

"You think he did. I'm not convinced."

"The ledger tracks thefts and tallies the subsequent sales of the jewelry. You can't ask for much clearer indication."

Della glared at him but couldn't come up with a decent argument.

Nick gave her a sympathetic look, but he only said, "Travis won't be doing anything but busting his ass over his current case for a while. So we're on our own. At least for now."

"What about asking the Dallas cops? The ones in your department."

He looked at her sharply. "You were listening to my conversation with Travis."

"A little," she admitted. "And don't even think about blasting me for it. You did the same thing to me."

"My partner is caught up in a case and there's no one else there I want to talk to."

"You could call another Dallas police department, couldn't you?"

"Why are you so gung-ho for me to talk to cops?"

"Why are you so determined not to?"

"It's a long story. One which I have no interest in discussing. So drop it."

"You're awfully touchy."

"So are you."

"True enough. Okay, I'll drop it." But that didn't mean she wouldn't wonder.

A little while later, Mary Lou came by and Della told her about the cast-iron pots and pans. Her friend promised to research them to get an idea of their worth. Della also told Mary Lou that Nick agreed to help investigate Charlie's murder. Finally, she told her about the ledger and what Nick thought it might mean.

"No way. Charlie wasn't a criminal," Mary Lou said.

"Not since we've known him, but what about before? Did he ever talk to you about his past?"

Mary Lou shook her head. "I always got the idea something bad happened and . . ." Her voice trailed off. "But Charlie, a fence for jewelry? How could it be true?"

"I don't know. I don't want to believe it either, Mary Lou, but I saw the ledger and I'm afraid Nick's right."

"Even if it's true, Charlie was a good man. Nothing will make me think otherwise." Shortly afterward, she left.

Della worked until late, with Nick helping her sort the cookware and taking pictures of each piece on his phone so Mary Lou could put them on eBay.

Her phone rang just as she was getting ready to leave for home. "Hey, Mary Lou. What—" Before she could get another word out Mary Lou began talking.

"Della, can you come home? Right now." The usually unflappable Mary Lou sounded scared and almost hysterical.

"What happened? Is Allie all right? Are you?"

"Allie's fine. Just get home. Please, Della."

"What in the hell happened?"

"The house was broken into. It's . . . Oh, God, Della, it's awful."

"I'm on my way."

CHAPTER THIRTEEN

KINGSTON KNIGHT was pissed. Not only had his search of Della Rose's residence turned up nothing, but King had fucked up. The babysitter and the kid had showed up just as he was leaving. He thought he'd picked a time when he wouldn't be interrupted, but they'd come back sooner than he'd expected. His face and hands had been completely covered so he wasn't too concerned about being recognized. But the babysitter had been standing stock-still in the middle of the doorway, so he'd had to push her out of the way. He couldn't be sure, but he thought she'd fallen down as a result.

King didn't hold with hurting women, children, or animals. Men didn't bother him. He figured they could hold their own, and besides, most of the men he arrested were lowlifes anyway. He'd had trouble arresting women in Houston, especially the crazy ones who were on drugs or just plain nuts. Even so, he didn't believe in hurting a woman unless he absolutely had to.

The jewels could still be somewhere in the Last Shot, but

there was a very real possibility that Della had found them and taken them home. If so, they would still be there, since a million dollar bracelet wouldn't be easy to fence. Someone had to search the residence, and Hayes sure as hell couldn't do it. The chief's shape made him completely recognizable no matter how he tried to disguise himself. So the job fell to King.

When he'd found nothing to lead him to the jewels, he had taken a few things he could carry off in a backpack. The laptop, a video game system, some trinkets from each room. Not that any of them had anything much in the way of jewelry or electronics either. He'd wanted to imply that this break-in had been unconnected to anything concerning the Last Shot, and to do that, something had to be stolen. Even though it was unlikely the two occurrences wouldn't be connected, at least the burglary made it a possibility.

The nine-one-one call had come in while he was changing back into his uniform. Easy enough to pick up his cruiser and head over there to make sure he hadn't left any obvious clues as to who had broken in.

The babysitter, Mary Lou Meadows, was sitting outside beneath the light on the front porch, holding an ice pack to one side of her face when he arrived. The kid was seated next to her, unharmed. The ugly little dog sat on the girl's lap. He'd made friends with the dog, opening the laundry room door, and giving it a treat before he shut it back in the laundry room.

He schooled his features to solemn compassion instead of the irritation he felt at things not going as planned. He'd met Mary Lou briefly before, but hadn't really noticed her since he'd been more focused on her boss. According to Hayes, Sheridan and Della were involved, and since there had been definite vibes between the two both times he'd seen them together, he suspected that was true. It made no difference to him who he got cozy with, Mary Lou or her employer. One or both of them might have some useful information. Whether either woman could lead him to what he wanted, who knew?

King felt more than a twinge of guilt when he saw Mary Lou. She must have tripped, fallen, and landed partially on her face. Even with the incipient bruise, she was pretty. Not flashy, but subdued. Blond hair pulled back in a ponytail, a shapeless T-shirt and shorts showing nice-looking legs, with blood trickling from a scrape on one knee. King usually went for the more flamboyant type, but if he needed to get close to the woman, at least she was decent-looking.

"Ms. Meadows? I'm Officer Knight." He offered his hand as she looked up, clearly startled.

She took his hand, lifting her eyes to his and said in a soft voice, "Call me Mary Lou. And this is Allie," she said, giving a nod to the kid.

Holy shit, the woman has the foxiest eyes I've ever seen. Cat eyes. Emerald green, sparkling like the stones in a priceless bracelet. One with a honking big emerald and a lot of ice. Getting close to Mary Lou wouldn't be a hardship at all.

"Do you need a paramedic? Dispatch called them. They should be here any moment." Possibly any moment, he amended silently. He finally let go of her hand, satisfied to see the flush creeping up her neck.

"No, don't bother. I'm okay. I've had worse," she said.

"When, Mary Lou?" the kid asked. "You never said anything."

Consternation flooded her eyes, making them even more brilliant. Damn, how had he not noticed her before now?

"It was a long time ago," Mary Lou said. "A—a car accident."

King caught the hesitation, but he didn't think the girl had. "Do you mind if I sit?"

"Oh, sure." She scooted over on the step to make room for him.

"Can you tell me what happened here?"

"Allie and I—Allie is Della's daughter," she said, interrupting herself. "We came home a little while ago, and I had just opened the back door when someone—the burglar—came through and shoved me out of the way."

"Sophia was barking," Allie put in. "But Mary Lou wouldn't let me go in to see about her." She sounded annoyed.

Mary Lou gave her a stern look. "For all we knew, the robbers were still in there."

"They weren't, though. Sophia was in the laundry room, and I was worried about her."

"Sophia is fine, Allie." From Mary Lou's weary tone, King suspected this wasn't the first time Allie had brought that up.

Allie hugged the dog. "Mary Lou fell down and hit her head. She's bleeding. I think she needs a doctor."

Again, Mary Lou waved the suggestion aside. "Scrapes and bruises," she said. "It's not a big deal."

"I think Allie's right and you need to see a doctor, or at least let the paramedics check you out when they get here."

"Oh, all right. Anything to make you two stop nagging."

"Did you see anything suspicious outside? Did he get in a car or truck?"

"He was on foot. I think. I didn't see a car. Did you, Allie?"

"Nuh-uh. He ran off that way." She pointed north.

"No, it was that way," Mary Lou corrected her, pointing south.

King breathed another sigh of relief. These two would be typical witnesses, meaning they didn't notice a lot, and what they did, was likely to be wrong. "What did the intruder look like?" he asked. "Can either of you give a description?"

Both of them started talking at once. They disagreed on almost everything. Both said he'd been covered in black, head to toe. Other than that, everything one said was contradicted by the other one. Which was a good thing for him. Not that it really mattered, since he was the one in charge of the investigation.

By the time King had taken their statements, the paramedics had arrived. So had Della and Detective Sheridan. Interesting that Della had left the bar unguarded, but not totally unexpected. Too bad he was tied up here and couldn't get over there to look around some more.

Della was busy hugging the kid while Sheridan scanned the house. King hoped Sheridan wouldn't be a problem, but King had a bad feeling he would be. The Dallas cop was a homicide detective. It wouldn't be long before Sheridan started nosing around. And the detective wasn't stupid. Not at all.

Chief Hayes came off as a dumbass, but he worked at it. King had reason to know the chief was anything but as dense as he appeared. Crafty and calculating was a much better description. And as hard-assed as they came.

As he'd expected, here came Sheridan. After they exchanged greetings, Sheridan got right to the point. "Were you able to get a description of the suspects?"

"Not much of one. They both described the clothing, but other than that, they didn't agree on the description."

"Damn. Neighbors see anything?"

"I've got another officer talking to them, but so far nothing." He paused and added, "Don't expect something to happen quickly on this. We're a small force without a lot of resources."

"I take it that means you won't be running extra patrols here."

"I can try, but the Chief has to okay it." King left it at that, but Sheridan's expression told him he knew the chances of that. As with the stupidity, Hayes took pains to seem lazy. But he was only lazy when it suited him.

"Charlie's murder, the break-in and vandalism at the Last Shot, and now a break-in here. Whoever is behind this is still looking for something," Sheridan said.

It wouldn't hurt to admit it. Anyone but an idiot would know. "It appears that way. Although it's still a possibility that the break-in at the house is a coincidence."

Sheridan shot him a cynical look. "Do you really believe that?"

"No, but I suspect Chief Hayes will have to be convinced. I'll dust for prints now. I suggest you take all three of them back to the Last Shot." Which would be ideal, leaving him time to look through things more thoroughly.

Sheridan shook his head. "Della won't go for that. She's already trying to get into the house to see the damage."

"It's going to take a while. I'm the only one who can dust for prints. Other than the Chief."

Sheridan grimaced and went off to talk to Della.

As he entered the house, King passed Mary Lou, arguing with the paramedic, who wanted to take her to the hospital. King had gotten a better look at her face when the paramedics began to treat her. She looked like someone had really whaled on her. He felt like a shit, even though he hadn't hurt her purposely.

King didn't call in the Crime Scene Investigators since they only came out for major crimes. A home invasion with no injuries didn't rate that. Their small police force handled most problems themselves. Before Charlie and Leon, Freedom had only had one murder in its history, and that had taken place in the late nineteen-fifties.

Now there'd been three. And his own chief had committed one of them. King wasn't happy about that, but there was no way to take down the chief without going down in flames himself. Not to mention, he wanted the money. A million dollar emerald and diamond bracelet was too tempting to give up.

A conscience was a damned inconvenient thing to have.

"HOW ARE YOU holding up?" Nick asked Allie. He sat down beside her on the back step. "You've been awfully brave." Most kids would still be freaking out. Allie hadn't, though she'd cried. But the face she turned to him was angry rather than sad.

"I should have kicked him where it hurts."

Nick was careful not to laugh. "I didn't realize you had the chance."

She shrugged. "Still. I could have tripped him or something. He ran right by me after he shoved Mary Lou."

"Mary Lou is all right. You were better off doing what you did and staying out of it. Besides, you might have made him angry enough to turn around and come back. He could have hurt Mary Lou worse. Or you."

"I guess. But I should've done something. Mom and me and Mary Lou took a self-defense course. They taught us all sorts of ways to hurt the bad guy and to get away. What's the point of that if I didn't even think about it when something happened?" she asked with disgust.

Interesting. Though not surprising, really. Della wasn't one to close her eyes to the bad things that could happen. She'd want her daughter and friend to be able to protect themselves. "Didn't a lot of what they taught you involve someone grabbing you?"

"Yeah."

"No one grabbed you," he pointed out. "I'm sure you'd have remembered if you needed to."

"Do you think so?" She sounded hopeful.

"I do. Do you practice?"

She nodded. "Mom and me and Mary Lou all practice. Mom says better to be safe than sorry." Her face fell. "But neither me or Mary Lou did anything this time." She stood up and began illustrating some of the moves. "You jam your elbow up into his chin, like this. And if he's facing you, you gouge out his eyes. And if you have keys in your hand you use those to poke in his eyes or hit him." Sounding pleased with that grisly description, she showed him those and several other moves. "But they said the most important thing to remember was to yell for help. And when you do, you don't yell help."

"What do you yell?"

"Fire. That was the name of the course. 'Yell Fire'. You're supposed to stomp hard on the bad guy's foot and yell fire, to startle him. He should loosen his grip, and then you run away as fast as you can. Even if he has a gun," she added. "The teacher said it's harder to hit a moving target."

"Sounds like a good course."

"I guess. But next time I'm gonna remember what to do."

"Let's hope there's not a next time," Nick said.

"WHAT DID HE SAY?" Della asked Nick as soon as he came back from talking to Knight. "When can we go in?"

"He's dusting for fingerprints now and said we can go in as soon as he's finished."

"What about the—" she hesitated, not sure what to call him, since he was clearly no ordinary burglar. "What about the man who broke in? Does Knight know anything about him?"

Nick glanced at Allie and pulled Della a short distance away. "Nothing useful."

"Allie and Mary Lou didn't give descriptions?"

"Oh, they gave them. But their descriptions were miles apart."

"Damn it," Della said. "Then that's no help. What about the neighbors? They didn't see anything either?"

"Not so far. Don't pin your hopes on witnesses, Della. Even when they see something, it might bear no relation to what the person really looks like or what really happened."

Officer Knight let them in some time later. "Did you get any good prints?" Della asked him.

Knight shook his head. "Almost every print was smudged, and if the burglar wore gloves, which is likely, then we wouldn't find anything from him. But we might get lucky."

After a quick inspection, the only things obviously missing besides a few trinkets were Mary Lou's laptop and Allie's video game console. The intruder had tossed Della's room thoroughly, although there was nothing of value in there. But damn, why did the bastard have to take the video game player? Charlie had given it to Allie for Christmas a couple of years before. He'd known how badly Allie had wanted it and that Della couldn't afford it. *Don't think about*

Charlie. If she did, she'd lose it and she couldn't allow herself to do that.

"What about my computer?" Mary Lou asked Officer Knight, an edge of hysteria to her voice. "I keep the books for several businesses. And even though I have the data backed up, any decent hacker can get past my firewalls. Even if they don't, my clients will have to change all their account numbers. What if they fire me? What if the thief gets hold of their information and steals them blind before I can warn them?"

"You can call them tonight. They should be able to reach their credit card companies immediately, and their banks first thing in the morning," Knight said. He patted Mary Lou on the back and added, "I might be able to locate the laptop at one of the local pawn shops."

Nick looked unconvinced but he didn't contradict him.

Della brought up what had been on her mind since the moment she heard the house had been broken into. "Chief Hayes will have to admit now that everything—Charlie's murder, the Last Shot being vandalized and now this—is connected."

Knight frowned. "He . . . might."

"Might? Are you kidding me? These people are looking for something and they obviously think I have it. Whatever the hell it is."

"Assuming you're right," Knight began, "do you have any idea what they're looking for?"

"Not a clue." She didn't want to tell him about the ledger. Or about Detective Taylor—Nick's cop friend who was going to look into it. She didn't hate Knight like she did the chief, but she didn't trust him either. Of course, Nick was the only cop she'd managed to trust even a small amount, so that was no surprise.

Della wondered if she trusted Nick because he'd saved her life or because she . . . Well, shit. She couldn't delude herself any longer. She had the hots for him.

Focus, she told herself. And not on Nick Sheridan.

She looked at Mary Lou and Knight. Speaking of focus, they'd moved out of earshot and seemed totally fascinated with each other. *Oh, damn. Mary Lou is hanging on his words like they're diamond drops. I hope to hell she doesn't fall for this guy.*

Although Mary Lou had been burned very badly by her ex, she was still susceptible to a good-looking man. Even Della admitted Knight was a damn fine looking man. And she remembered her friend had shown interest in the cop recently.

Allie's room had been spared major upset, and Della convinced her to go to bed. Sophia tagged along, and Della didn't have the heart to make her sleep in the laundry room. She hadn't been able to enforce that rule very well, anyway.

"I'm going to my room," Mary Lou said, walking through the living room with a plastic bag full of ice.

"You should get some sleep," Della said. "How's your face?"

Mary Lou shrugged. "It hurts, but I'll live."

"Are you sure you don't need to go to the ER?"

"Nothing's broken. I'm not going to the hospital for bruises. Stop fussing, Della. I'm fine."

Knowing that when Mary Lou made up her mind, Della couldn't change it with a crowbar, she let her go without further argument.

Now she had to face her bedroom. After a brief glance earlier, she'd put off dealing with it. She sucked in a breath and pushed open the door. The "burglar" had been more thorough here than anywhere else in the house. Drawers were pulled out, her things rifled through, the sheets and blanket on the bed had been stripped and tossed on the floor, and the mattress itself had been moved.

"Shit." It was all she could think of to say.

Nick, who was right behind her, put his hand on her shoulder. "Steady. It's not as bad as it looks."

Della shot him a disbelieving glance. "Yes, it is." She looked back at the mess and shook her head. "You don't need to come in here. I can handle it by myself."

"You can," he said, "but there's no reason you have to."

She didn't have it in her to argue. The damn "burglar" had pulled out every drawer and scattered the contents everywhere. He'd rifled through her closet. Her business papers, which were kept in a couple of cheap accordion files, were scattered over the closet floor. Della and Nick worked silently for a while, putting clothes and other things back in the drawers and the drawers back where they belonged. Her stomach hurt. She felt sick, thinking of a stranger's hands touching all of her stuff. Even her underwear had been pawed through. Sitting down heavily on the bed, she put her head in her hands and took in deep breaths, garnering her strength to deal with this latest blow.

She felt the mattress give beside her. "I'm sorry," Nick said.

"Me too."

He put his arm around her and gave her a comforting hug. She wanted to turn into him, as he'd done with her earlier, take solace from him and hide from yet another body blow. But she wouldn't. She knew better than to count on anyone but herself. Instead of moving toward him, she turned away, shrugging off his arm. "I'm okay."

"You don't have to be strong every minute, Della."

"Yes. I do." Being strong, walling off those feelings of help-lessness, rejecting the role of victim, that was how she coped. If she didn't, if she allowed herself to feel despair, to really feel it, she would break. Once she broke, she didn't think she could put herself back together.

CHAPTER FOURTEEN

OVER THE COURSE of his career, Nick had dealt with countless victims. Everything from homicide to petty theft. Many of those people hadn't liked or trusted cops and resented having to deal with them. Some had wanted police help, some hadn't. But he'd never seen a person as determined as Della to take it all on her shoulders and not accept help from anyone.

Damn it, he wanted to help her. He wanted her to let him in. To trust him. Maybe she did, at least a little. She'd asked him to come with her after Mary Lou's call. And she'd stopped totally flipping out every time he was around Allie. Progress, of sorts.

Della had returned to the closet, but instead of straightening up, she stood in the doorway, clutching the doorjamb with a white-knuckled grip. "I need a break."

"You need sleep."

"That too," she agreed. "Do you think he'll be back?"

That was the crux of it. And what could he say but yes? Still, he temporized. "No one has been back to the Last Shot."

"You've been there 24/7. If these people are in town, they'd have heard you're a cop and you're armed," she pointed out. "Do you think this burglar will come back to my house?"

"Yes," he said reluctantly. "At least, I think there's a good chance someone will. Which means you need protection both here and at the Last Shot. And I can't be two places at once. You need me at the bar to help you with labor." He decided to feel Della out about another possibility. "I could look for someone else to watch the house. There are bound to be security companies around here. Or a retired cop. They like this sort of gig."

She stared at him as if he'd lost his mind. "Are you crazy? Let some strange man I don't even know—a cop—stay in my house? With Allie and Mary Lou here? Absolutely not."

He sighed, having expected that reaction. "Are you ever going to tell me why you hate cops so much?"

"No." She added, the words dragged out of her, "It's not a pretty story."

"I've seen bad, Della. I've seen beyond bad," he said, remembering the candlelight, the music, the blood.

"You're thinking about it now, aren't you? Your last case."

He shrugged in answer.

"You won't talk to me about that. Why should I talk to you?" she asked.

"I have a damn good reason not to share. I don't want to give you nightmares."

"Do you think I don't have them already?"

Not like his. Bad as they obviously were, she had no concept of the nightmares he was fleeing. "This is pointless. We've gotten off on a tangent. The security we hire won't be in the house. They'll be outside."

"Not a chance in hell," she interrupted.

"What about tonight? Are you going to take me back to the Last Shot?"

She seemed surprised. "I hadn't . . . thought about it."

"Do you really think I'll leave you alone here after a break-in?"

"No," she said, taking in his expression. "But at least I know you."

"Yeah, but do you trust me?" Why had he asked that? He knew the answer.

"That's not the point. Obviously, I must trust you or you wouldn't be here. But surveillance is out. For one thing, 24/7 surveillance would cost way too much. You know it will."

He couldn't deny that. "I could help—"

She interrupted. "Do not dare offer to pay for it. I'm not comfortable with people spying on me. Can't we leave it at that?"

She must be hiding a hell of a story, he thought. But he didn't push. "All right. Then I think the best course is to install an alarm system at both places. Your house and the bar are five minutes apart, at most. I could be at either place depending on where you need me."

"Those cost too much. There's some monitoring fee, isn't there? Not to mention what the system costs."

"There are do-it-yourself systems. No monthly fee. We'll get ones with cameras and alarms that feed either way."

"How much are we talking for each alarm?"

"Consider this an investment. It will be cheap compared to hiring surveillance. I'll go over to Bay City tomorrow and pick up a couple," he said, naming a nearby larger town. "It shouldn't take long." She still looked undecided. "It wouldn't hurt to have an alarm system in place, whatever happens."

"Who is going to look at the camera feeds?"

"There will be two stations, one at the bar and one at your house. You'll be able to monitor both."

"And so will you."

"Yeah, isn't that the point? Didn't you hire me in the first place to be a night watchman?"

"I don't want cameras inside the house. Especially not the bedrooms."

He stared at her. What the hell did she think he was? "Good God, Della, I'm not a pervert. The cameras are to record intruders, not to spy on you and your family in your underwear, for God's sake."

"Sorry. I'm a little . . ." Her voice trailed off and she shrugged.

"Paranoid? Insulting?"

"I'm not paranoid. And I didn't mean to insult you."

"Really? You just accused me of getting off by spying on you."

"I said I was sorry."

She sure as hell didn't look sorry. "What happened to you as a kid, Della?"

"Nothing I'm ever going to talk about."

As she'd pointed out, he didn't want to discuss his issues either. "Your choice. I'll sleep on the couch. But I don't think he'll be back tonight. Too much activity."

"I'll get you a pillow," she said.

"Mom?" Allie stood in the doorway wearing a T-shirt and pajama pants, looking much younger than her years. "Can I sleep with you?"

Della's demeanor softened. "Of course you can."

"Okay. Is Nick gonna stay here?"

"For tonight."

"Good." She walked into Della's bedroom, pillow in hand.

"That's convenient," Nick said when Della shut the door behind Allie. "Now you don't have to worry about me breaking into Allie's room tonight."

He should have kept his goddamn mouth shut. Her expression, stricken at first, changed to anger. "I won't apologize for being a decent mother. Don't you ever try to make me feel bad for protecting my daughter."

Nick wanted to kick his own ass for his thoughtless words. He might not know exactly what had happened to Della, but he knew enough to wish he could cut out his tongue. "You're absolutely right. I'm sorry. I didn't mean that. I'm an ass."

"You got that right," she said, turned her back, and left him.

IN THE MORNING, Nick tried to think of a way to apologize for being such a jerk the night before. Since he had no clue how to do that, he opted for honesty. After Allie had left for school and Mary Lou had disappeared into her room, he approached Della.

"Can we talk about last night?"

"No."

He plowed ahead regardless. "I was way out of line. I wasn't thinking."

"You keep saying you know bad, but I'm not sure you do. Otherwise, you'd know better than to say what you did to me."

"Yeah, and I do. Normally. But—" he grimaced, searching for the right words. "It really bothers me that you don't trust me. I don't want you to feel that way. That's not an excuse, it's the truth."

"Why does it matter to you whether I trust you or not?"

"Because of this." He took her face in his hands and kissed her. He felt her surprise, then her lips softened and she kissed him back. After a long, intense moment, he pulled away and added, "I really like you, Della. Damned if I know why, but I do."

"If I tell you something, will you promise not to overreact?"

"Okay."

"Damned if I know why, but I like you too."

The only answer to that was to kiss her again. She went back into his arms willingly, her body snug up against his. He swept her mouth with his tongue and she returned it, their tongues tangling. He wanted to lay her on the closest surface, strip off her clothes and feast on that curvy body. Wanted to—

"Della, what are you—" Mary Lou broke off as they both came up for air. "Sorry. I didn't realize . . . I didn't mean to interrupt."

"You're not," Della said, moving away from him.

"Yes, she is," Nick said.

Della gave him the evil eye. "What did you need, Mary Lou?"

"Have you made your list of what's missing yet?"

"Yes, I made it last night. There wasn't that much to steal."

"Except my computer and the video game console," Mary Lou said. "I thought I'd take our list down to the police station."

"Good luck with that. Hayes couldn't find his butt with a map."

"King can. He said he'd find my laptop, and I believe him."

"King?" Della asked. "You mean Officer Knight?"

"Yes, he asked me to call him King. He was so great last

night. He even said he'd try to send extra patrols by the house."

Uh-oh, Nick thought. Looked like Mary Lou was falling for Knight. If she hadn't already, he suspected she would be soon. Something told him Della wasn't pleased. Maybe the fact she was biting her lip to keep from talking.

"Why are you looking like that?" Mary Lou asked Della. "You don't like him, do you?"

"I didn't say that," Della protested.

"But you thought it. I thought you'd gotten over your aversion to cops," she said, looking from Della to Nick. "I guess that only goes for one cop."

Nick interrupted before Della lost her temper and said something she'd regret. "Why don't you come with me to Bay City, Della?"

She gave her friend an irritated look before she turned to him. "Come with you? Why?" Before he could speak, she continued. "You want to take my car. My car that you called a piece of crap last time you were in it."

"That was the drugs talking." Not to mention, the truth. "But no, we'll go on my bike."

"Your motorcycle?"

"Sure. Have you ever ridden a motorcycle before?"

"No."

"You'll like it. Motorcycles are fun."

"Leave Mary Lou alone here?"

"I'll be fine," Mary Lou said. "Don't make me your excuse." She left the room before Della could respond.

Della scanned his face and asked, "Why do you want me to go with you?"

"It'll give you a break. You need to have a little fun after all the crappy things that have happened to you lately."

She didn't answer, which he took for assent. "We'll stop by the Last Shot on our way out of town."

DELLA HAD MADE a big mistake going with Nick to get the alarms. Since she knew nothing about motorcycles, she hadn't considered what it would entail. He'd given her a helmet, gotten on that monster thing he called a bike, and told her to get on behind him.

She tried to get comfortable but kept sliding on the seat until she was smack up against him. "What am I supposed to hold on to?"

He laughed and turned his head to look at her. With sunglasses and a motorcycle helmet, she couldn't see much of his face. And nothing of his eyes, but she knew damn well they were laughing too. "Me, what else?" He flipped down her visor. Then he turned on the bike. It rumbled, it roared, it sounded like a living thing.

She rode all the way over to Bay City and back, her front smashed up against his back, her arms wrapped around his waist, and that monster machine rumbling between her legs.

Oh, my God, she had a blast. Nick was right, riding a motorcycle was fun. Holding on to him, however, was disturbing, though not in a bad way. It made her twitchy, being so close to him, feeling the muscles beneath his clothes, smelling the hint of his aftershave. Wait a minute. Surreptitiously, she sniffed his neck. Baby powder. He smelled like baby powder.

Only one argument marred the day, and it took place at the hardware store.

Della sighed regretfully. "I can't afford these two systems."

"Can you afford to have your home or business broken into again?" Nick asked.

"Why can't I get the cheaper one?"

"Because it's basically useless. This one is the best bang for your buck."

Della rolled her eyes. "That doesn't make them affordable."

He gazed at her for a long moment. "Okay," he finally said. But he didn't put them back. Instead, he started carrying them to the front of the store.

Della grabbed his arm to stop him. "I thought you understood what I just said."

"I did. So I'm buying them. You can pay me back. Or not."

"No. Absolutely not. I don't want you to buy them."

Ignoring her, he started toward the front again.

"Nick, I don't want you to buy them. Are you deaf?"

He stopped again. "Not your call. Damn, Della, you'd argue with a stone."

"I would not. I'm being perfectly—"

"Hold this," he interrupted. He put the basket, overflowing with gadgets, in her hands.

"What are you do—" Della broke off because Nick took her face in his hands and kissed her. "You—" He kissed her again, longer this time. Oh, man, she really shouldn't have ridden on that damn bike with him.

"Are you finished?" he asked.

Della nodded.

"This is for your safety and that of your family. As a friend, I'm helping you out. So deal with it and come on." He took the basket from her and walked off.

She shut her mouth and followed him. But if he thought they were finished with this discussion, he had another think coming.

DELLA SAT AT HER kitchen table waiting for Nick to finish putting in the alarm system at the house. After which they were going back to the Last Shot where he'd install the other system. Nick said he'd installed alarm systems before, so it wouldn't take him too long. She had not won the argument over him buying the alarms, though she'd tried everything she could think of. Finally, she gave up.

"Mom?"

"Hi, Allie. What's up?"

"Brooke asked me to spend the night tomorrow night."

Oh, God, not this argument again. "Why can't she spend the night with you?"

"Because she's having a slumber party. All my friends are going. Besides, all my friends think I'm weird because you won't ever let me spend the night with anyone."

"You know I'm not comfortable with that, Allie."

"You never told me the reason, you just say no. It's not fair."

Della started to say she didn't know Brooke's parents well enough, but that wasn't true and Allie knew it. She should let Allie go. She knew Brooke's mother fairly well and had met her husband several times. They seemed nice.

But appearances were deceiving sometimes. "I'm sorry, Allie."

"But why? Why can't I? I'm twelve, I'm not a baby."

That was part of the problem, but she couldn't tell Allie that. Maybe she should come clean to Allie. Yet every time Della thought about telling her sweet, innocent daughter anything about her past, she wanted to throw up.

"Maybe next time," Della said. And they both knew that was a big fat lie.

"Next time you'll say no too. You're ruining my life! I hate you!" She ran out into the back yard before Della could respond.

Della knew Allie didn't mean it when she said she hated Della. Lots of kids said that to their parents for flimsier reasons than this one. It still hurt and made her feel like a shit. She couldn't tell Allie why she had reservations, yet she couldn't bring herself to let her go either.

A little while later, Della was still sitting at the table wrestling with what to do about Allie. Hearing the door close, she looked up, hoping it was Allie, but Nick stood there. "Are you ready to go back to the Last Shot?" she asked him.

CHAPTER FIFTEEN

"NOT YET," HE SAID. He took a seat at the table, trying to think of a way to bring up Allie's problem without Della getting pissed and defensive. Della's parenting style was none of his business. But damn, when Allie had turned those tear-drenched blue eyes up to his and asked, "Will you talk to my Mom? She listens to you." What else could he do? Nick doubted he had much, if any, influence over Della, but he felt like he had to try.

"Nick? What is it?"

He opted for bluntness. "Why are you so determined to keep Allie from spending the night with a friend? She's twelve years old. What do you think's gonna happen?"

Immediately defensive, she snapped, "I know exactly how old my daughter is. And I don't need you butting in to my business."

"Apparently you do. Allie asked me to talk to you."

"What?"

She looked so shocked he'd have laughed if he hadn't felt sorry for the kid. "You heard me. She was sitting out in the backyard with her dog, crying her eyes out. I asked her what was wrong, and it all came spilling out."

"I'd think you'd have better things to do than run interference for a twelve-year-old. Something like, oh, I don't know, like finding out why Charlie was killed. As far as I can tell, you haven't done a damn thing since you talked to your friend. Was Detective Taylor really busy or did you just tell me that to pacify me?"

That pissed him off. His eyes narrowed and his mouth hardened into a thin line. Della was a pro at attacking and deflecting. She'd hit him where it hurt. Square on his guilt.

"I've looked on the Internet, using my phone, which sucks. I found some jewel heists that his murder might be related to, but Travis will be able to find out a lot more than I can. I can't learn anything about whether the case is active/inactive, who are/were the suspects, nothing, without Travis."

"You're a cop. Why can't you access the case files?"

Della was a civilian. How would she know how it worked? "I'm not a Houston cop. It's touchy talking to another department and saying, hey, you're doing a crappy job on this case and I need to look at it. I need Travis's help to look into it. Not to mention, I need him to help me figure out what case this is related to."

"The Internet doesn't help? Everyone always says you can find out anything on the Web."

"Maybe. If your specialty is computers. Mine isn't. Plus, the Internet via my phone is almost worthless. Cold case files, possibly from years ago, won't be online. Even if they were, I can't access them from just anywhere. And current cases have restricted access."

He ticked off the questions, none of which he could answer without access to police files. "Who were Charlie's known associates? Leon Rivers was one of them. Who else could have been connected? What has Rivers been suspected of recently? How do the two thugs who killed Charlie come into it? Were they working with Rivers? For Rivers? They had to be working for someone, or someone else knew what they were doing. Otherwise you wouldn't have had two break-ins. And the biggie, what the hell are they looking for?"

"You're full of questions, but you don't have any answers."

"I have a few. I know that Leon Rivers and Charlie were connected in the past. I know that the men who killed Charlie believed Leon and Charlie had been in touch with each other recently. And I know one other thing. Leon Rivers was killed in an abandoned warehouse in Freedom, down by the water-front. He was murdered the same night Charlie was."

"How did you find out that Leon Rivers was killed?"

"The local newspaper dated the day after the murder was in the hardware store. Charlie's murder was the main article, but there was also one about the dead man in the warehouse. And that was Leon Rivers."

"I don't see how that helps us much, if any."

"I could go to Houston myself and investigate more thoroughly, but I have no idea how long it will take to get the information I need. And I'd have to leave you alone here after your house has just been broken into, the bar vandalized, and your boss killed. So pardon the hell out of me if I don't feel comfortable leaving you on your own."

"You don't need to take care of me. I can take care of myself."

He sighed and glared at her. "You need help, and I'm going to give it to you. Why do you think I insisted on the alarm systems? Because I thought it was fun?"

"Because you're pig-headed. And you think you're always right."

He laughed, then sobered. "Unfortunately, Della, I'm usually right about homicide. This case started with murder. I don't want the next one to be you, or Allie, or Mary Lou." She paled and he felt bad for scaring her. But it needed to be said.

"God, no," she said. "I don't either. But why would there be another murder? They've searched the Last Shot and my house and found nothing. I don't know anything. I don't even know what they're looking for."

"It doesn't matter what you know. What matters is what they *think* you know."

"So what you're saying is I'm screwed no matter what."

"I'm saying I'm not leaving you alone for days at a time. And one other thing. We need to make sure we've searched everywhere there might be something hidden. Jewelry, cash, maybe drugs. It can't be too large, or why would the last guy who broke into your house bring only a backpack?"

"Maybe what they want isn't even here. Or it doesn't exist. Have you thought about that?"

"Yeah. It exists, Della. And there's a reason they think it's in your possession."

"So what, we sit around and do nothing until your buddy comes through?"

"We search again. And we continue putting the Last Shot back in order. I'd have an easier time looking on the Internet if I had a computer instead of just my cell phone."

"Mary Lou's computer was the only one I had access to, and I think it's long gone, no matter what Officer Knight says." She frowned and added, "I don't like how cozy he's getting with her."

"She seems to like him." Nick didn't. There was something off about Knight, even if Nick couldn't put his finger on it.

"I know. Even if I said something, she'd just blow me off. She'd put it down to my feelings about—" She broke off before finishing the sentence.

"Don't hold back on my account. Your feelings about cops are damned obvious."

She simply shrugged. After a moment, she changed the subject. "Why are you helping me?"

Why are you so suspicious? "Because you need help, and I don't want to see you hurt. Because Charlie deserves someone to find who killed him, and Hayes is sure as hell not going to put himself out."

"I really don't understand you sometimes."

"I'm a cop. It goes with the territory." He was still a cop. For a while, he'd worried about that, but now he knew. He would always be a cop. None of it, not the nightmares, the flashbacks, the endless questioning of his actions could change that.

"Since you won't talk about it, I don't know what you have against cops. But I can tell you that most of them are decent, hardworking people who really care. Some of them are no good, but there are losers in every profession. Cops are no different." Before she could respond and take them even further off track, he said, "Now that we've settled that, we need to get back to Allie." She glared at him. "Did you think I'd forgotten?"

"You've forgotten that Allie is none of your business."

"Allie made herself my business when she asked me to talk to you. She just wants to spend the night with a friend. It's a normal thing for kids to do."

"Normal or not, she can't go. I didn't have a normal childhood. Which I'd have thought you would know by now."

"I know you had a crappy childhood and you hate cops. But you haven't told me anything else."

"Why should I?"

Because he wanted her to trust him. Because he was falling for her. "Does Allie know it? Does she know anything about your childhood?"

"No, and she's not going to, either." Nick didn't say anything, he just looked at her. "What's wrong with wanting my daughter to be safe?"

"Nothing. Why do you think she won't be safe? Do you know the girl's parents?"

"Yes," she admitted grudgingly.

"Well?"

She shrugged and wouldn't answer, which he figured meant yes. "Does the girl's father seem off to you? Or her mother?"

"They're fine," she said shortly. "There's nothing wrong with them." She hesitated and added so quietly he had to strain to hear, "I'm afraid."

Her hands were clasped in front of her, the knuckles white. Did he have a right to push her? Could he help by listening? He covered her hands with his. "Why are you afraid?" he asked quietly.

Her anxiety communicated itself through her hands. He thought it was a good sign she didn't yank them away. "I left home at fifteen. Before that, I never had friends over. I never played sports. I never went to a dance, or a party. I didn't play in the band or work on the yearbook, or do anything after school but go home. To a miserable home." She continued matter-of-factly. "My mother detested me. Don't try to tell me she didn't. She did. Ask anyone who lived here when she was alive. She wasn't shy about bad-mouthing me."

He believed her. He'd known people, arrested people, who should never have had kids. "What about your father?"

She laughed without humor. "She would never tell me who he was. Probably because she didn't know herself. I didn't leave home voluntarily. My mother threw me out when she caught her boyfriend trying to rape me. She said it was my fault, that I must have asked for it." She shrugged. "At least she came home before he could do the deed."

Damn it. He'd known her story would be rough, but he hated what she'd been through. "What kind of mother does that? You were just a kid."

"Not to her. I was fifteen, but I looked eighteen. I dodged her boyfriends for years." She shuddered. "Until the last one."

"Is he Allie's father?"

"No. I told you *he* didn't rape me."

Did she know what she had revealed with that inflection? "Not all men are like him."

"I know that. In my head, anyway."

"Was he a cop?"

"No. I don't think he had a job." After a moment she said haltingly, "Am I wrong? Am I so terrible? I want her to be safe."

He squeezed her hands between his. He wanted to hold her, to make her feel better. To drive the bad memories away. "You're not wrong. You feel the way you do for a very good reason."

"That doesn't help Allie. I hate upsetting her. Right now, she thinks I'm the meanest mom in the world."

"You love her. You want to protect her. Nothing wrong with that." He tried to think of a way to change her mind without making her feel worse. "Allie doesn't understand where you're coming from. Can you tell her?"

She shook her head. "God, no. She knows my mother was no good. And that I left home young and had her when I was fifteen. That's it."

"Nothing that happened was your fault. You were a child."

"I was never a child."

"Yes, you were. Stop beating yourself up over events you couldn't control."

"Like you have? Isn't that what you've been doing? Isn't that why you're here?"

He let go of her hands and sat back. Damn, she'd done did it again. "No, it's not the same. I'm not a child, and I should have been in control. I should have stopped him before he—" Nick broke off.

"Murdered her?" Della asked softly. "You couldn't stop the man who murdered Angelina. And you think it's your fault."

"It *was* my fault. Once again, we weren't discussing me, we were talking about you."

"You know, Nick, I think you need to talk every bit as badly as you seem to think I do."

He'd tried to talk. But he couldn't, not really. The closest he'd come was talking to his sister Alex, a bomb unit detective who'd lost a partner. But he couldn't tell even Alex the worse of it. Nothing helped. "That's not happening," he said abruptly. He changed the subject. Again. "What are you going to do about Allie?"

"You think I should let her go."

"It's not my call. But if you want my opinion, I think you should trust yourself. If you know the kid's parents, and you like the kid's parents, and you think they're decent people, then why can't you trust that Allie will be okay with them?"

"I trust myself. It's other people I have the problem with."

"You can't live your whole life not trusting anyone, Della."

"I haven't. I trust Mary Lou. I trusted Charlie." She looked at him and added. "I trust you."

"Do you? Trust me?"

Della lifted a shoulder. "Sort of. Mostly."

Nick laughed. "No one can accuse you of lying to spare someone's feelings."

"Does it really hurt your feelings?"

He sobered. "Yeah. I think it does." He shouldn't have admitted that, but what the hell.

"I trust you more than most people. Even if you are a cop."

"Damned with faint praise," he said. "On that note, I'm leaving."

"Nick," she called when he reached the door. "Are you mad?"

He turned around and smiled at her. "No. I'll survive, don't worry."

KING WAITED until he was sure Mary Lou was home alone. He wanted to return her computer, but he thought it best to wait. It would be more believable if it took at least a few days to find it. He rang the doorbell and waited. The house had an alarm now, he noticed. Sheridan must have put it in.

"Who's there?"

"It's Kingston Knight."

He heard her disabling the alarm. Mary Lou opened the door and stepped back to let him in. "What can I do for you, Officer?"

"Call me King." He could tell she'd been crying. Those

pretty green eyes were red and puffy. She was wearing shorts and a T-shirt, highlighting a surprisingly curvy body. Her blond hair was pulled back in a messy ponytail. One cheek and eye had turned black and blue. Every time he saw her, he felt like a shit for hurting her. But he'd make it up to her.

"I have something for you." He opened the briefcase he was carrying and took out the laptop. "I believe this is yours."

She put her hand over her heart and gazed at the computer with a stunned expression. "My computer? How did you find it? Are you sure it's mine?"

"It fits your description. I don't think there are too many around with an artistic masterpiece on the laptop cover. She'd put some sort of impressionist cover with lots of colors on the thing.

"Hardly a masterpiece," she said, taking it from him. She stared at it for several moments, then tears welled in her eyes and ran down her cheeks. She set the computer down and hugged him. "You have no idea what this means to me," she said against his shirt.

King had thought she was shy, but maybe she was only quiet. "You're welcome," he said. He settled on patting her back. It was much better for her to make the moves. He sure as hell didn't want her calling the chief to complain about him. Even Hayes couldn't ignore that.

She stepped back, her face flushed. "I'm sorry. I shouldn't have done that."

King laughed. "The day I mind a hug from a beautiful woman, I'll be dead."

She laughed too. "I'm sure I look gorgeous with my lovely bruises. But thank you."

"You should ice those bruises."

"I have been. I know the drill, I've been here before."

"With a home invasion?"

"No. With my ex."

"Sorry. Didn't mean to bring up bad subjects."

"There's a reason he's my ex," she said. "But let's not talk about that. I can't believe you found my laptop so quickly. Or at all. From what I understand, once it's gone, it's gone forever."

"Normally that's true. I got lucky. I'm not sure anyone even looked at it. Usually by the time I find them, if I find them, they've been wiped."

"Where did you find it?"

"A pawnshop over in Bay City. You should change your passwords and keep an eye on any accounts you had listed." He found it decidedly odd to investigate a crime he himself committed. King knew there would be no stolen account numbers or sensitive information leaked, but he had to proceed as if there were.

"I've already started the process of changing all the account numbers." She sighed. "My clients aren't happy with me. I'm sure I'll lose at least one of them."

"It's not your fault your computer was stolen."

"No, but that doesn't matter. Bottom line is, their businesses have been put at risk, and at the least, it's going to cost time and money to change everything. The files were password protected, each business with its own set of passwords, but a pro could have gotten into them, I'm sure."

In order to give the illusion that the break-in might have been a robbery, he'd had to take something, and the computer seemed ideal. Damn, he hadn't thought about what it would mean to Mary Lou to have her computer stolen. "I'm sorry."

"Thanks. Can I offer you some coffee, or do you need to go right back to work?"

King glanced at his watch. "Well, look at that. It's time for my break."

"What a coincidence," Mary Lou said, smiling. "Why don't you come to the kitchen and talk to me while I make a fresh pot?"

This meeting had turned out even better than he'd expected. With any luck at all, he could be tight with Mary Lou in a matter of days. And oddly enough, the more he saw her, the more he liked her for herself and not just a means to an end.

CHAPTER SIXTEEN

SATURDAY MORNING dawned, the day of the slumber party. Allie was ecstatic, and even though she wasn't leaving until afternoon, she had already started getting ready. Della tried to cope and silently cursed Nick for talking her into it.

Mary Lou came in and said, "Who are you and what have you done with Della Rose?"

Della knew exactly what she was talking about. Mary Lou had tried to talk her into the very same thing many times. "Oh, you're funny. Not."

"You're really letting her go. I just knew you were going to back out, but you're not. Are you?"

"I said she could go and she's going." Even though it might kill Della with anxiety. "It's not a big deal," she added, lying through her teeth.

"It sure seemed like it in the past. What changed your mind? Or should I say, who?"

"You're just a laugh a minute today."

"Thanks. I aim to please. How *are* things with Nick and you?" she asked brightly.

Della ground her teeth. "I don't know what you think is going on between—"

"Give me some credit, Della. I know exactly what's going on." When Della didn't respond, she continued, "The two of you have the hots for each other. And it's about damn time you were interested in a man, by the way. You're dithering and stressing and trying to decide what to do. Nick is waiting patiently—more or less—for you to come to your senses."

"There's nothing sensible about the situation." It's a crush, she reminded herself. The world didn't stop turning and implode when they kissed. *Liar, liar.* The world might not implode, but when he kissed her, it made her crazy. Her own body was betraying her. How the hell Nick had managed to make it wake up, she didn't know. No other man had been able to elicit even a twinge, but every time she was around Nick, especially close to him, or worse yet, kissing him, she . . . Oh, crap. She tingled.

Mary Lou put her hand on Della's arm and patted it. "Della, this is a chance to have fun. Nick's a great guy." Della shrugged. "He's ridiculously hot," Mary Lou continued. "He's been working his butt off here and at the Last Shot. What are you paying him, by the way?"

Della gave her a dirty look. "You know I'm not paying him." She had tried several times to do so, but he simply ignored her.

"And yet here he is, doing whatever you need him to do, and worrying about your safety," she said, waving a hand at the alarm.

"Fine. Nick is wonderful, and I should rip off his clothes and have my way with him. Are you finished annoying me?"

"What are friends for? And while I'm at it, you'll be on your own tonight. You should take advantage of it."

"Why, are you going out?"

"Yes. King and I are going to dinner."

King? Oh, shit, Mary Lou was going out with Officer Knight. Other than "Are you nuts?" Della couldn't think of a thing to say, so she kept her mouth shut. It didn't matter, though.

"I thought you'd gotten over your irrational dislike of cops?"

"I didn't say anything," Della protested.

"Your face said it all."

Della shrugged, not denying it. "It's not irrational. Just because I tolerate Nick doesn't mean I love cops now."

Mary Lou laughed. "You do a lot more than tolerate him, honey. But that's beside the point. I'm going out with King tonight, and I plan to have a wonderful time. Don't wait up."

"You're not going to sleep with him. . . . Are you?"

"Oh, I hope so," she said with a martial light in her eye. "If you start in on how I can't trust him, blah, blah, blah, I'm walking out right now."

"You're an adult. I'm not your keeper. If you want to go out with him, or sleep with him, or have wild sex in the ocean, you will."

Mary Lou eyed her warily. "But—"

"But nothing. I hope you have fun." *And I hope you're not making a terrible mistake.*

"I will." She started to leave but stopped in the doorway. "Can I give you some advice?"

"Sure. Why not. Everyone thinks I need it."

"Stop worrying about what's going to happen or what might happen down the road. Enjoy the moment."

Great advice, Della thought. Or it would be if she could follow it.

AFTER DROPPING off Allie at the party, Della went to the Last Shot. By the time she'd spent half an hour talking with the Palmers, she felt a lot better about leaving Allie with them. Of course, she was still nervous, but she had a good feeling. Jackie and Dwight had gone to a lot of trouble to make sure the girls had fun. They'd farmed out their other kids, and now there were six twelve-year-old girls screaming, giggling, running in and out of the house and being amazingly loud. It was a totally new experience for Della. Allie had friends over, and occasionally they spent the night, but she'd never had more than one at a time.

Jackie invited her to sit and visit, offering her a soft drink. Since she seemed to mean it, rather than simply offering to be nice, Della did.

"We have movies—don't worry, they're age appropriate," Jackie said. "Dwight is picking up pizza, and we have ice cream and other assorted junk food, makeup, and music. Don't be surprised if Allie comes home with a stomachache and looking like it's Halloween."

"Halloween? Why, are they dressing up?"

Jackie laughed. "No, but they're pretty heavy-handed with the makeup. Probably because none of their parents will let them wear it to school."

"That's good to know. To hear Allie talk, everyone else in her grade gets to wear makeup all the time."

"She's playing you," Jackie said with a laugh. "A few of

them do, but none of their particular friends do. Have you given in yet?"

"No, but I was feeling guilty. Now I don't have to."

Dwight came in with the pizzas and sat down to visit with her a bit. She'd talked to him several times before, and had never gotten any bad vibes from him. Still, she'd made sure Allie had fully charged her phone and she had promised Della she would call if anything happened to make her uncomfortable.

Allie had rolled her eyes, but promised. "I'm twelve, Mom," she'd said. "I'm not a baby."

No, she wasn't. Allie was growing up, and Della had been hiding her head in the sand about it.

Della went home and picked up Sophia, taking her with her to the Last Shot. Mary Lou had left on her date, and Della didn't want to hang around in an empty house, feeling lost without Allie or Mary Lou. She figured Sophia wouldn't either.

To Della's surprise, she'd fallen in love with the little dog too. Sophia was always so happy to see her, acting as if she hadn't seen her in a month when it had only been hours, or even minutes. Now that she was clean and Allie brushed her daily, her fur was soft, silky and soothing to pet. Who knew it would be so relaxing to pet a dog?

Della wanted to get together a liquor order and estimate how much it would be so when the insurance money finally came through, she could order it right away. She wanted to get the place back up and running soon. She'd already lost one cook, who'd moved to another town to find work. He said he couldn't afford to wait until the Last Shot reopened. The only reason the others hadn't quit was because they couldn't find a job elsewhere. But they could go at any minute, which would leave her in a bind. Cooks—dependable ones, anyway—weren't easy to find.

Nick was nowhere to be seen when she and Sophia walked in. Della figured he was either in the apartment upstairs or maybe he'd gone on a run along the beach. He seemed to like to do that, though Della could think of a lot of things she'd rather do.

Sophia began scratching at the swinging doors and whining to get into the kitchen. She wasn't strong enough to open them herself, though she tried, hurling herself against them. Pushing them open, Della let Sophia in and followed her.

"Son of a bitch!" Nick cursed.

"What are you doing?" His head and upper body were under one of the kitchen sinks. His shirt had ridden up and she could see tanned, muscled abs, rippling as he worked. She remembered he had a lot of those beautiful muscles all over his body. *Oh, man. Don't think about that.*

"Trying to fix a goddamn leak." He paused and asked, "Is Allie here?"

"A little late, aren't you?" She laughed. "She's not here. Cuss all you want."

"Somebody doesn't know shit from shinola about plumbing."

"Do you?"

"More than whoever fixed this last."

She sat on the bar stool by the island, enjoying the view. Hey, she was human, wasn't she? "That would be the plumber. He comes to fix it every month or so."

"Planned obsolescence," Nick said. "Or he has the hots for you."

She laughed again. "It must be the first one. He's gay."

Sophia, who'd been dancing around his legs waiting for Nick to notice her, decided she'd waited long enough and jumped onto his stomach. His upper body rose and she heard a thunk, followed by, "Shit! Ow, that hurt."

Della didn't even try not to laugh. "Don't be a baby. She can't weigh more than ten or fifteen pounds." She'd laughed more in the last fifteen minutes than she usually did in a week.

He pushed himself out from beneath the sink, glaring at her balefully, while rubbing his forehead. "The dog isn't the problem. Smash your head against that leaky steel pipe and tell me how you like it."

Still perched on his stomach, Sophia was now jumping up and licking his face madly. He removed her and set her beside him. "No, Sophia. I have a rule. I don't kiss dogs on the mouth." He smirked at Della. "Only women."

"She doesn't seem to care much about your rule," Della observed.

"Can I help it if she loves me?"

"She does, you know. She must know you saved her."

"Not me. Allie saved her." He gave her a last pat and stood. "Sophia looks better every time I see her. She's really filled out."

"I'd be worried if she hadn't. Allie and Mary Lou feed her constantly. I swear she eats as much as a Great Dane."

"Mary Lou and Allie? Not Della?" He grinned when he asked it.

"I feed her. At mealtime." He raised an eyebrow. "A few scraps here and there. When she looks hungry." Which was always.

Nick laughed at her. "Oh, yeah, you're the tough one."

"She turns those big, brown puppy dog eyes on me, and I

remember that scrawny little thing we first brought home. I can't resist. I'm afraid she'll get big as a house."

"Just make sure she gets enough exercise and she'll be fine. Her appetite will level out when she feels more secure. Probably."

"I'm not sure about that. I think she feels pretty secure now. She sleeps in Allie's bed every night and is treated like the queen of the household."

"Why didn't Allie come with you?" He wasn't looking at her but had squatted down to pet Sophia again. "She usually does on Saturdays."

"Very subtle, Nick. She's at the slumber party."

He looked up at her and smiled. "I'm glad you changed your mind."

"I'm not sure I am. Except Allie was so happy . . ." She trailed off. Allie's reaction had made Della feel like a jerk for not letting her go before now. "I don't want to talk about it. I came here because I didn't want to be home alone. And because we need to work," she added belatedly. Which sounded lame even to her.

"Mary Lou have a hot date?"

"Yes, as a matter of fact." She frowned. "With Kingston Knight."

"Knight, huh? I wondered if he had a thing for her when he found her computer so quickly."

"Why?"

"Stolen laptops are seldom recovered." He shrugged. "Maybe he knew which pawn shop to look at."

"Are you saying he's a dirty cop?"

"On the basis of recovering a laptop?" He shook his head. "No. But I do think it's conveniently lucky."

"I tried to talk her out of it, but she told me to butt out. Not in those exact words, but that's what she meant. I don't trust him."

"That's no surprise, considering how you feel about cops."

"Not all cops," she said, then winced. Damn, she hadn't meant to say that.

Nick smiled, that slow, killer smile she imagined made a lot of women's hearts beat faster. *It's just a crush,* she reminded herself for about the thousandth time. No big deal. He moved even closer, so he stood directly in front of her.

"That means you trust me."

If she hadn't been seated, she'd have backed away. As it was, she felt trapped. But she wasn't panicked. More like—oh, crap. Aroused.

"Don't get excited," she snapped. "All that means is that I don't think you're a pervert."

"You flatterer," he said, and kissed her.

His lips were soft, but firm. He kissed her slowly, his tongue touching hers and retreating, allowing her to feel each thrust and parry. It still shocked her, what he could do to her with a kiss. She couldn't remember a single other man who'd made her feel this way. Excited, stimulated, aroused. Hell, she couldn't even remember a man she wanted to kiss, much less have sex with.

Maybe this was what normal women felt.

Della ordered herself to stop thinking. To just feel and enjoy. She stood, wrapping her arms around his neck and getting closer to him, breast to chest.

Nick moved from her mouth to her throat, murmuring against the rapidly beating pulse, "You like me."

"Maybe."

He kissed her mouth again. "You like me a lot." Laughing blue eyes invited her to answer.

His mouth cruised her jawline, sending shivers up her spine. "How do you . . . figure?" she finished as his hand closed over her breast and gently kneaded it.

He drew back and looked at her. His eyes crinkled at the corners and his mouth lifted in a smile. "I wouldn't be kissing you if you didn't."

She smiled too. And then, damn it, she started thinking again, her smile fading. *Let it go. See what happens. Don't question.*

"What's wrong, Della?"

"Nothing." She tried to stop talking but her mouth had other ideas. "Where do we go from here?"

NICK KNEW WHAT *he* wanted. Della, he wasn't so sure about. "Where do you want to go?"

He kept his arms around her, running a hand up and down her back.

She looked at him, her eyes like dark, liquid chocolate. Deep. Full of secrets. "I want to be with you."

"Good, because I know I want to be with you. I have since the first time I saw you." He kissed her mouth again, taking his time, feeling her heat in his arms. Her body was pliant against his. Her mouth softened, inviting him to take what he wanted. Her arms lifted to wrap around his neck. She kissed him back, a long, impossibly hot kiss. Nick considered boosting her up on the kitchen island, but if he did, this would all be over far too soon.

Della moaned, then turned her head away. "Nick, wait. There's something you—something I have to tell you. Something you should know before we take this any further."

He kissed her neck and murmured, "Honey, don't you think we can talk later?"

"I don't like sex."

That got his attention. He raised his head and stared at her. She looked serious. "Come again?"

"I hate sex."

Now didn't seem to be the time to point out that she was all but melting beneath his hands. "You don't hate kissing."

"No."

"You don't hate it when I touch you." He put his hand on her breast and caressed it gently. The nipple hardened in response and she stifled a moan.

"No, but—"

"You've never had sex with me."

"What does that mean?"

He smiled at her. "We'll be good together, Della. Trust me."

She gazed at him, her eyes wide and . . . frightened, he could swear. He cupped her face in his hands and said, "We don't have to do this. Say the word and I'll stop right now."

"I don't want you to stop."

"Then I won't." Slowly, very slowly, he lowered his mouth to hers. Kissed her until she melted again. "You liked that, didn't you?"

"Yes," she whispered.

He kissed her again, pulling her against him and running his hands lightly up her body, stroking her back, stroking that lush little rear of hers, knowing that this would be a slow process. *Patience*, he thought. She needed time. She needed to be aroused, to be savored.

"Let me take you to bed, Della."

She didn't speak, but she took his hand and started for the

stairs to the apartment. Which was exactly the answer he wanted.

SHE STOPPED in the hallway, hesitant to move forward. "What about Sophia? Don't we need to—?"

"Sophia is asleep in the kitchen," he said, smiling a knowing smile. "She'll be fine."

Stop acting like a virgin when you're anything but, she told herself. *There's nothing to be nervous about. You know what happens.*

But did she? She'd never had sex with a man she wanted. Because she'd never wanted a man until she met Nick. Anyone who knew her history would laugh, but that was the truth.

"What are you afraid of, Della?" Nick asked, holding her hand and looking at her. "That you'll like it?"

She knew what he thought. He thought she was afraid of feeling too much. But she wasn't. She was afraid of feeling nothing. Silent numbness. Nothing. And once, just once in her life, she wanted to feel pleasure. From a man.

His hand cupped her cheek, slid down to caress her throat in slow, rhythmic circles. Fluttering, gentle touches of his fingers that should have been soothing. But they weren't. They were arousing, and judging by the knowing smile on that talented mouth, he knew exactly what he was doing.

She stared at him as her senses reeled, realizing what was so different about him, about them together. She'd never felt that numbing void with Nick. She'd been angry, amused, scared . . . aroused. But not numb. Not from the first time she'd seen him, the first time he'd touched her, when he'd laid his fingers on her wrist in the bar.

She liked it when he touched her. Liked looking at him. Lusted after him, but she didn't know if she could follow through. She liked kissing him. A lot. Liked it so much she was terrified of what would happen if she made love with him and . . . Oh, God, she couldn't deal with the void.

A couple of years ago, she had met Michael. He was from Houston, with friends in Freedom. He'd been nice. Very nice, and obviously interested in her. She'd thought it was worth a try, worth seeing if she could be like other women. She hadn't wanted him, but he was kind and earnest and she figured what the hell. So when he wanted to take her to bed, she'd let him.

He hadn't reminded her of her past. No harrowing flash-backs. No demons springing out to haunt her as she lay beneath him. She'd felt nothing. No pleasure, no pain. Just . . . nothing. As if she wasn't there at all.

She couldn't bear to go through that again. Especially with Nick.

CHAPTER SEVENTEEN

NICK OPENED the door to the apartment and led her to the bedroom. He started slowly, leisurely. Long, drugging kisses that made her ache. Hands caressing her through her clothes. Hands that gave pleasure rather than pain.

He sat on the bed, pulling her down until she straddled his lap. "Open your eyes," he said, his voice husky.

Bracing her arms on his shoulders, she did as he said. His mouth, the lips that looked so hard but felt so wonderful, curved in a wicked smile.

"Watch," he said, and began undoing her buttons.

She'd never been this intensely aware of a man before. She felt his hands at each button, but kept her eyes on his face until he parted the fabric and slid the blouse off her shoulders. She looked down at her cotton bra. Plain, white, serviceable, it was no man's fantasy. But then his hands closed over the fabric and the sight of those masculine hands, large and dark but oh, so gentle, sent her pulse into overdrive. He flicked the catch open, swift and sure. She knew he'd done it hundreds of times. She wondered if this time was different for him.

He spread the fabric and simply looked at her, concentrating until she felt the warm flush of arousal spread over her chest. "What?" she asked when he said nothing, simply stared.

"Your breasts are incredible." Finally, he took her breasts in his hands, stroking her, gently, until his fingers rested on the nipples. "I knew they would be."

It was unbelievably erotic, watching him, seeing the heat in his eyes, feeling the stroke of those strong fingers on her flesh.

Her bra slipped off, almost by itself. Instead of rushing, hurting, taking, he lingered. He cupped each breast, lifted it, stroked all over, the friction of his palms bringing her nipples to painful points. His fingers plucked at her nipples, rolled them until she was biting her lip, struggling not to scream.

More, she thought, as his mouth consumed hers, lips and tongues and teeth met, feasted, parted. She'd never imagined the heat. The blood roared in her ears. She wanted, wanted, wanted like she never had before. Her back arched, thrusting her breasts upward. Her fingers dug into his shoulders. "Nick," she managed on a strangled groan. My God, that he could do this to her simply with his hands on her breasts and his mouth on hers. Suddenly, she wanted more, wanted to feel his mouth at her breasts, his hands on her body.

"Relax," he said. "We can take our time."

Take their time? She wasn't going to last another five minutes. Their gazes met and she saw the slow smile reflected in his eyes. He knew exactly what he was doing to her.

"Watch," he whispered again, and bent his head to take her in his mouth.

He didn't, though. He teased her, stroking his tongue lightly around the aureole, tracing it over the skin, coming back to the peak that was throbbing now in anticipation. His tongue rasped over her nipple, his hair so dark against the skin of her breast. When he drew her nipple into his mouth and sucked, she gasped, her head falling back, offering him more as her back arched. His hands across her back kept her from falling. She was panting, wild to feel more. To feel, the heat, the desire, the thrill of passion.

He spoke into her skin as his lips moved across her chest, words like "beautiful," "soft," and then, "I want you."

Oh, God, she wanted him too. But he didn't hurry, he moved to her other breast and began again. The stroking, the teasing, then the sweet-hot, painful pull as he suckled her breast.

"God, Nick," the words burst from her on a gasp. "Don't you want . . ." She let her sentence trail off as he raised his head from her breast.

"Oh, I want. But getting there is half the fun."

"Take your shirt off, then. I want to touch you."

He smiled. "You do it."

So she unbuttoned his shirt, carefully slid it off, watching as his bare skin was revealed. It was obscene, she decided, that a bullet had marred that lovely flesh. Sleek, tan skin over sleek muscles. She spread her fingers over his chest, much as he had hers. Touched her lips to his chest, spreading kisses across it. He groaned and hauled her against him, gripping her rear until her sex rested against his. Through the layers of fabric she could feel him, hard and throbbing with potent arousal.

"Take off your shorts," he spoke in her ear.

Her stomach jolted. It had been too good to be true. Yet she'd already known more pleasure with him than she ever had before. Disappointment swamped her, that now it would end. He would find the pleasure and she would be left with . . . nothing.

But she stood as he helped her off his lap. She stepped

away and unfastened her shorts, sliding them slowly down her legs as he watched. She didn't know why, but the feel of his eyes caressing her as she stripped made her feel hot, shaky. She hadn't expected that. She stood for a moment in just her panties, again, plain, white, functional bikini underwear.

Tucking her fingers into the elastic, she slid them down her legs and stepped out of them. And again, he surprised her. Although she could see from the flesh straining against his zipper that he was more than ready, he didn't strip, didn't make a move to end it. Instead, he held out his hand and pulled her back to the same position, straddling his lap. Only this time, she was naked. Vulnerable. And so hot and achy she was about to die.

He kissed her mouth, sent his tongue inside in a teasing foray that turned hotter, deeper. His hand swept over her breast, slid down her stomach and rested at the delta of curls between her thighs. He drew back to watch as he sent a finger over her clitoris, rubbing gently, watching her all the while. She couldn't help watching too, her fingers flexing into his shoulders, her breathing rapid and uneven. He spread his thighs, which spread hers even farther. His finger probed, then slid inside, then back out before she could react. She whimpered in protest.

"Come," he said, and smiled, flicking his thumb over the cluster of nerves. "I want to see you come," he said, then thrust his finger inside her again.

Feelings she'd never thought to have battered her. Arousal rushed through her, the pleasure/pain throbbing in rhythm to his questing fingers. His hand mimicked the motions of lovemaking, withdrawing, thrusting back inside, and all the while his thumb tormented her.

"Come," he said again, sent his finger deep, and she shattered and screamed as her body throbbed and pulsed and spasmed endlessly.

When she opened her eyes, she didn't know how much later, he was still stroking her, soothing and arousing at once. "My God," was all she could manage.

He smiled. "Next time you come," he said, "I'm going to be inside you."

She believed him. And she wanted him, now, deep inside.

Rising with her in his arms, Nick laid her on the bed, then stripped off the rest of his clothes. Not slow now, but impatient, as she was. If she'd thought him impressive when he wasn't aroused, the sight of that awesome erection blew her mind. She reached out and touched him, stroked him, watching him grow even more as she did.

He groaned. "Better not. I won't last." She paid no attention, cradling him in her hands as she continued to arouse him. "You little devil," he said with a choked-off laugh. Opening the bedside table drawer, he reached inside and withdrew some condoms, tossing them on top of the table. She picked one up and opened it, rolled it down slowly until it covered his length. Then he was beside her on the bed, holding her close, skin to skin, sex to sex, and kissed her deep and hot.

He rolled her to her back and spread her legs, settled in between, waited a moment until she looked at him. "Wrap your legs around me," he ground out, and she did. His gaze locked on hers, he entered her, thrusting inside her and withdrawing. Doing it over and over until she felt the sweet edge of orgasm and exploded as he spilled himself inside her with a final deep lunge.

"DID I FAINT?" she wondered aloud.

"I don't think so," he said, smiling down at her. He rolled off her and she thought, *here we go*. Now he'd want to get away from her as fast and far as he could. He'd hustle her out of there so quick her head would spin. It couldn't possibly have been as good for him as it had been for her. Oh, she knew he'd gotten off. That wasn't the problem. Now that he'd gotten what he wanted, he'd want her to split. She wanted to stay. Wanted to just . . . be with him.

What did normal people do after sex? Did they talk? Go to sleep? She had no idea, with only one voluntary experience to measure it against. It had taken her years to find the courage to even try to be with a man after her teens. After she had, rather than risk feeling nothing again, she had no longer cared if she ever had sex again.

But then she met Nick. Sex with Nick had blown her mind. She'd had an orgasm, for God's sake. Twice. Finally, it made sense to her why people actually liked sex.

She lay with her back to him and waited, waited to see what he'd say to get her to leave. She heard him doing something, getting rid of the condom, she thought. Then the bed gave and his arm came round her to turn her to face him and pull her to him. Her head on his chest, his arm wrapped around her, he stroked her bare skin, petting her. Soothing. It felt nice. He felt nice. All warm, solid. Naked. Weird, Della thought, but nice.

"What are you thinking?" he asked her. His voice was a deep husky rumble in his chest.

"What do your—you usually do? After sex."

He was silent for a while, then said, "Leave."

She didn't like that it mattered. She didn't like the disappointment. "Okay, then I'll go."

But he didn't turn her loose. He pulled her closer and kissed the top of her head. At least, she thought he did, but she couldn't be sure. "I want you to stay. I want to sleep with you."

A treacherous contentment settled in her breast. "You just want to have sex again." Sex she could understand. This other —well, that was something else. Something dangerous.

Nick didn't deny it. He laughed. "That too. But I was thinking of sleep right now. Go to sleep, Della. Sweet dreams."

KING COULDN'T remember the last time he'd put himself out for a woman. Usually, he didn't need to. Either they came to him, or he forgot about them. Mary Lou was different, and he wasn't sure why.

She balked at the entrance to the restaurant. "King, I had no idea you were taking me somewhere so nice. I've heard about Riggiato's," she said, naming the nicest Italian restaurant in Bay City, "but I've never been here. I'm way underdressed."

"You're wearing a dress," he said. "You look fine."

"I look like I have on a three-year-old sundress. Which I do."

"I like it." He ran his hand up her bare arm and smiled. He liked it a lot. The dress showed a lot of skin, but not in a slutty way. Not that he'd have minded slutty, but Mary Lou was classy. He looked at the swell of her breasts above the low-cut top. Classy and sexy too.

He had a little fantasy going on about stripping that pretty little dress off of her when she said tartly, "Eyes up here."

Unabashed, he grinned. "Come on," he said, taking her arm and giving the hostess his name.

King made sure she had plenty of wine. Not to seduce her, though he had that in mind. But he suspected she didn't have the opportunity to sample good wine very often. If ever. And he wanted her to enjoy herself.

They talked while eating their salads, and after some urging, she told him a bit about her life before coming to Freedom.

"You've probably heard the story a hundred times," she said. "After all, you are a cop." She sighed and was quiet for a moment. "My ex-husband hit me. A lot. Black eyes, broken bones, bruises everywhere. Which is one reason he's my ex."

"I suspected that from what you said after the break-in."

"I'd almost forgotten what it was like," she mused. "It's been several years. But things like that come back to you real quick."

"Does he still harass you?" If he did, King would put a stop to it real quick.

"No. He's in prison. He's been there for years."

"Why is he in prison?"

"Drugs. He was selling crystal meth. I divorced him when he went to prison."

Her tone was curiously flat. "You're well rid of him. You don't need scum like that around."

"Tell me about it," she said in a more normal tone. "Anyway, that's my sad story. Now tell me yours."

"Why do you think it's sad?" He'd never had anyone say that to him before.

She considered him. "It's your eyes."

"My eyes look sad?"

"You look like you've seen a lot of pain."

King shrugged. "Goes with the territory."

"It's more than that, isn't it? More than your job."

King never talked about his past. Never. No one cared about that. No one except this woman. This very sweet, kind woman. "My father was a real bastard. Loved to hit people. Used to whale on my mother for the hell of it. I couldn't stop him, and I couldn't get her to leave him." He shrugged. "He threatened to kill her if she left him. She didn't leave, and he killed her anyway."

Mary Lou put her hand over his. "Oh, King, I'm so sorry. How old were you?"

"Seventeen. I'm surprised she lived as long as she did."

"Did he go to prison?"

King shook his head. He'd killed the son of a bitch before the cops came. As always, when he remembered, he felt the guilt. Not for killing him, but for not getting to the bastard in time to save his mother. He left before anyone knew he was the shooter. But he wouldn't tell Mary Lou that part of his story. "Someone meaner than he was shot and killed him."

"Good," she said softly, and squeezed his hand.

Killing his father was what made him decide to become a cop. He wanted to stop people like his old man from doing what they did best. Hurting and killing. He wanted to do it legally, so no kid would ever have to do what he had done to protect his mother. And failed.

Now King was one of the good guys. Except that he wasn't. He was an accessory after the fact to murder. He'd broken in to the Last Shot and Della's home. He'd stolen things. After killing his old man, he'd sworn never to cross the line again. Yet he had. The deeper he became embroiled in his chief's scheme, the more conflicted he felt. Would the money be worth it? King wasn't at all sure that it would.

King had thought long and hard before leaving the Houston PD. But he'd worked vice for so long, he had burned out. He was sick to death of what he saw daily as a vice cop. He was tired of dealing with the dregs of humanity. So when the opportunity for a complete change came up, he took it. Even though Hayes had a bit of a rep as an asshole, being an officer in a small town with little crime had sounded like just what King needed. And it had been. Until now.

After dinner, they drove back to Freedom. King stopped at the pier. They got out and walked along it, then sat and talked while the waves lapped against the wood and the soft ocean breeze blew over them. He kissed her and she kissed him back, her arms going around his neck and her soft breasts cradled against his chest. He sensed the heat and fire just beneath the surface and he could have eaten her alive.

If she'd been another type of woman, he might have taken her right there. Unzipped his pants, pushed up her dress, ripped off her panties, and thrust himself deep inside her. Have her ride him until she screamed. The risk of discovery, of doing her out in the open, would have been almost irresistible.

Mary Lou wouldn't like it. She might acquiesce, but she'd be nervous, afraid someone would see. She was intrigued, he knew that. But no sense risking scaring her off. He ended the kiss and heard her sigh. "I'd better take you home," he said regretfully.

They walked to the car, his own car, not the police cruiser he usually drove. He started the car and backed up.

"King, I don't want to go home."

He stopped the car and looked at her. Her lips were swollen from his kisses, her hair down around her shoulders, messy from the wind, looking like she'd just rolled out of bed. His body clenched. "What do you want to do, Mary Lou?"

"I want to go to your home."

King smiled and put the car in gear. "Anything you want, darlin'."

CHAPTER EIGHTEEN

DELLA WOKE UP slowly to feel Nick's hand caressing her breasts. Spooned together like real lovers, she thought. God, maybe they were real lovers. She didn't know what to think about that.

"What's wrong?" Nick murmured in her ear. "You were all soft and relaxed, and now you're stretched tight as a drum."

"Nothing's wrong." Nothing she could talk about anyway. *You're overreacting*, she told herself. Nick doesn't want permanent either. Why else would he still be single at his age?

He turned her over, propped himself up on his arm, and looked down at her. "Do you regret last night?"

"No." She traced his mouth with her finger. "I had fun." Della had never, ever thought she'd describe sex as fun.

"Yeah? Fun is good." He kissed her. "Fun is great." He kissed her again, longer, deeper and heat flooded her body. Just as it had all night, every time he touched her.

Della pushed him over on his back. "My turn."

"Works for me," Nick said, pulling her head down for a kiss.

Della looked over at the nightstand and grabbed the last condom. "Last one. What are we going to do about that?"

"Buy more. But first . . ." His hands closed over her breasts.

Della's head fell back. "First," she agreed.

Later, Della looked at her phone. "I didn't realize how late it was. It's almost time for me to go get Allie."

"Reality strikes."

"Listen, Nick, last night was great. But I'm not sure how—"

"Don't even try to tell me last night was it," he interrupted.

"I'm not. Exactly. But I'm not sure how this will work. Allie's twelve. She notices things now."

"Things like her mom sleeping with a man?"

"Things like her mother having sex, yes." She would sure as hell notice if Della started having men "friends" stay over. Thinking about her own mother's choice of men had her stomach rolling.

"You don't want Allie to know about us."

Nick isn't like that. You'd never have had sex with him if he was. "That's not it, exactly. I've just never had to worry about it before." The look he gave her made her realize what she'd said and how it must have sounded. "I'm not my mother. I'm not going to bring home a new 'friend' every two weeks."

His expression changed. "Damn, Della, I'm sorry. I should have thought about your childhood."

"Yeah, well I try not to."

He sat up and swung his legs out of bed to sit beside her. "Hey." He put a hand under her chin and looked deep into her eyes. "I would never hurt Allie, Della. I protect children, I don't hurt them." A shadow crossed his face and she wondered what he was remembering.

"I know," she said huskily.

"We'll work it out. Try not to worry." He kissed her, brief and hard.

Nick got up and walked to the bathroom. *Damn, he has a killer body*, she thought. Surely they could find a way to keep seeing each other.

You just want to have sex with him again.

Of course I do. Who wouldn't?

That wasn't all, though. She liked him. Really liked him. And that, she thought, was even scarier than the sex.

DELLA LEFT FOR home, taking Sophia with her, as soon as she could tear herself away, anxious to change clothes before she picked up her daughter. Mary Lou was gone when Della got there, which didn't surprise her. Mary Lou had probably gone to pick up groceries. Then Della remembered, Mary Lou had a date last night. With Kingston Knight.

Della's phone chimed, Allie's ring. She snatched it up and answered. "Allie? Are you all right? I'll be there—"

"Mom, can I stay at Brooke's tonight too? Please? Mrs. Palmer says it's okay. Please, Mom. Remember, we don't have school tomorrow."

She'd forgotten Monday was a teacher in-service day. "But —don't you want to come home?" After all, Allie had just spent her first night away from home.

Apparently, she didn't. She launched into a long list of everything they had planned. One of the other girls was staying, and Brooke wanted Allie to as well. Della knew this because not only did Allie tell her but she could hear Brooke in the background saying, "Please, Ms. Rose. Please let her stay."

"Let me talk to Mrs. Palmer."

Jackie took the phone quickly. "Della? We'd love to have Allie for another night."

"Are you sure? I can't imagine you aren't ready to get rid of all those kids." She paced the room, torn between a number of emotions. Obviously, Allie was fine and having fun. If Della hadn't felt good about leaving her with the Palmers, she wouldn't have. To her surprise, though, she'd only worried a few times last night. Partly because Nick had distracted her the rest of the time.

Della wanted Allie to experience a normal childhood. But that meant letting her grow up, and she wasn't quite ready for her baby to grow up. *Too bad. Allie's ready and that's what matters.*

Jackie laughed. "They're not all staying over again. Just two of them."

"All right. If you're sure," Della said, taking the plunge. "Thanks, Jackie. I know she's excited about it." She hung up and sat staring into space.

She heard a noise in the kitchen, and then the sound of the alarm being disarmed. She didn't like arming it all the time but she'd promised Nick she'd do it. At least for a while.

Mary Lou walked into the living room, stopping when she saw Della. They eyed each other in silence for a moment.

"You slept with him," they both said at the same time.

Mary Lou laughed. "I did. And I'm planning to do it again as soon as possible. Oh, Della, I really like him." She hugged herself, looking impossibly happy.

"I can see that." Della didn't know what else to say. Cautioning Mary Lou was pointless, because really, she had nothing concrete against the man. Just because she had a feeling that Knight wasn't what he seemed didn't mean she was right.

"You still don't like King, do you?"

"I don't know him." Della didn't point out that neither did Mary Lou.

"You think that because I screwed up and married my abusive ex that I don't know a good guy from a worthless one."

That summed up what Della had been thinking, but she sure as hell couldn't say so. "Why are you being so defensive? I haven't said a thing."

"You thought it," Mary Lou muttered, a little shamefaced. "But never mind me. What about you? I wondered if you were ever going to admit you had the hots for Nick."

Della shrugged. "It's just sex. Not a big deal." *And that's as big a lie as you've ever told.*

"Right. Which is why you've barely had a date in years, much less had a fling with anyone."

Before Della could think of a response, Mary Lou's phone rang. When she looked at the screen her face lit up like a Christmas tree. "It's King," she said unnecessarily, and went off to her room to talk.

Leaving Della with thoughts of not one, but two disturbing revelations. From the looks of it, Mary Lou was already in deep with Kingston Knight.

And having sex with Nick had meant far more to her than she'd bargained for.

KING WAS POSITIVE that the goods were in this town. A fortune in jewelry, including, if the man Hayes had killed was right, a fucking million dollar bracelet. Hayes hadn't done much of anything useful. He'd been too busy harassing King, asking what he'd discovered and how he planned to find the supposed fortune from this heist. Truth was, King didn't know. And the longer it went on, the less happy he was with his role in the scheme.

He'd searched the Last Shot, though maybe not as thoroughly as he could have. He'd searched Della's house and come up with zip. He didn't really believe Della knew where the stuff was, because if she did, why the hell hadn't she taken her daughter and the jewels and gotten out of the country?

It stood to reason that while Della and Sheridan might not know for sure what the robbers had wanted, they knew it was valuable. If and when Della and Sheridan found the goods, they would waste no time getting the law involved. Then he and Hayes would really be up a creek.

Hayes had been scheming to compel Della to not only find the stuff, but to hand it over when she did. The chief had told King about Della's history in Freedom. She was the daughter of the town whore and had left town when she was just a kid —and come back a few years later with a kid of her own and very little else. No telling what she'd done to survive. King had carefully questioned Mary Lou and would do so again, but either Mary Lou knew Della's secrets and wouldn't spill them, or Della didn't talk about her past to anyone, not even her best friend.

At Hayes's request, King had begun to look into Della's past. She had no criminal history as an adult, but her juvie record was sealed. Records that included some of the missing years. A sealed juvie file was standard operating procedure, but a law enforcement agency could ask that they be unsealed.

He knocked on the chief's office door, entered at the command, and shut it behind him. "Della Rose has a sealed juvie record."

Hayes continued flipping through the magazine he held. "So?" he asked without looking up.

"You need to ask a judge to unseal it." The judge would be more likely to grant the chief access than plain old Officer Knight.

The chief tossed the magazine aside and said irritably, "Damn, do I have to do everything myself?"

Since in King's opinion, Chief Hayes hadn't done much of anything—other than kill a man—King didn't answer.

"Shit. I'll take care of it," Hayes said. "That woman you're screwing hasn't told you anything useful?"

King's jaw tightened with the effort to stay silent. Mary Lou wasn't some random whore he was screwing. She was different. She was . . . decent.

"What's the matter, boy? Don't tell me you're falling for the babysitter. What's she got, besides big tits?"

Hayes was deliberately trying to piss him off. If the chief knew King had started to fall for Mary Lou, that could only be a bad thing. Hayes had plenty to hold over King's head as it was. He didn't intend to give him more ammunition.

Feigning indifference, he said, "Nah, she doesn't know squat. I keep thinking she'll let something drop, but so far she hasn't."

"Don't dump her too quickly," Hayes advised him. "You never can tell what she might find out that could help us."

Since King had no intention of dumping Mary Lou, he agreed readily. He couldn't deny he was worried about the chief's plans once they did find the stash, though. Any man, cop or not, who could put a bullet in someone as easily as Hayes had done and not suffer a twinge of remorse, was a dangerous man. And King was involved with him up to his eyeballs.

CHAPTER NINETEEN

WHEN DELLA returned to the Last Shot Sunday afternoon, she and Nick started working on another one of the tasks she had to do in order to open. Taking inventory of the dishware, barware, and other glassware, and figuring out the bare minimum of those she needed to buy. It would have helped if Charlie had kept better records of how much of what he ordered. But other than the liquor, he really hadn't. So while she wasn't quite flying blind, she was at least pretty damn nearsighted.

"What are you pissed off about?" Nick asked Della after they'd been at it for several hours.

"Who says I'm pissed off?" Della snapped.

"You've been slamming things around and muttering under your breath since you came back."

"I'm not upset." How did he read her so well when no one else could? "I'm annoyed, that's all."

He walked over to her and removed the coffee cup from her hand. "You don't have enough whole ones to break this one too. Who's annoying you?"

She shrugged. "Mary Lou. She's sleeping with Knight."

"That's no surprise. Anyone could see they were headed that way." He sat on the bar stool by the island.

"I don't like it. I don't trust him."

"Did you tell her that?"

"No. I didn't have to. She knows what I think."

"Which is . . . what?"

She picked up the notebook, then set it down with a bang. "I think he's bad news, and she's naive as hell, although how she could be after her piece of shit ex, I don't know."

"What did her ex do?"

"Beat the crap out of her and damn near killed her before she got away from him. He's in prison now on drug charges."

"Sounds like a winner."

"I didn't even bring him up. She did that. Said something about just because she made one mistake didn't mean she couldn't tell a good guy from a worthless one." She sat on the other stool and asked him, "Do you think I'm overreacting? Am I seeing problems where there aren't any?"

"Maybe. Maybe not."

She considered him carefully. "You don't like him either."

Nick hesitated. "He's better than Hayes."

"Which is saying absolutely nothing. What do you really think about him? No bullshit, just your gut feeling."

Nick rubbed the back of his neck. "My gut feeling is something's off about him. Nothing concrete. Just a feeling."

"That's exactly what I think. We need to find out more about Knight. We can't both be wrong."

"Sure we could. But I don't think we are. I asked Travis to find out what he could about Knight, too. He came here from the Houston PD. Not the same division as Travis, though."

"Isn't it weird that he came to Freedom from a big city police department?"

"Maybe. That's one of the things I've wondered about. What's in Freedom for him? Did he leave Houston voluntarily or was he asked to leave?"

"Knight is the one investigating both break-ins. If there's something wrong with him, I need to know about it."

"You'll know as soon as I do. There's one other thing that bugs me."

"What?"

"I don't like him hitting on you."

Surprised, she stared at him. "Knight hasn't hit on me. He's hitting on Mary Lou." Now he was, anyway. She remembered the break-in at the bar and how nice and helpful Knight had been. Could Nick be jealous? Nick? "Is that why you were like a dog with a bone when he was here investigating the break-in?"

"That's not how I'd describe it. But yeah."

"You were jealous." She nearly laughed, but Nick was giving her the evil eye, so she didn't.

He lifted a shoulder. "Call it what you want."

She wanted to tell him the truth. As much of it as she could. "Nick." She put her hand on his arm and pulled at him until he looked at her. "I haven't been with anyone in a long, long time. Whatever happens between us, I'm not going to play you."

He searched her face. "I wouldn't be here if I thought you were."

Della didn't know what to say, so she kissed him. He kissed her back, picked her up and started up the stairs. Della didn't argue.

"I KNOW WHAT you need," Nick said later.

"Me too. I need to get more work done." She'd put on shorts and a T-shirt, but her hair was still messed up from rolling around on the bed, and she was barefoot. He thought she looked great.

"Nope. You've worked enough for today. You need a walk on the beach."

She blinked. "Why?"

"Because it's sunset. It's beautiful. And because I want to romance you by the ocean."

Della looked stunned. Nick was a little surprised himself. He liked women. Didn't mind indulging them, even romancing them, occasionally. But a part of him couldn't help thinking of them cynically. Questioning what they wanted from him. And always, always questioning their truthfulness. The only exceptions to the rule were his mother and sister. They had no problem at all being truthful, no matter whether he liked it or not.

Other women, he couldn't trust. When you didn't trust, you didn't get involved. He knew why. The fact that it had happened years ago didn't seem to matter. Lucianna, the woman who had damn near made him swear off women completely. He hadn't thought about her in years. She'd tied him up in knots, taken his heart out and stomped on it with stiletto heels. He might deserve that now, but he sure as hell hadn't back then.

God, he'd been so young. So stupid not to have realized she was playing him. Her real quarry had been a super wealthy hedge fund manager. Nick had been a means to make the guy come up with the diamond. Lucianna hadn't been sucker enough to marry a struggling cop.

Every time he thought about walking in on her in bed with another man, he winced. Naked, except for the huge diamond ring on her hand. Having a great time, apparently. He'd hauled the man out of bed and done a number on him, but Lucianna had threatened to call the cops. On Nick. That would have been great. He'd have been the laughingstock of the department.

So he'd left the two of them and done his best to forget the bitch. First with booze, and when that didn't work, he'd settled on women. Lots of women. Women who just wanted a good time. He'd been content. Hell, he'd been happy with that. There were a lot of beautiful women who didn't want permanent any more than he did. If he got tangled up with someone who was picking out rings, he ended it the minute he realized where she was headed.

Nick never told his family what had happened, or anyone who didn't already know. His family knew he was commitment-shy, but they didn't know why.

He wasn't a total prick, even though he'd been told more than once he was a cold, unfeeling bastard. He let women know up-front what to expect. And he beat it if things got too serious. Which he always told them would happen before he ever slept with them.

Della was the total opposite of the women he usually went for. A curvy brunette with liquid chocolate eyes. Eyes that held a lot of secrets. Something about her had gotten to him from the first. He fell in deeper every moment he spent with her. He'd learned his lesson long ago, though. Tell her, up front, the way things were.

But he couldn't do that with Della. He simply couldn't get

the words out, and he wasn't sure why. On the surface, Della wasn't fragile. Anything but. Yet there was a part of her she kept back, just as he did. A part of her he didn't believe had been given much—or any—romance. He wanted to give her romance. He wanted her. More than he should.

They held hands and walked along the shoreline, the tide lapping at their bare feet.

"I don't ever do this," Della said.

"What? Hold hands and walk along the beach?"

"That too. But I was talking about enjoying the sunset on the ocean."

"You should give yourself a break more often. Let's sit." She started to walk away from the shoreline, but he tugged her back. "Here, in the water."

"I'll get my clothes wet. I don't have a bathing suit."

He smiled. "Yeah, I know."

She laughed and let him pull her down to sit between his legs, cradling her in his arms. "Blues and purples and pinks and gold," she said as they watched the sun sink into the horizon. "So beautiful. I've seen a lot of sunsets, but I'm usually doing something. Working, driving, worrying. I don't ever relax and watch the sun set."

"I don't very often," he admitted. "At least I didn't until I came down here."

"Why did you come down here? Because of that case? The case you can't forget?"

Just like that, the spell was broken. He got up, held out a hand and hauled her up. He started walking back to the bar.

"You're not going to tell me, are you?"

"No." She already knew more than he wanted her to know. For God's sake, he'd cried when he found out Angelina's mother had committed suicide. Cried while Della held him.

"It might make you feel better."

"No, it won't. I told you, I've tried. The last thing it made me feel was better."

"Maybe you weren't ready then. Or you didn't talk to the right person."

He let go of her hand and stopped walking. "I'll tell you what, Della. I'll tell you my nightmare if you'll tell me yours."

Her eyes widened. "I don't have nightmares."

"Bullshit. You had one last night." He stepped closer. "Why do you hate cops, Della?" he asked softly.

Her gaze hardened. "Don't go there, Nick. You don't want to know."

"Then stay out of my nightmares. Trust me, you *really* don't want to know."

She didn't say another word, just turned her back and headed for the Last Shot. So much for romance, he thought.

BOTH NICK AND Della pretended they'd never had the flare-up on the beach. They went back to the Last Shot and made dinner. Della had thawed out a frozen lasagna one of the cooks had made, and they still had enough ice cream to send them both into sugar shock. Then they'd gone upstairs, made love in the shower, and fallen asleep.

Nick didn't know if *she* dreamed, but he did. Blood, guts, gore. A madman's eyes, blood dripping from the knife he held. The smile on the killer's face. Nick pulled the trigger and the smile disappeared. That's when he woke, sweating, stomach roiling, shaking. Christ, he needed a drink.

He got out of bed and strode naked to the kitchen. He didn't need to turn on the light, he knew where the bottle was.

Exactly where he'd left it a few nights before, so that maybe, just maybe, he could get back to sleep after the dream woke him. Could he drink away the nightmare? He hadn't managed it yet, and besides, since he'd come to the Last Shot, he limited himself to one shot. He didn't want to be sloshed in case something happened.

He splashed two fingers of Jack Daniels into a jelly jar, picked it up, and tossed half of it back. It burned going down, burned in the pit of his belly. If he kept this up, he'd put a hole in his belly, and he didn't even like to drink that much. He scrubbed a weary hand over his face. Besides that, it didn't work. An entire bottle couldn't make that dream disappear.

"Bad dreams?" Della asked from the doorway.

He glanced up and saw her in the back glow from the hallway light. With her hair tousled, her eyes slumberous, and wearing his T-shirt that skimmed her thighs, she looked soft, sexy, and damned inviting. He shrugged without speaking.

Della walked toward him, took the glass from his hand and set it on the counter. "I don't know what demons are driving you, Nick, but I can tell you for a fact, drinking doesn't work."

"Nothing does." He picked up the glass, and finished off the bourbon, watching her over the rim of the glass. "You got a point?"

"Maybe you should try something else."

"Got any ideas?"

She smiled and stepped closer. "One or two."

What the hell, he thought, setting down the glass and reaching for her. Sex was a lot more fun than his previous efforts to relieve the pain. She put her arms around his neck and brought that curvy, lush body next to his. He went from half aroused to hard as a rock inside of a minute. Then she kissed him and he turned to concrete.

No finesse. He slid his hands beneath the shirt and cupped her bare rear, lifting her up until his aching flesh rested against nirvana, covered only by the thin scrap of cotton. He thrust his tongue inside her mouth, heard her groan as he gave her the rhythm they both craved. Before he lost it and simply buried himself inside her, he ripped his mouth from hers. "Put your legs around me."

"What?" She looked dazed.

"The bedroom. I don't have—"

She squirmed, working her hand in between them and pulled a condom from the pocket of his shirt. "Here. Now."

He let her slide slowly down him, wringing a groan from them both before he took it from her and ripped it open. Fifteen seconds later, he backed her against the refrigerator door, ripped off her panties, lifted her and plunged inside. She was wet. Tight. Real.

God. He'd died and gone to heaven.

NICK WOKE WITH a start when Della kicked him. He sat up and looked at her in the moonlight. She was moaning, thrashing around, but clearly still asleep. "No! No!" she screamed and sat up in bed.

Her turn now, he thought. The past with its demons haunted her as much as his demons tormented him. He drew her into his arms. She didn't resist, but allowed him to give her comfort. "Bad one?" he asked softly.

"You have no idea."

"One of those nightmares you don't have?"

"I don't have them every night," she said, as if that made a difference. She drew in a shaky breath, and he could feel her gathering her strength. How did she do that? When he had his flashbacks—or dreams or whatever the fuck they were—he was often shaky for hours. Too many memories.

"It's okay," he told Della, stroking a hand up her arm. "You're okay." He wondered why Della brought out his protective instincts. He was used to feeling them for victims of crimes he investigated, for his family. But he'd never felt that way for someone he'd been involved with. He didn't let it go that far. He'd learned that lesson early and well.

She sighed and said with her cheek against his chest, "Do you believe in monsters?"

"Yeah." He thought about Crazy Larry. "Absolutely."

"Not fairy tales. Real ones. They look like ordinary people but they aren't." She drew back and looked at him. "They lived in my house. And when I left, I found out monsters were everywhere. You can't get away from them."

"You're safe now. Those monsters are in the past." Like his were?

"Are they? I'm not so sure of that."

He wanted to tell her he was sure. Wanted to tell her he'd protect her, keep her safe. But he'd sworn he wouldn't lie to her, and he knew without a doubt that he could fail again. So he said nothing. He kissed her, made love to her again, and hoped it would be enough to drive the monsters from both their dreams. At least for tonight.

CHAPTER TWENTY

NICK'S PHONE rang early the next morning. He wouldn't have answered, but he not only knew Alex's ring, he knew his sister. She would keep calling until she got through to him. He sat on the edge of the bed and reached for his phone.

"Yeah. What?"

"Hello to you too. Did I catch you at a bad time?" Alex asked.

"No, I'm always awake at the crack of dawn."

"Don't be so grumpy. Call me back. And don't put me off too long. I'll keep calling until you talk to me."

"Like I didn't know that."

"Soon, Nick," she warned. "I love you."

"I love you too. I'll call you later."

He hung up and turned around, reaching for Della.

She clobbered him. Hauled off and socked him. Not a love tap, either. It hurt. He grabbed her hand before she could hit him again, just in case she wasn't through. "What the hell was that for?"

"Because you're a lousy two-timing bastard. I did what that poor dumb woman on the other end of the line would do if she could see you now. And don't try to tell me you weren't talking to a woman. I heard her voice."

He started laughing. Laughed so hard he had to hold his stomach.

Della glared at him, the death ray look. When she sat up, the sheet had fallen away and she was naked, her beautiful breasts bare and beckoning. Distracting as hell. He tried to focus on why she was so bent out of shape. He needn't have worried. Judging by the anger on her face, she sure as hell meant to tell him.

"You son of a bitch. You may think it's funny, but you can bet she—"

That sent him into fresh laughter. He knew he was only pissing her off more, but he couldn't help it.

"You told her you loved her."

He managed to stop laughing long enough to say, "I do love her."

"Then why aren't you with her? Why are you here with me? You lying, cheating—"

Della tried to jerk her hand away, but he held on. Looked into those brown eyes spitting fire. "I was talking to my sister."

"Do I look that stupid?"

He let go and got out of bed, digging in his dresser drawer until he found what he wanted. He walked over to the bed and tossed the snapshots down, grinning as she picked one up. "My sister Alex. That's her husband, Luke, and their baby daughter, Jenna. Do I have to call her back to convince you?"

Della stared at the photos like they were alien beings. He sat on the bed and pulled her onto his lap before she could clobber him again. Nuzzling her neck, he said, "I think I like this jealous streak."

"Don't flatter yourself." But she sighed when his hand closed over her breast. "I don't like being lied to."

He kissed her and said against her lips, "I won't lie to you, Della."

"Good," she whispered. And kissed him back.

LATER, THEY TALKED. "So, what does your sister do?" she asked, trailing a hand down his chest. Della had amazing hands, hands that could lead a man to heaven.

"When she's not on maternity leave, she's a cop. A bomb unit technician." He felt Della tense. Again, he wondered what it was about cops that she hated so much.

"Another cop."

"Yep. Our dad's a cop too. Beat cop. Retired."

"What about your mother?"

"She isn't a cop. She's a judge. Retired now, too, like our dad."

"God. A whole squad of law enforcement in one family."

"Not quite, but we're working on it. They'd like you. Maybe you can meet them sometime." Now where had that come from? He'd never before felt the desire to introduce any of the women he'd slept with to his family. If they met them, fine. If not, who cared?

She rose on her elbow and stared at him like he'd just suggested she crawl into a rattlesnake den. "Meet your family? Are you kidding? I can't meet your family."

"Why not?"

"They're cops. And I'm not the type of woman men take home to mother."

He knew what she meant, and it pissed him off. "Why do you do that? Talk smack about yourself? Why wouldn't I introduce you to my family?"

"Why would you?"

He wouldn't. Unless she meant something to him. And he was beginning to realize she did. "Della—"

She laid her fingers on his lips. "Don't tell me lies. I'm here because I want to be, and so are you. Let's just leave it that way. Besides, just because I have the hots for one cop doesn't mean I can deal with a riot of them." Sitting up and swinging her legs to the floor, she picked up her shirt and bra from the floor and began getting dressed.

Don't go there, he thought. *She said she has the hots for you. Be happy with that.* Damn it, he went anyway. "Is that all it is to you?"

She glanced over her shoulder before pulling her shirt over her head. "What?"

"Sex. Is that all this is to you?"

She looked puzzled, then smiled. "No. It's great sex."

"You're dodging my question."

"Why are you bringing this up?" She rose and stood beside the bed. "Isn't the sex all you want out of it?"

Wasn't it? It had always been enough before. But now, with Della . . . God, what was going on? "I'm not sure."

She turned away, pulled on her jeans. Finally, she turned back to him. "I'm not—I don't do relationships. Look, Nick, the sex is fantastic. Can't that be enough?"

It should have been. He couldn't have fallen in love with her. He liked her. Liked her mouthiness, her toughness that she used to cover up any vulnerability. Liked her quick mind and smart ass mouth. He really, really liked having sex with her. But love her?

What if he did? She obviously didn't feel the same. He was beginning to understand what the women in his life had felt like. All of them but Lucianna, anyway.

"Why are you staring at me like that?" she asked.

"Usually I'm giving that speech, not receiving it. I can't say I like it."

She shook her head. Laid a hand against his cheek. "You don't want to get involved with me, Nick. There are things . . . things I can't talk about. It wouldn't work."

"I've got baggage too, Della. Everyone does."

"Not like mine."

"Tell me." Another first. He'd never cared enough to hear about anyone's emotional baggage. Hell, he couldn't deal with his own, why did he think he could help her?

She gazed at him for a long moment. And he, who was so good at reading between the lines, reading what a person didn't say, couldn't see a thing beyond the blankness of her gaze. "No."

What could he say? "If you ever—"

"I won't," she interrupted. "And unless you want to make a deep, dark, confession and come clean about your baggage —" She broke off, waiting for his answer.

Gritting his teeth, he said, "No. Not a chance." He didn't intend to ever tell her about his "baggage."

"I didn't think so," Della said.

And that settled that. For now, anyway.

NICK WAITED UNTIL Della left the apartment to call Alex back. He'd told Della he'd be down to help shortly. Talking to Alex usually didn't take long, since something was invariably going on with the baby.

He reached her voicemail, of course. "Alex, it's Nick." Before he could hang up, she answered.

"Hi. I just put Jenna down for a nap. Talk about perfect timing."

"How's my beautiful niece?"

"Absolutely perfect. Well, mostly."

Nick laughed. "What do you need?"

"When are you coming back? We miss you. The department misses you too."

"I don't know. I've got a kind of a . . . situation here." Not to mention he still hadn't figured out what he was doing with his life. If anything, the nightmares were getting more frequent, not less. How could he go back to work when he didn't know where the hell his head was? Did he miss Dallas? No. Because for him, being in the Dallas PD brought back too many memories. Problem was, working in Dallas wasn't the only thing that brought back the memories. Almost anything— and nothing—could do it.

"Let me guess," his sister said. "A tall, blond, big bazookas kind of a situation?"

Thinking of Della, he laughed. "Nope. Not even in the ballpark. Brown, brown," he said, using cop shorthand for brown hair and eyes. "Five-five. Curvy. Beautiful."

"Doesn't sound like your usual type."

"She's not. Her name's Della. Della Rose."

"Are you involved with her?" Alex demanded. "Is she important? If she is, why haven't you told me about her? Oh, never mind," she said before he could answer. "Tell me she has a brain."

"Yeah. Della's damned smart."

"Whew. For a minute there, you had me worried. I thought you might have actually fallen for her."

"I have. I'm so in love with her I can't think straight." That was the truth he'd been avoiding. Something he hadn't admitted, or even realized, until just now.

"Wait a minute." Alex smacked the phone against something. "The world as we know it is coming to an end. Did you just say you were in love? You, the original I-just-wanna-have-fun guy?"

"You always said I was riding for a fall. Well, I took one."

Her voice changed, became more maternal. Motherhood agreed with Alex, he had to admit. "Nick, that's great." When he didn't speak, she added, "Isn't it?"

He smiled wryly. "Not exactly. She's not in love with me."

"Are you sure?"

"Oh, yeah. She made it crystal clear where she stood, and it wasn't hearts and flowers." She just wanted him for his body. Some people would have said he'd gotten exactly what he deserved. Some people were assholes.

"Maybe she'll change her mind. Women are always falling for you. Make her fall for you."

He had to laugh. "Make her? I wish I could." His smile faded. "Alex, this is—Jesus, nobody told me it would be like this. I never—it's never mattered before, you know?"

"I do. Remember, I fell for my chief suspect in a bombing case."

"Yeah, but Luke was innocent. And you married him."

"Are you thinking about marriage?" Alex sounded shocked as hell. Understandable, since he was too.

"It's pointless to think of marriage when I can't even get her to commit to a relationship that's about more than sex."

"What's wrong with her?"

Nick laughed again. "Because she doesn't want to get involved with me? Nothing." He sobered. "She won't talk. There's a door she won't open. I'm not sure she ever will. Della's not like other women."

"Obviously not, or you wouldn't have fallen in love with her."

"Behind the door, she's got secrets, problems. A bad childhood. A hard life, nightmares. She's a single mom working her ass off to take care of her kid. And she won't open up to me."

Alex was quiet for a long moment. "Nick, have you opened up to her?"

His sister knew about the case. She knew what Crazy Larry had done to his victims. And she knew Nick had flipped out after shooting the bastard. Alex was a cop. She understood in a way only another cop could.

"How can I? Do you think I'm going to put those pictures in her head? She has a twelve-year-old daughter, for Christ's sake. A sweet, bright, beautiful little girl. A blond-haired, blue-eyed little girl," he added unwillingly. He heard Alex suck in a breath. "I can't do it to her, Alex. Even if I could, it would be wrong."

"Oh, Nick. I hate what this is doing to you. I understand why you feel you shouldn't tell her, but you have to open up to someone sooner or later."

"No, I don't. I'll get past this. I just need some more time."

She didn't answer, but she didn't argue either. After a silence, she sighed and said, "At least you're getting some rest down there. And no murders to worry about."

"About that," Nick said, and told her the story.

Alex didn't have much to say other than she'd have to see what Travis came up with, and offered to look at whatever Dallas PD files she could lay her hands on.

Just before they hung up she said, "Be careful, Nick."

"I will. 'Bye." Nick hadn't told her he'd already been shot. For one thing, it had been a flesh wound. For another, Alex might be a cop, but she was also his sister. A sister who worried about everyone in her family. She didn't need to worry about Nick any more than she already was.

After he hung up, he stood staring at his phone, thinking. If Travis didn't call him by tonight, Nick was calling and asking him if he'd discovered anything. These things took time, but it wouldn't hurt to remind Travis that they needed some answers. Della wasn't the only one getting impatient for some facts.

ON HER WAY HOME, Della replayed her last conversation with Nick over and over in her mind. She didn't want to, but she couldn't stop herself. What had he meant? Did he really want to be involved with her? It had never entered her head that Nick might want more than sex—that she might mean something to him, that he might want something beyond the great sex.

What did he mean to her? She wasn't in love with Nick. She couldn't be. She was no good at relationships. Had never wanted one. Oh, maybe she'd thought about it once or twice, but God knew she'd never met a man, besides Charlie, who was worth much.

But Nick was different. Like her, he wouldn't talk about the case that haunted him. It had to be bad. Nothing minor would give a man like Nick nightmares. And his nightmares were doozies. She felt compassion for him. Wanted to help him. That's all.

So what if the sex was more than she'd ever imagined it could be? So what if she felt alive with Nick, like she never had with another man? That didn't mean anything except that he was a good lover, and she'd obviously had poor experiences with sex in the past. She'd never let anyone close. Nick had done it without her even realizing it. He'd gotten to her, damn it. He cared about her. About Allie. He wouldn't tell her, because he knew she'd spook. But since they'd become lovers, she'd caught him looking at her from time to time. Looking at her like . . . She couldn't describe it.

Like she was the light at the end of the tunnel. And goddamn it, he was a light in the midst of all the crap. She couldn't trust it. Couldn't allow herself to trust him. Allie was too important for Della to make a mistake. She couldn't risk it.

But she wanted to. God, she wanted to.

CHAPTER TWENTY-ONE

THE WEEKEND came, and Mary Lou had another date with Kingston Knight. Della told herself that Mary Lou deserved a break. Her friend had taken care of Allie at all hours for years, thanks to Della's job. Now, with the bar being closed indefinitely, there was no reason Della couldn't take care of Allie herself.

Mary Lou had been out every other night since her first date with Knight. Della considered that a bit excessive. When the hell did the man work? She loved the time with Allie, not that she had her all to herself. Allie was involved in a lot of activities, both after school and on weekends.

When her daughter wasn't busy, she was playing with the dog or on the phone to one of her friends. Her cell was glued to her ear. She wanted a Bluetooth so she didn't have to hold it, but Della vetoed that, knowing that if possible, she'd be on the phone even more. Finally, Allie and Brooke had recently started "studying," getting together after school and alternating houses where they did their schoolwork. They claimed they studied, but Della thought there was an awful lot of laughing going on for that to be the case. Allie was happy, though, and that meant a lot to Della.

Damn it, she missed being with Nick. And not just because she missed the sex. They managed to sneak in a little time together during the day occasionally, but she missed him at night. How did that happen when she'd only spent two nights with him? Not to mention, it had only been a few nights since she'd been with him.

Mary Lou came through the living room and stopped when she saw Della sitting on the couch. "Oh, good, you're home. I have to leave in a minute. Allie's at Brooke's."

"Don't rush off," Della said. "I feel like we never talk anymore." Which they didn't. because when Della wasn't working, Mary Lou was spending time with Kingston Knight.

"We've both been busy," Mary Lou agreed, but she sat beside Della. "I've been going on ride-alongs with King. Research for my book."

"What book? Are you writing a book? When did that happen?" Della knew writing had long been a dream of Mary Lou's, but Della didn't realize it had gone beyond dreaming.

Mary Lou nodded happily. "I've wanted to forever, but I've been too scared. You know how long it took me to get up the courage to submit to magazines. But I talked to King about writing a book, and he convinced me to try. It's a romantic suspense."

"I guess that's reasonable since you've always got your nose in a book, and it's usually a suspense of some sort."

"It's hard, but the ride-alongs are so helpful. King has been great."

Goody for King, Della thought, but managed not to say it. "What's a ride-along?"

"It's when you get to ride with a police officer during a

shift. Sirens going and all that. You wouldn't believe the things I'm learning."

Please God, don't let me throw up. Struggling, Della tried to block the image Mary Lou's words conjured.

Why are you stopping? Where are we? The cops laughed. "We're going to have some fun," they told her, dragging her out of the back of the cruiser and into the woods.

Della put her head in her hands and sucked in deep breaths. *Don't think*, she chanted to herself. *Don't remember. All this was over years ago.*

"What's wrong? You look terrible," Mary Lou said. "Are you sick?"

"No. I'm fine. I haven't eaten today, and I got a little dizzy." Mary Lou gave her a sharp look, but she didn't call Della a liar.

Regaining a shaky control, Della asked, "Isn't that risky? Does the department know about it? What happens if he has to answer a dangerous call?"

"Of course they know. Most police departments have ride-alongs. Or a lot of them do. So far, we haven't had any problems. The actual shifts have been pretty tame, but King has been telling me about all sorts of cases that are exciting, so I can use them in my book."

Della couldn't think of a word to say. Other than, watch out for that son of a bitch, and she knew that wouldn't go over well. Maybe she was being unfair. But she remembered catching Knight watching her a few times when he'd processed both break-ins. Especially when he came to the house. Scrutinizing her as if she knew more than she was saying. The expression had come and gone so quickly she couldn't be sure she hadn't imagined it.

"You still don't like King, do you? What's it going to take

for you to admit he's a good guy? If you'd forget your—your prejudice for once and just talk to him—"

"I have talked to him, Mary Lou. I can't help it, I don't trust him." Fair or not, that's the way she felt.

"You trust Nick. Why Nick and not King?"

"Well, for one thing, Nick took a bullet for me. He's helping me find out the people behind Charlie's murder. And you know what he's been doing for me at the Last Shot. You said yourself I should give him a chance."

"All the more reason to give King a chance too." Della didn't answer. "Sophia likes him," Mary Lou said, reaching down to scratch the dog behind her ears.

"Oh, for—Sophia's a dog. What does that have to do with anything?"

"Dogs are good about recognizing people who mean harm."

Della laughed. "Sophia? That dog is so friendly you could break into the house and shoot a gun, and all she'd do is roll over on her back and beg to have her tummy scratched. And probably pee," Della added.

"Last time she barked. A lot."

"That's true. And we're lucky the burglar didn't shoot her to shut her up."

"Della, that's a horrible thing to say."

"Why? It's the truth. I don't want anyone to hurt the little dog, but for God's sake, Mary Lou, criminals are not generally nice people. The people who wrecked the bar and robbed the house are criminals." Della felt something wet on her bare foot. Looking down at the groveling dog, she realized Sophia had peed on her.

"She just peed on me. Yeah, she's very discerning."

Mary Lou laughed. "Serves you right for maligning her." She stood and said, "And on that note, I'm leaving."

"Mary Lou, wait." Della grabbed her hand before she could leave. "You matter to me. I can't help worrying about you."

Her friend's expression softened. "I know you do." She squeezed Della's hand and let it go. "But you need to trust me on this. King's a good guy."

Della wished she could believe her. But saying anything more would only alienate Mary Lou, and that was the last thing Della wanted.

AS SOON AS MARY Lou left the house, Della left too. She stopped by the hardware store and picked up sample paint colors for the Last Shot's main room. She really liked them and thought they'd cheer up the place. She was no decorator, but she knew what she liked and she wanted something upbeat. There were a lot more things she wanted to do to the bar, but paint was the easiest, quickest, and cheapest way to change the looks. To do much more, she had to wait until the insurance money came in. Restocking and replacing would take a huge chunk out of the cash Charlie had left her.

"Are those your only color choices?" Nick asked Della when he came into the bar and dining area from the kitchen.

"Why? Don't you like them?" Della asked as she finished painting a big patch of the fourth, and last, color on the wall. She stepped back and considered the colors. "I think this one works best," she said, pointing to a bright orange-yellow color. "And then this one for accent on the south wall." Muted red-orange.

"They're . . ." His voice trailed off and she glared at him, daring him to say something negative. "Interesting."

"I know they're bright. That's the point. I'm sick and tired of gloominess. I couldn't ever get Charlie to change anything." Damn. She closed her eyes, seeing Charlie at the bar, telling her the Last Shot had been doing fine for twenty some-odd years, and he didn't see any point in changing the dull tan color of the walls. Besides, he liked it. When he'd had it repainted, which had happened once several years ago in Della's memory, he'd stuck with the original color. Which, in her opinion, had been blah to start with. Now it was blah, dull, and extremely grimy.

But it reminded her of Charlie.

"Are you okay?" Nick asked.

"I feel guilty wanting to change anything."

"Why? Charlie left the place to you. From everything you've said about him, he wouldn't expect you to make a shrine to his memory."

"There's a big difference between making a shrine and changing everything about the place."

"You're over-thinking this." He looked around. "The place needs a paint job. You might as well paint it a color you like."

"You think the colors I picked are ugly."

"No, I don't. I think they're, uh, bright."

"Which in this case means ugly." What was wrong with her? She couldn't even make a simple decision about paint? What did Nick's opinion matter? Why did she even care?

"What's up with you? You've been second-guessing yourself all morning. You haven't made one decision without a boatload of angst. Pick a color and paint the damn walls. It's not life or death."

"It's important," she insisted. "I want the Last Shot to do

well. I need it to do well. This place has to support Allie and me."

"I get that. It did all right when Charlie ran it, didn't it?"

"Yes. But I'm not Charlie. I don't have any experience."

He sighed. "You've been working here for years. Charlie gave you managerial duties, even if he didn't call you a manager. Right?"

Della hunched a shoulder. She'd asked Charlie more than once to name her as manager, but he'd been content with the way things were. Although he had given her a raise when she pointed out how much more she did than waitressing. "What if I screw it all up?"

"You won't screw up anything significant."

"How do you know?"

He walked over and put his hands on her shoulders. "Because you're smart, capable, and you work your ass off. You're not going to fail."

"I might. I had a fight with the liquor store owner this morning." When he looked puzzled, she added, "The only liquor store in town. He used to cut Charlie a deal, so that's where we always got our supplies."

"So what's the problem?"

"He doesn't like me. Honestly, it's more that he didn't like my mother. Hell, I didn't like her either." Nick waited, remaining silent. "Instead of giving me the same deal he gave Charlie, he's gouging me for more. A lot more."

"That's crap. What are you going to do?"

"Find a new one." She bit her lip. "I burned my bridges with him. Mostly."

"Doesn't sound like a big loss. What happened?"

"I got frustrated. I told him to kiss my ass and I'd find another distributor who wouldn't charge me double what he charged Charlie. There are lots of other liquor stores, even if they're not in Freedom. Besides, I'm not going to give someone my money who hates me because of a woman I haven't seen in over twenty years and who I couldn't stand either. I know she was awful, but for God's sake, that was years ago."

"Sins of the mother," Nick said. "It sucks, but some people are like that."

"Especially in small towns," she said. Which was yet another reason why she wouldn't tell anyone about her past, or how Allie was conceived. Allie knew Della had never been married, as did anyone else in town who cared enough to ask. That was one thing. The rest of her past, that was quite another. Allie shouldn't have to suffer for something she had no control over.

Neither should Della, but it was nothing new to her.

"Is that all you're upset about?"

She shrugged. "Sort of."

"What does that mean?"

"We can talk about it later. First, help me move everything from against that wall. We'll leave the accent wall until last," she said, motioning to the wall where the old jukebox stood.

When they finished moving furniture and pictures, and covering everything with plastic sheeting, Nick climbed the ladder, refusing to allow her to paint the top of the wall. When she argued, he ignored her. Rather than dump perfectly good paint over his stubborn head, she started at the bottom. They were going to roll the middle, which should go faster.

"What else are you upset about?" he asked as they began painting.

"Charlie's case. I feel like we're doing absolutely nothing to find out what's been going on. When is your friend going to tell us something? Are you sure he's even looking? Maybe he's jerking us around. The longer we go without knowing why Charlie was murdered, the farther away we get from finding out the truth."

"It takes time to look into things like this, Della. Gaining access to files from other people's cases is difficult. It's never as quick as you want it to be. Added to that, Travis had to put to bed another case before he could devote a lot of time to it."

"Sounds like excuses to me."

"It's not. That's how things work. Besides that, Travis called this morning and said he'll be here tomorrow. He didn't say a lot, but he thinks he found the case your problems are related to. He'll tell us more when he gets here."

"Well, hallelujah. Finally. What kind of case is it?"

"A jewelry heist in Houston. A big one that took place at a charity ball. The majority of the haul hasn't been recovered. Several members of the gang are still free, as well."

"I sure haven't seen any jewels, and we've searched pretty thoroughly."

"Not thoroughly enough."

"Why does he think this case has anything to do with Charlie?"

"One of the thieves they caught ran with Charlie back in the day. Travis is going to talk to him today." He held up a hand. "That's all I know right now."

They'd know more tomorrow. So she just had to be patient for another day. "What about Officer Knight? You asked your friend to check him out, didn't you?"

"Travis hasn't had time to do much about that, but what he has found out is interesting. Knight left a police department in a Houston suburb voluntarily to come to Freedom. No one knows why, or if they do, they're not saying. The chief here has a rep for being a pain in the ass."

"That's no surprise. Knight must have had a reason for coming here."

"Yeah, but we don't know what. Travis is going to dig some more." He waited a minute and said, "You still haven't told me everything that's upsetting you. Spill it."

"Is this your detective skills at work?"

"No, this is my 'I have eyes' skills at work."

She sighed, thinking she might as well tell him. "I'm worried about Mary Lou. I think she's really fallen for Knight."

"Did you try to talk her out of dating him?"

"Sort of. I told her I didn't trust him. Which I don't. She kept talking about what a great guy he is and I should give him a chance. Oh, and get this." She stopped painting and stood, putting her hands on her hips. "Mary Lou said Sophia liked him. Like that's supposed to clinch the matter. She's a dog, for God's sake, not a psychic."

Nick looked down at her and smiled. "Dogs can be very perceptive. They sense things people often miss. All of the K9 officers I've known were extremely accurate in their judgment."

"K9 officers? You mean police dogs?" she asked incredulously. "Do you know Sophia? She's about as far removed from a police dog as you can get."

He laughed. "She does seem to love everyone indiscriminately."

"She might lick 'em to death, or trip them, but that's about it."

"Yeah. Which is why you should keep the alarm on as much as possible." He climbed down the ladder and moved it over to start on another area.

"I have been," she protested. "Most of the time," she added when he lifted an eyebrow.

He paused before climbing the ladder. "Alarms don't work if you don't turn them on."

"I'd go insane if I had to turn it on and off every time Allie and Sophia go in and out. Which is basically any time Allie is home. I can't tell you how many times Allie has set it off."

"No need. I get the feed, remember?"

She'd forgotten that, which was odd, considering. "After the fifth call from the neighbors, I quit turning it on when Allie's home. At least until she goes to bed." Nick's expression spoke volumes. "Do you really think he—they—would risk coming back in the middle of the day? We live in town. We have neighbors who are home a lot."

"Do I think it's likely? No. But Della, I can't guarantee anything." He set down his paintbrush then took hers and set it beside his. He put his arms around her. "I want you to be safe. You and Allie and Mary Lou. It's important."

"I know. I understand."

"I'm not sure you do." He kissed her, a long, slow, soul-stirring kiss, and then let her go.

With that cryptic comment, they went back to work.

CHAPTER TWENTY-TWO

NICK'S FRIEND came to town the next day. Della heard Nick talking to him in the bar area and, instead of going on in to meet him, she hid behind the swinging doors to the kitchen and gathered her strength. Since meeting Nick, she seemed to do nothing but deal with more cops. Nick swore Travis Taylor was a nice guy, but what did Nick know?

She peeked out to get a look at Detective Taylor. He had dark blond hair, short but not super short. He didn't particularly scream cop to her, which was interesting. His face was stubbled with a beard, like he hadn't shaved in a few days. She admitted he looked good. He wore jeans and a Houston Texans T-shirt. Sunglasses concealed his eyes.

Della sucked in a deep breath and pushed open the doors.

"Let me see where Della is," Nick was saying. "She'll need to hear this, and there's no sense you going through it twice."

"I'm here," Della said, coming up beside Nick.

"Hey, I was just about to come find you." Nick introduced them to each other.

Detective Taylor took off his sunglasses and offered his

hand. Cop's eyes, hard and astute, cataloging everything about her for further consideration. Then he smiled and she thought she'd imagined that sharp-eyed once-over. Della bet he found that transformative smile pretty damn useful. While it might soothe some people, it only made her more suspicious.

She didn't want to shake his hand. She didn't like to touch men, especially cops, unnecessarily. But he was doing Nick, and her, a favor so she sucked it up and did it anyway.

"We can go outside," she said, dropping his hand quickly.

"Okay. Be there in a minute," Nick said. "I'm going to get the ledger."

Which left her alone with Detective Taylor. *Gee, thanks, Nick.* It occurred to her to offer the detective something to drink. "We're not up and running yet, so there's no beer, but I can offer coffee or a soft drink."

"Coffee would be great. Need some help?"

"I'm a waitress. I think I can handle it myself." Be good, Della, she remembered belatedly. "But thanks. Why don't you go on outside and I'll be there in a minute?"

Though she took her time, thinking surely Nick would be back, he was still missing when she went out with three mugs. "Is black okay?"

"Black is perfect. Thanks."

Della set Nick's cup down between them and took the seat across from Taylor.

"How long have you and Nick known each other?" he asked.

Her automatic response was "none of your business," but she bit the words back. "Just a few weeks."

"I haven't been to Freedom before. I've heard it has great fishing. Seems like a nice place."

"It is when people aren't getting murdered, vandalized, or

robbed." God, she sucked at small talk. Taylor made a few more efforts to talk to her but she answered him as briefly as possible. Where the hell was Nick? "I don't know what's taking Nick so long. Maybe I should go—"

"Hey, sorry. I had to take a call. Here's the ledger." Nick handed it to Taylor and sat down. "Thanks for the coffee."

Impatient to get to the point, Della asked, "What did you find out about Charlie and this jewelry robbery you and Nick thought was connected?"

"Your hunch was right," he said to Nick. To both of them, he said, "Twenty years ago, Charlie Burke owned a pawn shop in Houston. He was suspected of fencing stolen goods, but never convicted, or even charged, for that matter."

"Maybe that's because he was innocent," Della said.

"Nice theory, but this"—he indicated the ledger—"says differently. Burke was successful for a number of years. He fenced jewels, predominately, and had contacts with several crime rings, we think, including a couple that specialized in stealing high-end jewelry."

"How high-end?" Nick asked.

"The top. Jewelry of the mega-wealthy. Burke's clients had a number of creative ways of relieving the wealthy of their jewels." He continued, "Then Burke's daughter died or was killed. It was ruled an accidental drug overdose, although there was evidence that there was more to it." Taylor's expression changed. Chagrinned, he said, "The PD didn't put a lot of manpower on it, so the ruling stood."

"Surprise, surprise," Della said dryly.

"It happens," Taylor said. "No one said it was a good thing. That's just the way things go sometimes."

"I'm still having a hard enough time believing Charlie was

a fence. What is it about the ledger that makes you think that's true?"

"The ledger tracks thefts and tallies sales." He flipped it open and showed her a page. "We'll be able to discover more and possibly link some of these heists to people involved in more current crimes."

"After twenty years?" Della asked. "Isn't that a stretch?"

Taylor shrugged. "It might be. But a lot of these people are career criminals. They don't change just because they get caught once or twice. They go to prison, get out, and do it all over again."

"If he was a criminal, Charlie changed. I never saw him do anything that wasn't on the up and up."

The cop looked unconvinced. "We'll be looking into that."

She started to argue, to insist she knew Charlie, but then sank bank in her chair. What was the point? Nick and his friend had made up their minds. Still, even if it was true, Charlie had cut ties with that life years ago. Over and done with.

Except whatever had gotten Charlie killed was very much the here and now.

"Was your boss involved with any shady characters? Did any of them come into the bar, especially recently?" Taylor asked.

"No, he didn't want—" She stopped abruptly. Oh, damn. Damn, damn, damn.

"What is it, Della?" Nick asked.

"Charlie had an argument with a man a week or so before he died. He got bent out of shape over it. At the time, I didn't think it was suspicious. He's had other people come in occasionally who he didn't like. But this guy seemed to really bother him. Charlie told him to get out and that he 'left that behind twenty years ago.'" She looked at Nick. "I can't believe I didn't remember that until now. You even asked me about suspicious people, and I still didn't connect it."

"Can you describe him?" Nick asked her.

She tried to remember. "He wasn't tall. He had brown hair, long, to his shoulders. But the main thing I remember is his face looked like a ferret." To Taylor she said, "Could that man be the one the killers were talking about?"

"It's possible. I brought a picture." Taylor opened his briefcase and pulled out a photo, tossing it on the table. "Look familiar?"

Della picked it up to look more closely. "That's him. So, you think he asked Charlie to hide this loot for him? Why? Charlie wasn't a crook. Besides, he told the man to get out."

"This is Leon Rivers."

"The man the killers mentioned. They said he'd been here," she remembered.

"I found out a little more about Charlie Burke and Leon Rivers besides the fact that they were tight years ago. Really tight," Taylor continued. "Partners, most likely. They had some kind of falling-out after Burke's daughter died, and Burke decided to retire. As far as I could find out, he didn't keep up with the old crews. He cut all his ties in Houston, moved to Freedom, and became a model citizen."

Della couldn't help but laugh. "I can see his face if anyone described him that way."

"The point is, he moved here and went straight. But Leon Rivers tracked him down for a reason." The detective reached in his briefcase and pulled out another photo. "And it's a doozy." He laid the picture on the table in between Nick and Della so they could both see.

"Good God, is it real?" Della asked. A picture of a bracelet on a woman's arm unlike anything she'd ever seen. Which, yeah, wasn't saying a lot. But this thing, she'd never even seen a picture of something like it. A huge emerald, maybe two inches by two inches, set in the middle of a wide band of so many diamonds she couldn't begin to count them.

"It's real, all right," Nick said. "This is from the Fitzweiler heist, isn't it?"

"You got it," Taylor said. "I suspected this could be the connection when you first told me about the murder. But I wanted more confirmation." He looked at Nick. "As you know, it can be hard to get information on a current case. And this one is very much current and unsolved. Someone, and we now believe it was Rivers, absconded with the bracelet and a good bit of the haul."

"It's called *L'émeraude Perfide*," Nick said. "The Faithless Emerald. It's supposed to be cursed. A man named Upshot had it made for his mistress in New Orleans in the 1920s. The day he gave it to her, he was killed in a freak accident. He fell out of a streetcar and was run over. The mistress died the next day, in a fall down the stairs. Wearing the bracelet. The story goes that Upshot's wife put a voodoo curse on it."

Della gaped at him. "You're telling me you believe in voodoo? You?"

"I didn't say I believed it. But everyone who's ever owned it, or had it in their possession, at least that I've heard about, has had some bad mojo. This time it was going to be auctioned off, because the owners had died in a boating accident and the heirs wanted the money."

"It was part of a jewelry heist that took place in Houston, at a charity ball, several months ago," Taylor said. "They had a model wearing the bracelet to stir up interest for the auction. She was killed during the robbery. The cops caught a few of those responsible, but a couple of the majors got away. With the stash."

"Houston PD traced them to a fence who was rumored to move high-end jewelry," Nick said. "But before the cops could move in, the jewels and the fence vanished."

"The Blasters planned the heist," Taylor told Nick.

"Shit. The Blasters are behind all this? Are they the ones who found Rivers and killed him?"

"We don't know. If they did, they're being more subtle than usual in coming after Della."

"The Blasters?" Della asked, her stomach sinking. "You mean the gang that's part of the Death Tangos?" *There's irony for you*, Della thought. She'd managed to avoid the violent gang when she lived in Houston. Only to have them after her now?

"Yes. But we're not certain that they're responsible for your boss's death."

"How much is something like this worth?" Della asked, looking at the picture. Thousands, certainly. Hundreds of thousands? For a bracelet?

"Here's where it gets really interesting," Taylor said. "The bracelet alone is worth a cool million. With the rest of the heist, we're talking close to two million."

Della dropped the picture like it was on fire. "A million dollars? A bracelet that costs a million dollars? Are you freaking kidding me?"

"Nope," Nick said. "That's a conservative estimate. So now we know what they're after. No wonder they killed Charlie when he wouldn't cooperate."

"Charlie didn't know anything about it," Della insisted. "If he had, he'd have told the cops. He and Hayes hated each other, but Charlie would still have gone to the cops."

"A million bucks, or more, is a hell of a lot of money," Nick said. "Not to mention, would he really rat out a former partner?"

"Detective Taylor said himself that Charlie had been straight for years. I don't believe he would help this Rivers guy."

"Call me Travis," he put in.

Della paid no attention. "And besides, remember what he told the men who killed him. Charlie said he hadn't seen Leon Rivers in twenty years."

"Which we know wasn't true," Nick said. "You just identified his picture as the man who had been here days before Charlie was murdered."

That stopped her short. "That isn't the point. The point is, those bastards think Charlie had the bracelet. Or that I do," she said with sickening clarity. Was that what the burglary at her house had been about?

"Or they might believe the jewels are here, somewhere that Burke stashed them, and that you don't know anything," the detective said.

"Damn, that's comforting," she said sarcastically. "Then why did they break in to my house if they think Charlie hid them?"

Taylor and Nick exchanged glances.

"Tell her the truth. She can take it," Nick said.

The detective lifted a shoulder in an "if you say so" gesture. "We believe whoever orchestrated the break-ins is waiting for you to find the jewels. To locate the bracelet, if not the entire haul that's still missing. They've hit the bar, the apartment, and now your house without finding anything. Obviously, you haven't either, or you'd have given it to the police or fenced it yourself, and then left town."

"I would never—"

"I'm sure you wouldn't," Taylor said hastily. "But the criminals might think you would."

Slightly mollified, she said, "We've searched. Everywhere. I don't know where else to look. What if it isn't here? What if they're wrong and it's in a completely different place?"

Neither Taylor nor Nick said anything. Which was answer in itself. "We're screwed," Della said. "Or rather, I'm screwed."

Nick put his hand over hers. "You had it right the first time. I'm in this with you, Della, and I'm not leaving."

Ever? *Don't do this to yourself,* she thought. *Don't hope for more than you're ever likely to get.* Be content with Nick helping her now, and let the future settle itself.

NICK AND DELLA stared at each other. He squeezed her hand again. "You don't have to do this alone, Della," he repeated.

She started to speak but her cell phone rang. Was it his imagination or did she look relieved?

"I have to go," Della said a few minutes later, after ending her phone call. "Mary Lou is going out. I'll be at home with Allie." She smiled wryly. "She's not happy that I won't let her stay there alone, or with just Brooke, but I'm not about to do that. Especially now that we think the Blasters could be involved."

"Don't forget the alarm," Nick reminded her.

Della rolled her eyes but she said, "I won't. Don't nag."

Travis laughed. "She's got you there, buddy."

"Shut up, Travis." But if he knew Travis, he wouldn't.

"We'll have to start the search tomorrow," Della said. "Unless you want to start without me."

"I'll wait," Nick said.

"I'm about to leave," Travis said, getting up. "It was nice to meet you, Della." He stuck out his hand, and once again, Della seemed to be searching for a way to get out of shaking it.

She finally took it, gave it a quick shake and dropped it quickly. "Yeah, thanks. I mean, thanks for finding the information. I'll see you tomorrow, Nick."

Travis waited until she'd left, watching her leave a little more appreciatively than Nick liked. Finally, he took his eyes off Della's butt and looked at Nick. "She's a looker."

"Yeah."

"Not your usual type."

"No."

His friend leaned back in his chair and put his hands behind his head. "You two together?"

For now, Nick thought. But he sure as hell wouldn't give Travis that opening. "Hands off."

"Just askin'," he said with a grin. "Because if you aren't—"

"We are." Nick scowled. His buddy, Travis, who rarely met a woman he couldn't talk into bed. Although he'd find it damn hard with Della. "Don't make me hurt you."

Travis laughed and sat up. "You and who else? Seriously, dude, why doesn't she like me?"

"Don't take it personally. Della hates cops."

"You're a cop."

"I'm the exception."

"Lucky you."

"Yeah." Lucky for now. But assuming he ever got his shit together enough to go back to Dallas, what would happen then?

CHAPTER TWENTY-THREE

L UCKY FOR HIM, Mary Lou liked to talk, King thought. He rarely had to ask a question, since she talked about anything and everything that affected her. And whatever affected Della Rose affected Mary Lou as well.

King had the night off, and after taking Mary Lou to dinner, they'd come back to his place and immediately hit the sheets. In most of his relationships—in all of them to date—King had been sick of the woman by this point. But it didn't work that way with Mary Lou. He wasn't sure why. Maybe because she seemed to genuinely care about him. Or because she was the first truly decent woman he'd been with. He hadn't ever been attracted to the decent type before. He liked his women raunchy and experienced.

To his shock, the sex was great with Mary Lou. Sex wasn't the only thing that was good with her, either. She listened to him like every word out of his mouth was fucking gold. God, he was falling in love with her. He had even been thinking of ways to take her with him once he found the damn bracelet.

She'd go for it—if he got her out of town before she found out he and Hayes were the ones behind Della's troubles.

And what's Mary Lou going to say when you take her to the Maldives along with your cut of a million dollar stolen bracelet?

His cut, assuming Hayes didn't somehow double-cross him. That was the problem dealing with people like his chief. You couldn't trust them. Which meant King needed to find the stuff first. Maybe he should cut his losses and turn in the bracelet once he found it. There was bound to be a reward. Unless he wound up being an accessory to murder.

Damn.

"King?" Mary Lou was snuggled up against his side. Warm and naked, just how he liked her. "Does it bother you that Della doesn't like you?"

"Not as long as you don't dump me because of her."

"I wouldn't do that. I keep hoping she'll change her mind. Did I tell you that Houston policeman—the detective—came to town today?"

King kept his voice carefully neutral, even though it worried him that Sheridan had brought a Houston cop into the mix. "You mentioned he was coming, but I hadn't heard what happened." He knew he'd covered his tracks, but there were still a lot of potentially harmful things the cop might discover.

"I don't understand why they won't talk to your department. Oh, I get why she won't talk to Chief Hayes, or let Nick talk to him either. I know Della really hates Hayes, but you're the law here too."

"Can't be helped. I can't totally blame them. The Chief hasn't been forthcoming with any of the investigations."

"Still . . . Well, anyway, Della told me about it. Travis Taylor —the cop from Houston—mentioned a robbery at one of those fancy balls not long ago. They think Charlie knew one of the thieves, one of them who got away. With a bunch of jewelry," she added breathlessly. "They think this man, I can't remember his name, they think he hid the jewels somewhere in the bar."

"So did Charlie know about it? Was he involved?"

"I don't believe it, and neither does Della, even though Nick and his friend seem to. No matter what they say, Charlie was a straight arrow as long as I knew him. Della says the same thing."

That, or he had the two women snowed. "Della doesn't know anything? Doesn't she have an idea where Burke might have hidden the stuff?"

"Why would Della know?" she asked sharply. "I told you, Charlie wouldn't do it. Della heard him tell the man to get lost. So they think that man hid the things without Charlie's knowledge."

That was Mary Lou. Loving and loyal. She'd be loyal to him too, until reality hit her in the face. He shook off his dismal thoughts and asked, "What kind of jewelry? Anything special?"

"That's the crazy thing." She sat up in bed, eyes sparkling. "Nick's friend thinks it might be some outrageously expensive bracelet."

"How expensive?" King asked.

"It's worth a million dollars. Can you believe it? A million bucks." She laughed. "Isn't that wild?"

"Pretty wild," King agreed. At least now Della and Sheridan knew what to look for. King was certain Della hadn't found the jewelry yet. If she had, she'd have fenced the bracelet herself, in which case, why was she still in town? Or she'd have turned in the loot to the cops. To Hayes? King couldn't see it.

Besides, he'd have heard about it if she'd turned it in to anyone.

So, she hadn't found it yet. Della needed the motivation to find the haul. He hadn't heard from Hayes about her juvie record. Hayes had connections. King would bet the bank that he'd gotten into those files. If he had, he hadn't shared his findings with King.

King wasn't sure what Hayes planned, but King intended to find the jewels first. That would give him the upper hand, and then he could decide what he'd do.

"What are you thinking about?" Mary Lou asked him. "It must be good since you're smiling so much."

By themselves, the other jewels were a sweet haul, but the emerald and ice bracelet was fucking orgasmic. *L'émeraude Perfide*. Even the name sounded like money. Enough to set him up for life. And the icing on this priceless cake was tasty little Mary Lou Meadows.

She was still looking at him questioningly. "I'm thinking about you," he said.

"Oh?" She smiled, a sweet, sexy smile. "You don't happen to be thinking about this, do you?" She stoked her hand up and down his cock and laughed as he instantly hardened. "Now what are we going to do about this?" she asked innocently.

"I don't know. What did you have in mind?"

She whispered a suggestion that had his eyes crossing. He lay back and helped her climb on top of him. "Show me," he growled.

"Oh, I will," she said, and began to ride.

DELLA SHOWED UP at the Last Shot bright and early the next morning, ready to begin the search.

"I didn't expect you until later," Nick said. "What did you do about Allie?"

"I called Mary Lou early and asked her if she could come home and stay with Allie. I told her I had business that couldn't wait." Della frowned and added, "I wound up telling Mary Lou what we found out from Detective Taylor. She probably went straight to Knight with the news. Do you think that's a problem?"

"Probably not. Unless he's involved somehow."

"Do you really think he is?" Della asked.

"I don't know," Nick said. "I have no reason to. All I have is a feeling that something's off about him."

"I wish she wasn't involved with him."

"Nothing we can do about that." Della still looked worried. Nick pulled her into his arms and kissed her, and when she would have spoken, kissed her again. Della didn't initiate spontaneous shows of affection often. It didn't bother him. Much.

"What was that for?" she asked him after she finally relaxed and kissed him back.

"Because I wanted to."

She smiled. "Work before play."

"I was afraid you'd say that," he said, but he let her go.

"Where do we start?" Della asked.

"Methodically. Start in one corner of the room and go from there."

"This is going to take forever."

Nick couldn't argue. "Pick your corner."

"You go ahead. I have a text coming in and want to make sure it's not about Allie. Or from her, although she's not supposed to have her phone on during school." She gave him a wry smile. "She's had it confiscated before."

Nick grinned. "Teenagers. Their phones are glued to their hands."

Della picked up her phone. "She's twelve, she's not—" She broke off abruptly, staring at the text message.

Her face went chalk white.

He crossed the room to stand beside her. "Della? What is it? Is something wrong with Allie?"

"Nothing. Nothing. It's not Allie." She turned it off so quickly he only had a glimpse of the text, not even enough to see what it was. Her skin color turned from white to a greenish cast. Without another word, she dropped her phone on the bar, clapped a hand over her mouth, and ran to the bathroom. He debated briefly, then shrugged, picked up her phone and followed, stopping outside the bathroom door.

Although he could hear her heaving, he didn't pound on the door. He didn't even check to see if it was unlocked. She wouldn't want him in there. If he knew Della, she was wishing he wasn't present at all. And she'd definitely be pissed if he checked her text, but as he intended to get answers whether she wanted to give them or not, he turned on the phone.

She hadn't locked it and the text, message and picture, came up immediately. *You know what I want. Give it to me and this disappears. I'll text you soon, and you'd better have it.* Nick recognized the picture for what it was immediately. Della's mug shot. She was young. Very young, but still, very clearly, Della. And just as clearly, someone had beaten the crap out of her.

So she'd been arrested. She'd said she left home at fifteen. Anything could have happened, from theft to things he didn't even want to think about. And now someone was blackmailing her with this information. Nick checked, and as he suspected, the Caller ID was blocked. Probably a burner phone. Della had to come out of the bathroom sooner or later, so he waited. He heard water running and then finally shutting off.

Long minutes later, Della emerged from the bathroom. She started and backed up when she saw him.

"Are you all right?"

"Fine. Something I ate. Food poisoning."

"Interesting timing." She didn't speak, but looked at him with stricken eyes. "Della," he said softly, "I read the text. And saw the mug shot."

"You had no right to look at my phone." Though she tried to sound angry, she sounded resigned, and miserable.

"No. But I did. You want to tell me why you were arrested?"

She wilted. It was like whatever had been propping her upright had been removed. "No, I don't want to tell you. I can't tell you."

"Is it that bad?"

Her eyes lifted to his. Tortured, desperate eyes. "Worse."

"Come here." He took her arm and guided her, firmly, over to the one booth they'd left uncovered when they began painting. "Sit." He made her sit, then slid in beside her. "Talk to me. Tell me what's going on."

She shook her head.

Nick handed her the phone. "Trust me, Della. I've heard it all. Nothing you can tell me will shock me. I've been a cop a long time."

"God," she whispered. "Oh, God, I don't know what to do."

Nick squeezed her hand but remained silent.

Slowly, she reclaimed her hand and turned on the phone. Brought the text up and handed it to him. "I was fifteen. Barely. My mother had kicked me out just a few weeks before this."

"Who beat you?" With the picture magged up, he could see one eye was swollen, her lip had been split, and her cheekbone as well. "You were just a kid. Who beat you?" It could have been anyone, from a mugger to . . . a john. *Ah, Christ, don't let it be a john.*

"The boys in blue," she finally answered.

"The cops did this to you?"

She shrugged. "Officer Carlisle and Officer Ames. I've tried to forget their names, so many times. But I can't forget."

"Why? Why did they arrest you? What were the charges?" Not to mention, was the mug shot the only thing the blackmailer had, or did he have the whole shebang? The entire file that should have been sealed when she turned eighteen.

"Prostitution. Resisting arrest. Battery of a police officer."

God. Exactly what he'd feared. Living on the streets. Surviving however she could. "Were the charges legit?" he asked, though he knew the answer.

"Yes. I was hooking. Although, I think selling your body for food shouldn't be considered a crime." She continued, speaking dispassionately. "I lived on the streets in Houston. I had no money, no skills, and I was trying to stay out of the foster care system." She shook her head. "I don't know why. I'd heard horror stories about it, but nothing could have been worse than living with my mother."

"A lot of kids end up doing anything they can to survive. You survived, Della." She simply shrugged again and looked away. "What about the other charges? Is that why they beat you? Because you resisted arrest?"

"No. I didn't resist arrest."

He had a bad feeling about this. A really bad feeling. He wanted to take her hand, but she'd put both hands in her lap and was sitting very straight. Her body language said very clearly, "don't touch me." "What happened, Della?"

She turned back and looked at him, eyes dead, face impassive. Expressionless. "I resisted being raped by the cops who picked me up. I fought back, scratched their faces, kneed one of them, spit on them, anything I could do to get away, so they added battery of a police officer to the charges."

"Goddamn it." He wished he could have just five minutes with the two bastards who had raped her. Five minutes to beat the bloody hell out of them. "They should have been shot." Nick knew things like that happened. They were the exception, but bad shit happened. Shortly before he'd come to Freedom, a cop in the Metroplex had been arrested and convicted of raping an eighteen-year-old girl in his squad car, for God's sake.

She continued, as if she hadn't heard him. Maybe she hadn't, lost in the past as she was. "At first I was grateful. People don't think of Houston as cold, but when you have no shelter, no coat, not even a sweater, and it's winter, it's damned cold. The car was warm and I was so cold. Teeth chattering, bone-deep cold. I figured they'd put me in juvie, and I wouldn't have to do it anymore. Hooking, I mean. The whores who'd been around told me I'd get used to it, and pretty soon it would be nothing. No big deal. But I never did. I hated it. Every single time a man put his hands on me, I hated it.

"Maybe I would have gotten used to it. I'd only been hooking a couple of weeks when they picked me up. We drove and drove, so long I fell asleep. Then they stopped. Pulled me out of the car and dragged me to the woods. I knew. So I fought. They beat me, but I kept fighting. Then they hand-cuffed me and raped me. Only, they said it wasn't rape because I was a hooker."

She'd been a kid. Just a kid. Why was it always the kids? "You know that's bullshit, don't you?"

"Does it matter?"

"Yeah, it matters a lot. You were the victim of a crime, Della. They should have been thrown in jail, not you."

"I was going to tell everyone I could when I got to the station. Shout it out, get them arrested." She smiled humor-lessly. "What can I say? I was still young and naive. Even after . . . But I learned quickly. They found a way to keep me quiet. Being Big Berta's bitch didn't sound like something I wanted to do. They showed me a picture of her." She shud-dered. "Just her picture scared the shit out of me."

God, it just kept getting worse. "The system failed you. The people who should have protected you, the police, victimized you instead. I'm sorry isn't enough, but it's all I've got. I am so damn sorry, Della."

"It doesn't matter. But this"—she tapped on her cell phone —"this is blackmail. Because whoever's behind it knows I'll do anything, *anything I have to* for Allie. To protect her."

God. Of course. Her daughter. "Allie's father—"

"Allie's father was a rapist. I think. But I can't even say that for certain."

"Allie doesn't know," Nick said.

Della shook her head. "She's never going to, either. How could I tell her? What would I say? Can you imagine saying, 'Sorry, honey, but your father was either a rapist or one of my johns.' Knowing how she was conceived would destroy her."

"It doesn't have to. You chose to have her. You chose to keep her. Allie knows you love her."

"Come on, Nick. How would you have reacted if your mother had told you such a thing?"

He couldn't imagine it. "You said your mother never told you who your father was. You survived hearing that and worse."

"Yeah, and I became a teenage prostitute. If I only had to tell her about the rape, that would be bad enough. But telling her I was a hooker?" She shook her head. "God, no."

"This clipping could be all they have. It could be a ploy to scare you."

"It worked. The thought of Allie finding out terrifies me. She'll hate me. Worse, she'll hate herself. Allie's twelve. The worst possible age to have everything you believed in turn out to be a lie."

"Not everything. You love her. That's not a lie."

"Everything else—"

Nick interrupted. "I heard you tell her that her father was a bad man. A man who hurt you. A man you'd never see again. None of that's a lie."

"It isn't a lie, but it isn't the whole truth either. And if I can't find the bracelet and the other jewels—because we know now what he wants—and he follows through on the threat"— she broke off, putting her head in her hands—"Oh, my God, Allie, my little girl, will be the whore's daughter. Just like . . . I was."

He moved her hands and made her look at him. "That's bullshit, Della. You're nothing like your mother, no matter what happened in your past."

She gave a strangled laugh. "Like mother, like daughter. Oh, God, I can hear the gossip now."

"You're imagining a scenario that might never come to pass."

"Do you really believe that?"

"Della, you were a juvenile. Your file should have been automatically sealed when you turned eighteen, unless you were arrested again."

"I wasn't. And apparently, my file wasn't sealed."

"Did you petition to have it sealed? Once you became an adult?" He doubted she had. She probably hadn't known she needed to do it.

"Are you kidding? I stayed as far away from any cops or courts as I could. Otherwise CPS might have come after me." She closed her eyes. "Oh, God, if CPS gets wind of this . . ."

"One thing at a time," he said, though the thought of Child Protective Services investigating Della worried him as much or more than it did Della. "If your records were sealed automatically, and it's likely they were, then those records would not be accessible to just anyone. But . . . anyone in the criminal justice system could request them."

Della stared at him, her face looking greener by the moment. "Meaning the local cops."

He nodded. "Hayes and Knight could have requested access. In fact, they're the most likely suspects. One or both of them could be your blackmailer."

"Hayes and Knight could be behind everything. And if they are, they'll take the information in my file and dribble it out, bit by bit, making me crazier each moment I can't find the damn bracelet." She buried her face in her hands. "They'll tell CPS. They'll tell them, and I'll lose Allie."

He wanted to reassure her, wanted to protect her from this, from every bad thing that had ever happened to her. He wouldn't fail. Not this time. "No one will tell CPS."

"They will if we don't find what they're looking for."

"Not necessarily. Even if they did, CPS needs a better

reason than what's in a supposedly sealed juvenile file to take your child."

"You can't guarantee that. No one can." Nick put his arms around her, gathered her in, even though she resisted. Held her. Just held her until she put her arms around him and whispered, "I'm so scared. I can't lose Allie. I can't."

"You won't. I swear you won't." They stayed like that, wrapped in each other's arms, for a long, long time. But Della never cried.

When they finally released each other, Della sucked in a breath and straightened her shoulders. Devastated, but dry-eyed. Once again, he was awed by her strength. "What can I do?" she asked. "Besides find the jewelry and let Hayes and Knight have it, I mean. Even if I do that, they could still blow up my life."

"I can ask Travis for help. The caller ID was blocked. I'm sure they used a burner phone, but Travis can run the numbers on your cell. He can investigate Hayes, and Knight again."

She looked at him like he was nuts. "No. I'm not going to the cops. *Any* cops."

"I know you don't trust him, but you trust me. Travis is a good cop, Della. He's a good person. He knows what life on the streets is like. He won't judge you."

To say she looked skeptical didn't even touch it. "Sure he won't. I bet he'll think it's awesome you're sleeping with a hooker."

"You're not a hooker."

"Right. Former hooker."

"Shit." He squeezed the bridge of his nose and tried to think how best to convince her. "Look, Della, we need help, and Travis already knows what's going on. He has resources I don't have right now."

"He's your friend." She shrugged. "If you don't care that he knows you're fu—"

"Goddamn it, Della, it's more than that."

She raised an eyebrow. "Is it?"

For him it was. For her? He didn't know. But he said, "Yeah, it is."

Della simply looked at him. She didn't deny it, but she sure as hell didn't agree with him either. "Della, it's not your fault."

"The rape isn't. But the rest of it . . . Nobody made me, Nick. I got into prostitution voluntarily."

"Damn, Della, you were a kid with no home, no family, no money. You had to survive."

"Nick, are you deaf? Men paid money to have sex with me. Twenty will get you off, fifty's your ticket to paradise. I was a hooker. There's no way to pretty that up."

He reached in her lap and pulled her hands up, placing them on the table, then covering them with his own. "Listen to me. I've seen thieves and murderers, crack whores and hookers. Drug dealers, rapists, child abusers. I've seen the dregs of humanity. You're nothing like that. You were a child who made a bad choice. A child who made the only choice she thought possible at the time."

"Can you really look at me the same, now that you know?"

"No." She tried to pull her hands away but he held on. "Knowing what you've been through, how you survived, no—not just survived but raised a great kid—it makes me admire you even more. You're goddamn amazing, Della."

"You're crazy."

Not the time, Nick. Not the place. Don't do it.

"No." He smiled at her wryly. "Not crazy. I'm in love with you, Della."

CHAPTER TWENTY-FOUR

ELLA STARED AT him, wondering if she could possibly have heard him right. She'd told him she'd been a hooker and he'd told her . . . he was in love with her?

"I know." He smiled ruefully. "Not quite the time or place I should have chosen. But"—he patted her hands, squeezed them—"there it is."

"Is this a joke?" she finally managed to ask.

"Do I look like I'm joking?"

"No. But you don't look crazy either, and you obviously are."

"Hell, Della, I didn't want to fall in love. I'm thirty-five years old, and I figured it was never going to happen to me. And then I met you, and you've been turning me inside out ever since."

"What's between us . . . It's just sex. You know that's all it is." *Wasn't it?*

"No. It's not. I know the difference, Della."

Oh, God, he really meant it. She didn't want to hurt him. But everything he said was terrifying to her. Enjoying sex was a miracle. Love? What did she know about love? "I don't—I don't love you, Nick."

He didn't seem shocked. Or even hurt, for that matter. "Maybe you don't. And maybe you just won't let yourself."

Their gazes met and held. A part of her wanted to believe him. The rest of her couldn't risk it. "I can't deal with this right now." Not on top of everything she'd ever dreaded coming to pass. "The only thing that matters now is Allie. CPS isn't my only worry. If this gets out, if Allie finds out how she was conceived, it will destroy her."

Thankfully, he accepted the change of subject. Not that this one was any better. "You've never considered telling her?"

"No! God, no." The very thought reduced Della to mindless panic.

"Telling her doesn't have to be a disaster. Knowing the truth doesn't have to ruin her life."

"Yes. It will."

"You don't know who your father was, do you?"

Her face hardened. "No, and that's undoubtedly a good thing."

"Did it ruin your life? Not knowing who he was?"

"No. My mother told me when I was little. I don't remember when. She said I was a little bastard, and she had no clue which lowlife was my father. She did it to hurt me." Even now, years later, Della could see the satisfaction on her mother's face when she'd told her. "She was good at that."

"You wouldn't tell Allie to hurt her. You'd make her understand."

"How? You make it sound simple when we both know it's anything but. How do I tell my sweet little girl that I don't know who her father is? That he's either a rapist or some random john?"

"Tell her the truth. Tell her you loved her from the moment you had her. From the moment you knew you were pregnant. Tell her you did everything in your power to keep her safe." He paused and asked, "How did you manage to keep Allie? It couldn't have been easy."

"It wasn't. After juvie, before I went into foster care, they found my mother and called her. Big shock, she told them she wouldn't take me back. I wouldn't have gone, I'd have done anything rather than go back to her. Oh, wait, I did." He said nothing, waiting patiently for her to go on.

"Heather and Tad Jones became my foster parents. They were . . . okay. They knew I was pregnant. They said I could keep the baby, that they'd help me."

"Did they?"

"They tried." Looking back, she knew she should have stayed with the Joneses. Her life would have been easier. "But I didn't trust them. I didn't trust anyone. Especially not . . . him."

"Did he—"

"No, he never touched me. I can see now that he wasn't like that. He'd never have hurt me. But back then, I couldn't stand to be around men. As soon as I turned eighteen, I took Allie and left. We were on our own for about six months, and then I got the call about inheriting my mother's house."

"That must have been a hard six months."

"It was miserable." Working odd jobs, mostly at night so she could take Allie with her. Sometimes she traded babysitting with another single mother, but she hated leaving Allie. "But the worst thing was worrying that somehow CPS would take Allie away from me. Thank God I wasn't on their radar. I would never give her up."

He took her hand again. "Then you'll tell her that. As long as she knows you love her, she'll deal with it, Della."

The thought of telling Allie the truth, all of the truth—God, no, she couldn't do it. *What if you have to? Hayes and Knight. The blackmailer almost had to be one of them.*

Don't think about it, Della told herself. *We'll find the bracelet and . . .* Her reasoning broke down at this point. What if they never found any goddamn bracelet because it wasn't even here?

What in the hell would she do then?

"I DON'T LOVE you, Nick." Della's words echoed in his mind as they started searching again. They'd been through the whole place but not as thoroughly as it was obviously going to take. Search every nook and cranny, pry up every suspicious board. This search gave him plenty of time to think. *Damn it.*

Della wasn't talking either. Thinking about Allie and how to tell her the truth if she had to, he knew. He couldn't blame her for not wanting to tell Allie about her past. But he had a strong feeling she wouldn't have a choice. Not because he thought the blackmailer would go through with his threat, necessarily. Secrets, especially terrible secrets, had a way of getting out.

Nick, dumb shit that he was, had to tell her he loved her at about the worst time a man could possibly pick. Since when had he become a moron about women? He'd never been that stupid before. Except with Lucianna, he remembered, but he'd been young then. If a woman had done the same to him, he'd have been out the door before she turned around. Della had no choice but to stick because of the blackmailer. But she obviously didn't want to talk about what he'd said. Who could blame her?

She didn't love him. Not a surprise. Every time he'd said anything to even imply they might have something together, something more than the sex, she'd pulled back. She was scared, and no wonder, with her history. How could he convince her that the two of them were worth a shot? Truthfully, how the rape and prostitution had affected Della, and helping her deal with the effects, was a lot more important to him than the fact that she'd been a teenage hooker. She'd survived, and he wouldn't fault her for how she'd done it. How could he convince her that her past was gone and what mattered was right now?

"I'm an idiot," Della exclaimed, rising up from behind the bar. "Why didn't I think of it before? The fish. Of course, it's in the fish." She took off for the kitchen.

"What fish?" Nick asked, following her.

"I put it in here until I could see what it would cost to fix it," she said, ignoring his question and yanking open the storeroom door.

"The sailfish? The fish that hung over the bar?"

"It's the obvious one, but there are others too." She stepped inside. "Thank God I moved it in here. And that I didn't have the money to get it repaired."

Nick didn't point out the bracelet might not be there. Inside a stuffed fish was as good a place as any to hide it. The tail and bill had broken off, but the body of the fish was intact. And there was room in its open mouth to put something small.

Della stuck her hand in before he could suggest using a flashlight. "Are you sure you want to do that without looking first?"

"Yes," she said impatiently. "Oh, God. There's something . . . I feel something—" Breaking off, she withdrew her hand and an object with it.

"What the hell?" Nick asked. "That's no bracelet. Or other jewelry. Is it a rock?"

Della turned it over, staring at it with a bemused expression. "I think it's an orange. Petrified."

"Why is there a petrified orange in a fish?"

She set it beside her. "I have no idea. It seems odd, even for Charlie."

"Odd? Weird as hell is more like it."

Della felt around again. By the time she finished there was quite a little treasure trove accumulated. Besides the orange, Della pulled out a quarter, several buttons, a can of chewing tobacco, a blow pop, a dog biscuit, and last but not least, a tiny stuffed King Kong. But no bracelet or anything of value.

"Well," Della said. She looked at him and they both began to laugh. "Oh, my God," Della said, still laughing, "This is so something Charlie would do."

"It's a strange assortment," Nick said.

"Some of this is Allie's. I guess he held her up there and let her put toys or whatever in it and then forgot about it."

"Why would she put an orange in a sailfish?"

"She was four years old when she started coming in. Why does a four-year-old do anything?" Della sobered. "I was so sure I'd found it." She stood up and sighed.

"I thought you might have too." He put his arm around her and hugged her. "Don't worry, we'll find it." He leaned in to kiss her, meaning to console.

Della's mouth softened, opened. Their lips clung together as her arms came around his neck. He tightened his hold on her, drawing her closer. Her soft breasts pressed against him, her lips doing wicked things against his. Her tongue darted into his mouth, teasing, taunting. Nick groaned, boosted her up on the table they'd moved in there because one leg was two inches shorter than the others.

What the hell was he thinking?

He pulled back and started to speak, but Della put her fingers to his lips. "Shhh." Hands on his cheeks, she pulled his head down to meet hers. She let go of his face, and, still kissing him, her hands got busy on his jeans, unbuttoning, unzipping, freeing him. Cradling him in her hands, stroking him.

He pulled her hands away and held them manacled together in one hand. If he hadn't, he'd have gone off like a rocket in another minute. He got rid of the jeans, thanking God he'd put a condom in the pocket earlier.

She laughed, letting him unfasten her shorts and yank off her panties. She wrapped her arms around him, her legs around his hips as he drove into her in a deep, fast lunge. Their eyes locked, he pulled out and drove back in, but slowly, drawing out the pleasure. Again. Slowly. Her pelvis rocked him, her softness drawing him in, squeezing him, making him crazy. With a last driving thrust he exploded deep inside her, and heard her cry and felt her come apart in his arms.

HER HEART FINALLY stopped hammering, her breathing slowed. Della opened her eyes and looked at Nick. "What the hell is wrong with us? What's wrong with *me*?"

"Nothing." He kissed her and stepped back, letting her slide down to the floor. "Not one single thing is wrong with you."

Finding her clothes, she pulled on her panties and shorts. Being a man, Nick didn't have to do much to redress. She couldn't even blame this on him. No, she was the one who'd had the serious lapse in judgment. She was the one who'd attacked him like a starving woman. Nick hadn't turned her down, but he was a man, after all.

"I'm being blackmailed. My life is about an inch away from completely blowing up in my face and ruining my daughter's life if it does. We're looking for some goddamn ridiculously valuable bracelet that might not even be here." She waved a hand at the table. "And what am I doing?"

Nick said, in a patient tone that made her want to smack him, "Having sex. What's wrong with that?"

Della stared at him with her mouth open. "Are you serious? Right in the middle of a desperate search, we decide to *do it* in a storeroom? You don't find anything wrong with this picture?"

He grinned. "No. I thought it was pretty damn great."

"You're insane."

"Della, having sex is a fairly normal reaction to extreme stress. Don't beat yourself up about it. It's not like we spent the afternoon going at it. We took ten minutes. Max."

She opened her mouth to blast him again when her phone rang. She fished it out of her pocket, thanking God it still worked after being pitched on the floor with her shorts, and answered. "Hello."

"Oh, good," Jackie said. "I was afraid you'd have your phone turned off. Look, I know this is last minute, but a friend of mine cancelled on me and I have an extra ticket to go to *So You Think You Can Dance* in Houston tonight. I'm taking Brooke, and she's dying for Allie to come with us. We'll stay overnight and come back late tomorrow evening."

"Houston? Overnight? So they'll miss school the next day? I don't know—"

"It's just one day. I know Allie is interested in dance. I'll take good care of them, I promise."

"I know, Jackie, it's not that." Della had become a lot more comfortable with Jackie, and to her surprise, that wasn't the reason she hesitated. But Allie loved dance? She hadn't mentioned it to her mother. Had she? Maybe she had and Della hadn't been paying attention. It dawned on her that since she'd been home more in the evenings, she knew Allie watched a lot of dance reality shows. But she'd thought they were for entertainment only. Did Allie have aspirations to dance?

While she hesitated, Jackie continued. Before Della knew it, she'd promised to bring Allie's overnight things and clothes for the next day over to Jackie's. She hung up, still wondering why she'd agreed.

"Everything okay?" Nick asked.

"That woman could sell popsicles in the Arctic. Jackie Palmer, Allie's best friend's mother, has tickets for *So You Think You Can Dance* in Houston. She wants to take the girls after school, see the show, spend the night, and stay tomorrow to shop."

"Allie will like that. She talks about that show a lot."

Well, hell. Did everyone know about Allie's latest craze but Della? "I said she could go."

"Now that that's settled," he cocked his head, "Are you finished wallowing in guilt?"

"Very funny. Yes, I'm finished."

"Good." He caught her hand and tugged her closer. "Spend the night with me tonight."

"You just think you're going to score again."

"That's what I love about you, Della. You're such a romantic." He kissed her. "Spend the night with me because I want to be with you."

What was the point of arguing when that's exactly what she wanted too? "All right. But as soon as I get back from delivering Allie's things, we're searching again."

DELLA WENT HOME to pick up Allie's things. As she was leaving, Mary Lou came in through the kitchen door. When she saw Della she—God, there was no other word for it—Mary Lou danced up to her.

"What's up with you?" Della asked. "You look like you just won the lottery."

"I did. The love lottery. Oh, Della, I'm so happy."

"Yeah, I can see that." What the hell was a love lottery? "Why?" she asked cautiously.

"Look!" Mary Lou thrust out her left hand, spreading her fingers. A diamond solitaire engagement ring sparkled on her hand. "Isn't it the most gorgeous, beautiful ring you've ever seen?"

Another one of my worst nightmares coming true.

Della hadn't trusted Knight before. Now that she knew he could be, and probably was, the blackmailer, she distrusted him even more. The only response she thought of was, "Holy shit, Mary Lou, have you completely lost your mind?" Della bit down on her tongue since, obviously, she couldn't say it without completely alienating her friend. Della and Nick only had suspicions. Whatever she told Mary Lou, Knight would know it a second later.

"Aren't you going to congratulate me? King and I are getting married."

She had to at least try to stop Mary Lou from making a huge mistake. "Are you sure you want to do this? You haven't known him very long."

Mary Lou deflated, though not much. "I know you don't like him, but that's just your prejudice against cops. Any cop but Nick, that is."

Della didn't take the bait. Instead, she said, "I'm worried. A few weeks ago, you barely knew him. Now you're talking marriage. I don't want you to get hurt."

"King isn't going to hurt me," Mary Lou insisted. "You need to trust me on this, Della."

You aren't the one I don't trust. But since she couldn't tell Mary Lou what she and Nick believed about Knight, she kept her mouth shut.

"You'll see. Once you get to know him, you'll see what a great guy he is."

"I want you to be happy."

"I love King and he loves me," her friend said. "I couldn't be happier." Mary Lou hugged her. "It's a dream come true," she said as she left the room.

More like a nightmare.

CHAPTER TWENTY-FIVE

AFTER DELLA dropped off Allie's stuff, she went back to the Last Shot. Nick was working in the main room, searching for the jewels. She went behind the bar and started prying up boards. She'd looked everywhere else around the bar, she might as well look under the floorboards.

"What's going on?" Nick asked her after a bit. "You haven't said a word and you look pissed."

"Mary Lou," she said grimly, "is in love."

"Ah."

"She's madly in love and engaged to Kingston Knight." And there wasn't a damn thing Della could do about that.

"Mary Lou's been with Knight almost constantly since your house was burglarized, hasn't she?"

"Whenever she isn't working. Every single chance she gets. I knew she was sleeping with him, but I hoped it wasn't serious. I kept thinking she'd realize it was just sex."

"Like you think it is between you and me," he said.

She stood up to glare at him but he wasn't looking. He appeared to be studying the floorboards, or pretending he was.

"Really, Nick? You want to talk about that now?" Because she damn sure didn't.

He looked at her and shrugged. "Maybe it isn't just sex for her."

"Maybe it isn't," she said, pressing a hand to her aching back. "But it's a freaking disaster waiting to happen, like her marriage was. I thought she might have learned."

"You didn't tell her that, did you?"

"I'm not an idiot, Nick. Of course I didn't tell her. Besides, anything I say is useless. She wouldn't believe anything bad about her precious King. Not to mention, I'm sure he knows everything we've told her. She can't keep her mouth shut at the best of times." Deciding she needed a break, Della sat in the open booth. "I'm worried about her. Which I did tell her."

"You haven't told her about the blackmail threat, have you?"

"Hell, no. Anything I tell her goes directly to Knight. If he's the blackmailer, I don't want him to know how worried I am. And if he's not, then I sure as hell don't want him to know about it."

"We don't know for a fact that Knight doesn't love her. And we don't know for a fact that he's the blackmailer. Knight could know nothing, and Hayes could be the one who's behind the blackmail and everything else that's happened."

"I don't trust Knight. Are you going to tell me you think he's completely in the clear?"

"No. There have been a number of things that bothered me, and now that we suspect him of blackmailing you, the odds of his guilt skyrocket. I had some problems with his investigation after the burglary."

"What kind of problems?"

"Shoddy techniques. He didn't follow protocol. Plus, he

wasn't very thorough. But Freedom's a small town without a lot of police manpower. And I figured he was just following Hayes's lead."

"Lead doing what? Being a lazy ass?"

Nick shrugged. "It's hard to find the perp in a home burglary like yours. Most cases never do get solved. And the chances of finding any stolen merchandise are slim to none."

"So the fact that Knight recovered Mary Lou's laptop so quickly is suspicious."

"Too quick and too easy," he agreed. "Most electronics aren't recovered at all, much less that quickly. Laptops are so easy to get rid of. You almost never find them. Knight found Mary Lou's in a couple of days, fully intact. She wasn't sure it had even been touched."

"She changed all the passwords, but I remember she never found any evidence that someone had hacked into it and had any information." Della stopped searching, or pretending to search. "How did he find it so fast?"

"I've been asking myself that question since he brought it back to Mary Lou. It's possible he found it at a pawn shop," Nick said. "But the easiest way would be he found it because he took it himself."

"But that means Knight was the burglar. How could he be? He pushed Mary Lou out of the way. Wouldn't she have recognized him?"

"Not necessarily. She barely knew him at the time, and from what she and Allie said, he was covered from head to toe in black."

"I thought you and Detective Taylor believed the Blasters were behind all this? Does that mean Knight or Hayes is involved with them?"

"It's possible. The gangs have been known to have cops on their payrolls."

"This is just great. Mary Lou is involved with a crooked cop. One who's been bought off by the biggest gang in the state."

He came over to the booth and slid in beside her. "It's still speculation."

"But you think it's true." She studied his face for a moment. "There's more, isn't there?"

"Yeah. Travis called yesterday and we talked about the case." Nick ticked off the points as he spoke. "Knight and Hayes found Leon Rivers, dead and tortured, in an abandoned warehouse near the waterfront. Next, the same men who killed Rivers hit the Last Shot. We believe this because all three men were connected in Houston. All three men dealt in stolen jewels. On top of that, Rivers's suspected killers asked Charlie if Rivers had been here. They were convinced he had and that Charlie knew where the jewels were."

"You think Hayes and Knight know all this too."

"According to Travis, Knight is likely to have recognized the thieves. They were all three well-known jewel thieves in Houston."

"If Taylor thinks all this is true, why doesn't he arrest Knight and Hayes?"

"We don't have any evidence. Nothing we can prove. Suspicion, no matter how well founded, isn't good enough. Even the suspect who was *conveniently* shot while in Hayes's custody isn't enough to make arresting either of them a possibility."

"I've told Mary Lou everything we knew or suspected up until I got the blackmail text. So Knight knows everything."

"Undoubtedly."

"God, why didn't I see this before? I should never have talked so freely to her after I knew she was sleeping with Knight."

"Hindsight," Nick said. "We can't be sure Knight's behind everything. Or Hayes either. But it's a damn good theory."

"How do we prove it?"

"I'll talk to Travis again. If he can find out who requested your juvie file, that will tell us the identity of the blackmailer. We still won't have enough proof for an arrest, but at least we'll know who it is. Then Travis and I will come up with a plan to expose him."

"But then Detective Taylor will know what's in my file. How do I know what he'll do with that information?" Della had no reason to distrust Nick's friend, except for the fact that he was a cop. Which, in her mind, was plenty of reason.

"He's only looking for information about who asked for the file. There's no need for Travis to see the contents of the file."

"I don't care, I don't like it. How do we know he's not as crooked as the cops here are?"

Nick took a moment to answer and she could see by the tic in his jaw that he was getting frustrated. But that was too damn bad. "Because I know him. I've known him for years. Not every cop is scum, Della. Travis is one of the good guys. I trust him."

"You trust him for you. How do you know he's trustworthy for me?"

"Travis is a good guy," Nick repeated. "Don't worry, he'll do the right thing."

"You're not giving me a choice, are you?"

"No. It's the only way we'll know who's behind all this. Once we know that, Travis and I can set a trap to expose whichever one is responsible."

"I don't know why I bother to argue. You're going to do what you want no matter what I think, aren't you?"

"We'll come up with a plan," he repeated. "A plan that doesn't put you or Mary Lou in danger."

"Good luck with that."

CHAPTER TWENTY-SIX

NICK HADN'T SAID anything about the two of them since he'd told her he loved her, and Della hadn't brought it up again either. She'd told him she wasn't in love with him. That should have been that. But damn it, she'd been thinking about it ever since he said the words *I'm in love with you, Della*. Which was probably what he'd intended.

What would it be like to trust a man enough to love him? To fall for him so hard that she didn't care about obstacles, she only cared about being with him? And honestly, what were the obstacles to her falling for Nick? Her fear. Fear of the past, fear of the future. Fear of giving herself to someone and becoming vulnerable. But hadn't she already done that? Hadn't she become vulnerable the minute she'd had sex with him?

Now Nick knew the worst about her. And as incredible as it was, she believed that her past truly didn't matter to him. How could that be possible?

They had searched about three-fourths of the bar area, very thoroughly this time, without unearthing a damn thing. They took another break, sitting on the barstools, and drinking water. Both had reached their quota of coffee hours earlier.

"Nick." When he looked at her, she asked the question that had been on her mind since she first received the threatening text. "What if we don't find the bracelet? What if it's not even here?"

"Come here." He held out a hand, and she came to stand between his legs. He looped his arms around her back. "We'll find it."

"You don't know that."

"No, I don't. But I know that if the bracelet is here, we'll find it. And if not, you'll find a way to tell Allie and call his bluff."

"He could still tell CPS."

"They have no reason to take Allie away from you. You're a good mother, you work hard, you're supporting yourself and your daughter. She's obviously healthy and happy."

"Right now she is." She shuddered. "God, I don't want to think about having to tell her. What if I do and she hates me?"

"Allie won't hate you, Della. Kids have survived worse. You did. Allie will know you love her and you chose to have her, you chose to keep her. Isn't that the most important thing?"

"I don't know. I only know that telling her is"—she closed her eyes, imagining the scene—"too awful to even think about."

"You told me."

"Only because I had no choice. Otherwise, I'd never have told anyone."

He sighed and ran a hand up her back, soothing, comforting. "When are you going to forgive yourself, Della? Do you think the rape was your fault?"

"No," she said automatically. "But . . . I put myself in that situation. I could have gone into the system. If I hadn't been on the streets—"

"Bullshit," he interrupted. "That's complete bullshit, and you know it. You were raped. You're not at fault, not in any way."

"You don't understand."

"Yes, I do. Do you think you're the only person who's ever made the wrong choice? A choice that you've regretted from almost the instant you made it? It happened. You made a choice you'd give anything to undo. But you can't, so you have to move past it. Forgive yourself, and move forward."

She put her hand to his cheek. "Like you have, Nick?"

His eyes filled with raw despair. "Some things, some failures, can't be forgiven."

"Do you really believe that?"

"In your case, no. But in mine? Hell, yes."

AROUND MIDNIGHT, they finally called it a night. "I know what we need," Nick said as they left the bar area for the kitchen.

"I bet I can guess," Della said dryly.

He grinned. "Good idea, but that's not what I was talking about." Instead of continuing upstairs, he opened the big walk-in freezer. "Emergency supplies," he said, and set a half gallon container of Blue Bell chocolate chip ice cream on the table. He opened a drawer, pulled out two spoons and handed one to her. "Dig in."

Why not? she thought. Ice cream wouldn't solve her problems but it wouldn't hurt either. Spooning the first bite into her mouth, she moaned. She realized she was starving, since she'd only picked at the sandwich she'd had for dinner. "I'd forgotten how good ice cream is." She sighed and got another spoonful. "I can't remember the last time I had any."

"Don't you buy ice cream for Allie?"

"Sure, but I try not to eat it."

"Why?"

"Why do you think? Why does any woman try to stay away from ice cream?"

"Don't tell me you're on a diet." He stopped with the spoon halfway to his mouth and looked her up and down.

"Okay, I won't tell you. Besides, I'm not exactly on a diet. But I would need to be if I ate ice cream all the time."

He took a big bite. "If you want my opinion," he said after he swallowed, "your body is perfect just the way it is."

She laughed. "Good to know."

"Ice cream is one of the wonders of the universe. You shouldn't deprive yourself."

"Well, if you insist, I guess I have no choice." She smiled and they ate some more in companionable silence.

She looked up to see him staring at her. "What? Do I have ice cream on my face?"

"As a matter of fact, yes. Come here and I'll wipe it off."

As she went to him, she thought he had more in mind than cleaning up ice cream, and she was right. He stroked his finger over her mouth, then put it in his. "Tasty," he said. Tugging her closer, until she put her arms around his neck, he kissed her, sliding his tongue into her mouth to dance with hers. "Even tastier," he murmured.

He kissed her again, his tongue making slow, sexy forays into her mouth. With a last thrust, a promise of more, he left her mouth and his lips trailed down her neck to the pulse now hammering at the base. His hands cupped her bottom, pulling her even closer. He took her mouth again, urgently this time. Without breaking the kiss, he picked her up and carried her to the stairs. And then up them, to the bedroom.

The window was open, the warm sea breeze blowing in. The moonlight spilled across the bed, bathing it in soft light. They stood beside it and kissed, long, deep, soul-stirring kisses. When she would have rushed, he stopped her. "This time we take it slow." His hands came up beneath her shirt, cupping her breasts, moving around to her back and unfastening her bra.

He undressed her a piece of clothing at a time, leisurely kissing each expanse of skin as he laid it bare. Caressing her breasts, gliding his hands over her stomach, slipping one between her legs as he peeled off her panties and pulled them down, following with his mouth. When she was naked, he guided her down to sit on the bed. She watched as he stripped off his shirt, unbuttoned and unzipped his jeans, pushing them down along with his boxers.

"You really do have a killer body," she murmured.

"No, that would be you," he said, smiling. "Lie back."

She started to scoot back into the middle of the bed, but he stopped her. "No, just lie back. Right here." He leaned over her and kissed her mouth, kissed her until she throbbed, kissed her until she could hardly breathe for wanting him. He trailed kisses down to her chest, licking and sucking her breasts, then continuing down, across her stomach, and down, farther still. Kneeling between her legs, he spread them apart and kissed her, where she throbbed and ached for him.

Della tried to say something, but all that came out was another moan. Her back arched, her hips lifted. His mouth, his tongue, his lips and hands played her, driving her up, pushing her over the crest and she shattered, crying out his name. The last tremor hadn't yet faded when she felt him slip inside her, a deep, slow glide. She wrapped her legs around his hips, pulling him in, demanding he go deeper, harder, and she climbed again with each thrust, until she hurtled over the edge of orgasm as she felt him spend himself inside her.

CHAPTER TWENTY-SEVEN

H E HELD HER as she slept. Just held her and looked at her . . . and wished he could do this every night. *Damn, who'd have thought it? Nick Sheridan, crazy in love.* Closing his eyes, he slept. And dreamed . . .

"Police! Open up!" Nick shouted, and kicked in the door. Swinging his gun right, left, straight ahead, he scanned the room, his gaze halting on a set of stairs leading to a basement. A dim light emanated behind a door near the bottom of them.

Music. He heard the sweet whine of violins in a classical arrangement he didn't recognize. Loud enough to mask the sound of his break-in? Nick crept silently down the stairs, moving toward the sound, his nerves wound to bowstring tautness.

The unmistakable smell of blood hit his nostrils before he reached the partially open door. Goddamn it, was he too late?

But maybe there was still time, maybe the child wasn't dead yet, maybe he could stop the psycho before it was too late. Silently, he edged the door open with his foot.

The knife gleamed silver and red in the muted glow of light

thrown by a ring of candles. Alone with his victim in the center of the ring, Crazy Larry was laughing, no, giggling, as he held a young child against his chest, knife against the little girl's throat. Blood dripped, a steady rhythm, flowing from her body as surely as her life.

At first, no thought formed in Nick's mind, no words issued from his mouth. Nausea built, bile bubbling in his throat. Nothing, not one of the grisly realities he'd seen in ten years of viewing the aftermath of heinous crimes compared to what he saw now.

And then she opened her eyes. Jesus God, she was alive. Tortured, bloody, but alive.

He leveled his gun at the killer. "Police. Drop the girl. Put down the knife. You're under arrest."

He laughed. The bastard laughed. "Make me." And he cut her again.

"Put down the knife and the child. Let go of her, you son of a bitch."

Blood dripped onto the floor from the fingers wrapped around the knife handle. Crazy Larry smiled, madness gleaming in his eyes. He dropped the child and came at Nick, knife raised. "You won't take me in."

Nick fired, double-tap, and the killer kept coming. He fired again, and again, until he emptied his clip. Crazy Larry dropped just before he reached Nick. Nick kicked the knife away and made certain the man was dead before rushing to the child.

She was alive, barely. He heard the death rattle of her breath as she drew it in laboriously and knew she was dying. She couldn't speak, though she tried. Her eyes locked on his, begging him for something he couldn't give her. Pleading with him to save her. He cradled her, whispered she would be all right, though he knew it was a lie. Her face was wet with blood, with tears. Her blood, but the tears were his. *God, don't let her die. Please, God, don't let her die.*

Nick stripped off his shirt, tried to stop the bleeding with it, but there was so much blood, he couldn't find the worst of it. Her face, her neck, her stomach, arms, legs. Blood poured from each and every wound. So much blood for such a tiny girl. He used his radio, called it in. Asked for a bus, knowing help wouldn't arrive in time.

He heard the last rattle. Felt her final, gasping breath. And cursed himself, God, and most of all, the madman who'd killed her. He'd been too late.

He couldn't let go. He held her, he didn't know how long. His partner knelt beside him. "Nick, she's gone. She's gone, man. You have to let go." He put his hand on Nick's arm, trying to get him to release her.

Nick stared at Brad. "I tried to reason with him. I told him to leave her. I tried to reason with a psycho. Why didn't I shoot the bastard when I came in? The minute I saw him with her? I could have saved her."

"No." Brad shook his head. "We were too late. She was too far gone when we got here. It's not your fault, Nick."

"She was alive when I came in. Alive." He was crying like a baby. Nick, the cop who never cried at the worst homicides. The cop who could look at the most vicious cases, do his job, and leave the horror of it in the field. The cop who could be calm and collected, dispassionate enough to tell his story to the jury and make sure the killer paid for the crime. He couldn't leave it this time. Not this time.

"I should have taken him out."

"GOD, NO!"

Della woke suddenly, with Nick's cry echoing in her mind. Unsure if she was dreaming, she reached out to touch him, jerking back when he came up swinging.

"Nick, wake up. Wake up," she repeated. "You're dreaming."

He stared at her blindly. "Jesus." Turning his back to her, he swung his legs over the edge of the bed and sat there, then buried his head in his hands. "Oh, God, no," he whispered.

Tentatively, Della touched him, putting her hand on his shoulder. When he didn't push her away, she moved closer, sitting beside him and sliding her arm across his shoulders. Such strong shoulders, bowed now with grief. "What is it, Nick?"

She thought he wouldn't answer. The moon shone through the window, lighting the room with a soft, iridescent glow. He tried to steady his breathing, tried desperately to regain a control she'd seen crack only once before. When he learned of the suicide of Angelina's mother. "Tell me."

When he raised his head and looked at her, she saw tears, not simply of sorrow, but of bone-deep despair. "Oh, God, Della. I remembered. I remembered what really happened."

"Tell me," she said again. "Let me help you."

He spoke haltingly, as if the words were wrenched out of him. "She wasn't dead. She was alive when I got there. Alive."

Angelina, she thought. He was talking about Angelina. His last case, the case that drove his demons. She rubbed his shoulder, waited for him to go on.

"The son of a bitch had her. His knife was at her throat. There was so much blood. So damn much blood. More blood than any child could have lost and still live." He looked at

Della. "I knew she was dead. She couldn't have survived what he did to her."

"Angelina was . . . a child?" Oh, God. Her stomach churned. He'd never specifically said and Della had assumed the victim had been an adult woman.

"Yes. A little girl. She looked like—" He stopped abruptly. "Just a child."

"I'm so sorry." She wanted to help, but she didn't know how. Other than repeating those useless words, I'm sorry.

He shook her off and got up. Silently stared out the window. He turned and faced Della. "She opened her eyes. Oh, Christ, Della, Angelina was alive when I got there."

She couldn't imagine. Never wanted to imagine something so horrifying. "What . . . what did you do?"

He gave an anguished laugh. "Do? What did I do? I fucking froze. I'd never seen anyone bleed that much and still live. And while I stood there, he cut her again. But she wasn't dead. Not yet. He dropped her and came at me. I shot him. I emptied my magazine into him. It wasn't enough. I could have shot him a thousand times, and it still wouldn't have been enough."

"Angelina?" she whispered.

He shook his head. "I tried to stop the bleeding. I couldn't even identify the worst wounds. I called for help. Called my partner. Brad came in, I don't know how much later. It seemed like I held her for hours, but I know she wouldn't have lasted longer than a few minutes." He sat down again, beside her on the bed. "Angelina died in my arms. I didn't save her. I couldn't save her. I failed."

"You didn't fail. You tried to save her. You did everything you could."

"It wasn't good enough. If I'd killed him sooner, gotten

there sooner, I might have saved her. Instead, I watched her die."

Della put her arms around him. Hugged him, held him, grieved with him. And she, who never cried for herself, cried for him.

CHAPTER TWENTY-EIGHT

NICK CAME OUT of the bathroom and she was still there, waiting for him. He'd have run like hell, but Della was stronger than he was. He'd blocked what really happened, which was pathetic. He couldn't handle it, so he'd convinced himself Angelina was dead when he came in. He believed that he'd killed the bastard *after* Angelina died. Taken him out instead of taking him in.

No wonder the Captain made him take a leave of absence.

He'd seen homicides. So damn many. Grisly, sad, disgusting, horrifying. But nothing as soul-crushing as this, nothing compared to helplessly holding a little girl in his arms as she died. He'd failed dealing with it as surely as he'd failed saving Angelina.

Since it was still the middle of the night, Della had turned on the bedside light, but on the lowest setting. She was wearing one of his T-shirts, sitting up in bed with her knees drawn up to her chest and her arms looped around her legs. Nick had pulled on his boxers and beat it to the bathroom as soon as he found a shred of control. And now she was sitting there looking at him, and he had no fucking clue what to say.

"Hoping I'd be gone when you came out?" she asked.

"No," he denied immediately.

"Liar," she said softly. "You're going to have to talk to me, Nick. You don't have the option of shutting me out now." She let her legs down and sat cross-legged, facing him on the bed.

Yeah, she didn't look like she'd let this go. She'd already seen him at his worst. He might as well talk to her. But it wouldn't help. Nothing would. He got into bed, propped a couple of pillows against the headboard and leaned back. "I don't know whether to apologize for telling you such a grisly story, or apologize for losing it."

"Why would you think you had to apologize for either one?"

He gestured helplessly. "I'm a homicide cop. I've seen the worst. I should be able to handle—" He broke off, unwilling to say the words again.

"There's no shame in having a hard time dealing with something so horrific."

She was serious. Obviously, she didn't understand. "Della, it's my job. The bastard was a serial killer. He liked to kill little girls. We—my partner and I—had been chasing him for years. Never in time, always seeing what—who—that psycho left behind.

"I dealt with situations like this all the time. But not this time, not this case. Instead, I completely lost it. For months, I've denied what really happened. I changed it in my head. I let myself believe she was already dead when I got there, because I couldn't face the truth." The truth that he had failed, and an innocent little girl had died.

"Don't you think there are other cops who have problems with cases that are so monstrous?"

"Brad—my partner—didn't. He'd been chasing the bastard for as long as I had. He saw what happened. He didn't lose it."

"Did Brad hold a little girl in his arms while she died?"

He didn't remember telling her that. God knows what he'd said and didn't remember. He shoved his hands through his hair, wishing his memory weren't so squirrelly. Was it true, not true? What had he said? What had he only thought he said?

Nick shook his head. "No, but he was there while I did." Wasn't he? He remembered, now, Brad telling him to let the EMTs have her. *She's gone, Nick.* But had Brad been there before, when Angelina was dying in Nick's arms? And what did it matter if he was or wasn't? Brad had kept his shit together, and Nick hadn't.

"Obviously, that's not the same thing," she said when he didn't answer.

He shrugged. Nick knew what was going on now. He'd failed, and rather than risk failing again, he'd retreated. He'd quit. And now, to top that off, he'd told Della about the worst case of his career. God knew he hadn't wanted to put that picture in her head. Just how graphic had he been?

"What did I tell you?"

"You don't remember?"

He shook his head. "Not exactly. I remember falling apart." And he remembered Della comforting him. Nick Sheridan, homicide detective, didn't fall apart. But Nick Sheridan, the man, had taken a hell of a dive.

Della put her hand on his arm and rubbed it comfortingly. She'd shown him more spontaneous affection since he'd freaked out than she ever had before. God, he must be pathetic.

"You talked about her bleeding, about how much blood there was, but you didn't get into every gory detail, Nick, if that's what you're worried about. You said enough for me to know that if anything was worth losing it over, this case was it."

"I shouldn't have told you. I should have kept it to myself. You're a civilian. You don't need to hear about serial killers and their horrific crimes."

"Keeping it to yourself worked out really well for you, did it?"

He gave her a dirty look. "There are other people I could have talked to."

"But you didn't," she pointed out. "You talked to me. And now you're busy beating yourself up because you did. Why?"

Nick didn't have an answer to that question.

"I see what it is," Della said. "You're embarrassed. You think talking about it makes you weak. But it doesn't, Nick. It just makes you human."

"I'm not embarrassed. I'm pissed. I didn't get to her in time. That's on me."

"You didn't save Angelina, but you did save more little girls from being killed by that maniac. That's a good thing, Nick."

"Too little, too late."

"Not for the other little girls he can't kill now. If you hadn't stopped him, he'd have gone on killing. You said I needed to forgive myself, but from where I'm sitting, you need to forgive yourself as much or more than I do."

CHAPTER TWENTY-NINE

ARLY THE NEXT morning, Nick and Della started the search again. In tacit agreement, neither mentioned Nick's nightmare or subsequent revelations. Nick would have to work through it himself, no matter how much Della wanted to help him.

Over the last two days, they'd been over every inch of the bar, kitchen, and apartment with a fine-toothed comb. After their talk, neither had slept much the remainder of the night, so Della had made a pot of strong coffee when they went downstairs. After they'd had their first cup, they took the second into the bar area to decide where to start. Again. Nick went directly to the jukebox. Picking out a song, Della thought with a smile. Allie and Nick both did that nearly every time they came into the big room.

"It's not working," Nick said after punching several buttons. "You'll have to get a repairman out here to fix it."

"A repairman? That's a laugh. No one but Charlie ever worked on it. There might be people to do it in big cities but not around here." Not to mention, Charlie wasn't about to pay someone to mess with his jukebox. He had loved the thing and seemed to enjoy fixing it almost as much as he did hearing the music.

"I could take a look at it. I've never worked on a jukebox, but I've worked on a lot of electronics."

"Knock yourself out. Don't cut yourself on that glass." Nick started looking for a way to open it up, first pulling it out from the wall. He stopped, turned around, and stared at her. At the same time both of them said, "The jukebox."

"Damn, how could we have missed it?" Nick asked.

"I don't know. How carefully did we look at the jukebox? You checked it early on, didn't you?" Della asked.

"I looked in the back and didn't find anything. But—"

"We didn't look inside. I remember thinking we should, but there was obviously nothing in the top, right beneath the broken glass. We'd have seen it. And I didn't think about it again until just now."

"How do you open it to change out the songs?" Nick asked.

"I have no idea. I told you, Charlie never changed the songs."

They stood side by side, feeling around the edges. "This is it," Della said, her fingers finding a catch. She opened the catch and they lifted up the top to expose the inner workings. Wedged into one corner was a gray cloth bag.

They both stared at it, then looked at each other. "Unbelievable," Della said. "What if that's not it?"

"What else could it be? Get it out and look."

Della reached in gingerly and pulled out the small bag. "There's another beneath it. And still another beneath that."

Nick picked up the other bags, while looking around to make sure they hadn't missed any more.

Della walked to the bar and pulled up a stool. "I think I'd better be sitting when I open this."

Nick took the seat beside her, waiting for her to open the pouch. But she hesitated and looked at him. "Rivers must have hidden them without Charlie's knowledge. Charlie never looked in the jukebox unless it was broken. I don't believe Charlie would have helped Rivers, least of all hidden the stuff in the jukebox."

Nick didn't know, and at this point it didn't matter. "If they find Rivers's fingerprints on the jukebox that will be a strong argument that he did it. But that's for later."

It fell out of the bag onto the bar, the sparkle of diamonds so keen it was almost blinding, hundreds of diamonds of all sizes set in a wide band. Dazzling, beckoning, and in the middle of all that splendor, as big as a baby's fist, was a single emerald glowing a deep seductive green. Vibrant color in the midst of ice.

"Holy shit," Della said.

"The picture didn't touch it. *L'émeraude Perfide*," Nick said as Della picked it up. "Treacherous emerald. Fits, doesn't it?"

"I can't believe it's real," Della said.

"Real enough to kill for." He opened the other two pouches and poured the contents onto the bar. A fortune in bracelets, necklaces, and rings tangled together. Stones of every type, set in gold and platinum, with diamonds and without. A feast of jewelry, with the *pièce de résistance, L'émeraude Perfide*. Nick had never seen anything like it in his life.

"Unbelievable," he said. "No wonder Rivers didn't want to give up these beauties."

"He could fence this?" Della held up the emerald bracelet. "And those?" she asked, motioning to the other gems.

"Or ransom them. Especially the bracelet," Nick said. "I'll call Travis. He'll want to take custody of these right away."

"Nick, wait." She put her hand on his arm, stopping him from pulling his phone out of his pocket. "If you do that, we'll never be able to prove who was behind all this. Or who is blackmailing me, either."

Damn, she had a point. "I'm a cop, Della. I have to follow the law. I'm obligated to turn this in to law enforcement."

"So what, we just let them get away with it?"

"No, once we have the contraband safe, Travis and I will set a trap. You'll get the hell out of here so you're not in danger."

"I have as much right to be here as you do," she said, looking at the mass of jewelry on the table.

"No. You don't. Look, Della, I'm not about to run a sting with you in the middle of it." He shook off her hand and pulled his phone out of his pocket. It didn't take long to fill in Travis. "He'll be here as soon as he can," he told Della. "He's in Houston, so it will be a while. In the meantime—"

The screen door at the front entrance banged. Mary Lou and Kingston Knight walked into the Last Shot.

KING DIDN'T NEED the gleaming mountain of jewelry or Mary Lou grabbing his arm and hollering, "Oh, my God, that's them. The stolen jewels!" to tell him he'd hit the jackpot.

He *felt* the thing. The bracelet, a cool million worth of emeralds and diamonds, sucker-punched him. It was lying there, waiting for him to pick it up and hit the road. He could be gone in thirty seconds. Not too long after that, he could be on a boat headed out to the Gulf. But he couldn't take Mary Lou with him, or return to the US once he left. There would be no turning back. He'd be the criminal instead of the man who arrested criminals. A con instead of a cop.

Goddamn it, you crossed that line when you let Hayes get away with murder.

"I'll take care of those," King said, stepping closer to the bar and pulling his gun from the holster.

"The hell you will," Sheridan said, pulling his weapon at the same time King did. "Don't come any closer. I'm not turning these babies over to anyone but Detective Taylor of the Houston PD."

"These are stolen goods. They were found in my city. If anyone contacts the Houston PD, it will be me. Now, you move away from the jewels."

"Do you expect us to believe you'll do that?" Della asked him. "To trust you with a fortune in jewels? Fat chance." She turned to Mary Lou, who was looking between him and the others, totally bewildered.

"He wants the jewelry for himself," Della said. "Knight and Hayes are behind everything. Charlie's murder, the bar being wrecked, our house being broken into, me being blackmailed."

Blackmail? Hayes must have managed to unseal Della's juvenile record file and was using it to blackmail her. The chief hadn't told him anything about that. And how the hell had she reached the conclusion that he or Hayes were responsible for Burke's death?

"I don't believe you. King wouldn't do anything like—Wait a minute, did you say you were being blackmailed?"

"That's right. Ask your fiancé," Della told her. "He should know, since either he or his boss is the blackmailer."

"King, what is she talking about? None of this makes sense. Tell her she's wrong."

He looked into Mary Lou's eyes. God, she was so trusting. He didn't want to be the one to destroy that trust. But what could he say? How could he possibly explain the fucking mess Hayes had dragged him into?

"Put those guns down this minute," Mary Lou said, looking from him to Sheridan. All the indecision had left her face. "This has gone far enough."

"That's not happening," Sheridan said. "Della, get out of here and take Mary Lou with you."

"Oh, this is great," Della said sarcastically. "Once you get the little women out of the way, you two macho cops are going to have a shoot-out? No way in hell."

"Do what he says, Mary Lou," Knight snapped. "There's no need for either of you to get hurt."

"No," she said, standing up to him with her full height of five-foot-two. "I'm not going anywhere until you explain this to me, Kingston Knight. What the hell are they talking about?" Della started to speak. Mary Lou held up a hand. "We've heard quite enough from you, Della. And you too, Nick," she said before Sheridan could chime in. "I'm waiting. Is what they say true?"

He could put an end to this in a heartbeat. All he had to do was grab Della or Mary Lou, gather up the jewels, and leave the bar. Sheridan would never endanger a woman. Neither would King. He'd never even considered it until all this shit with the stolen jewels had happened.

He sighed and holstered his gun. "Yeah, it's true. Most of it, anyway."

NICK LOOKED AT Della, who looked as surprised as he was. What the fuck was going on? Knight had admitted his guilt?

"You can put up your gun," Knight said. "Your problem is going to be with Hayes, not me."

"Thanks, I'll keep it right where it is. But I want yours on the floor. And the backup piece too." Nick stared at Knight, trying to figure out where he was coming from.

Knight put his guns on the floor without argument, which went a ways toward convincing Nick he was sincere. No cop gave up his weapon willingly.

"Move away from the guns. Explain. Why did you come clean? And why now?"

Knight took one of the barstools and looked at Mary Lou. Spoke to her as if she was the only one who mattered. Apparently, she was, to Knight, anyway. "For what it's worth, neither Hayes or I had any idea what was going on until we found Leon Rivers dead in the warehouse. We had nothing to do with Burke's death."

"Who did, then?" Della asked.

"The two men who broke in here."

"Why should I believe you?" Della asked.

Knight just shrugged and turned his attention back to Mary Lou. "I've had second thoughts all along. Especially after you and I got together. I didn't expect to fall for you, but I did. I wanted out, but with Hayes blackmailing me, I couldn't see a way to do it." He glanced at Della. "Hayes is your blackmailer, not me."

"That's convenient," Della said. "Especially since he's not here to call you a liar."

Ignoring Della, he looked at Mary Lou. "I won't lie and tell you I didn't want the money. Over a million bucks worth of jewels." He shook his head. "Who wouldn't be tempted? Even if I hadn't been, Hayes made sure I was on board. After the suspect from the shooting here at the bar told us what he knew, Hayes killed him. The chief threatened to frame me for his murder if I didn't throw in with him. He had the means to do it, too."

Knight continued, speaking mostly to Mary Lou, who looked more shaken by the moment. He went through the whole thing, starting with the call to investigate an abandoned warehouse, and finding Leon Rivers there, tortured and dead, and ending with now, when he'd decided he couldn't do what his boss wanted. Though a number of things were news to Nick, he and Della had been right on track.

Not that Nick trusted him. Knight had just admitted to being an accessory to murder, albeit reluctantly. He'd need a great lawyer, not to mention a lot of luck, not to do prison time.

Mary Lou hadn't said a word throughout Knight's entire confession. "You and me," she said quietly when he fell silent, "that was all a lie. You don't love me. You never have. I was a means to an end."

"No! I love you Mary Lou and I want—I wanted to marry you. I tried to figure out a way to have you and the money— the jewels—but today, I had to admit that would never happen. You would never go for it."

"No, I wouldn't," she said. Her eyes brimmed with tears and anger. "Goddamn it, King, you made me fall in love with you. I promised myself after I finally got free of my ex that I'd never again fall for a criminal." She laughed unhappily. "You're even worse. You're supposed to be one of the good guys. What a fool I've been."

Della put her arm around Mary Lou. "Don't blame yourself. None of this is your fault, Mary Lou. You're not the first woman to fall for the wrong man, and you won't be the last."

"This is so damn touching," Brumford Hayes said. "But I'm in a hurry. Quit dickin' around and hand over those stones, Knight."

CHAPTER THIRTY

NICK TURNED around to his worst nightmare.

Chief Brumford Hayes stood at the entrance to the bar, holding Allie by the arm, a gun pointed to her head. Nick's vision grayed, and for an instant he saw Angelina, dripping blood, held in a madman's grip.

But only for an instant. Allie was alive and struggling, and Nick was going to make goddamn sure she stayed that way.

"Let go of my daughter, you bastard," Della cried, lunging for Hayes.

"Della, stop!" Nick yelled, fear for Allie lending volume to his voice. "He'll kill her."

She stopped instantly, thank God. "Let her go," she repeated. "Please," she added, her voice breaking.

"Listen to Sheridan if you want her to live," Hayes said putting his hand on Allie's neck and shaking her viciously. "Stop squirming, brat. Do you want a bullet in your head?"

"No," she choked out. Tears tracked down her cheeks, but she subsided.

Hayes spoke to Knight. "I knew you were too much of a

pansy to follow through. Good thing I bugged the place, you double-crossing piece of shit. This pretty little thing"—he jerked on Allie's arm until she cried out in pain—"walked right into my hands."

"Let the kid go," Knight told Hayes as he stood up. "Are you crazy? Kidnapping? You don't need her."

"She's insurance. No one's going to risk shooting me when I've got a gun on the girl." Looking at the floor where Knight's guns lay, Hayes said disgustedly, "I see you already gave up your weapons, you dumb bastard."

Ignoring Knight after that comment, Hayes looked at Nick and smiled. "You know the drill, Sheridan. Guns on the floor, kick them away. King, while he's doing that, you put the jewels in those sacks there and hand them over. All of them."

While all this was going on, Allie had been looking at Nick intently. She signaled, making the okay sign with her free hand, inclining her head toward Hayes, then pointing to the floor. If he read her right, she was remembering her self-defense training, and hoping he remembered their talk. He nodded at her, very slightly as he started to put down his gun.

"Go on," Hayes said, gesturing at Nick with his gun. "I don't have all day."

With Hayes's gun pointed away from Allie, Nick knew he'd never have a better chance. He started to put down his weapon, but instead he yelled, "Fire."

Allie stomped on Hayes's foot, twisted out of his grasp as he lost his grip, and ran to her mother.

"Go, go, go," Nick shouted as Allie, Della, and Mary Lou ran out the front door. A loud crack of gunfire rang in the room, then three more volleys in rapid succession. Nick dove for cover behind the booth, firing at Hayes as he did so.

Realizing his side was stinging, Nick put his free hand to it and it came away bloody. *Just a graze*, he thought, or he'd have been in more pain. He wiped his hand on his shorts, put the injury out of his mind, and tried to figure a way to draw the chief out. Nick knew Hayes was hiding at the far end of the bar. Which meant he had straight, unobstructed access to either door. *Shit*. Della, Allie and Mary Lou were out front, available for Hayes to use as a human shield. No fucking way was he going to let that happen again.

Nick hoped like hell Knight hadn't gone over to the dark side again. If he had, they'd all be in deep shit. More gunfire erupted from either end of the bar. Nick could see Knight, close enough to tell that his shirt was soaked in blood at the shoulder. Another one of the chief's bullets had hit home, which ought to put Knight on Nick's side. He wondered if either he or Knight had managed to hit Hayes. If so, it clearly hadn't stopped the man.

Nick watched Knight reload. It was obvious from the slow, deliberate actions the man was hurting. Nick still didn't completely trust Knight, but since he needed help, the cop would have to do. Through a series of motions, Nick signaled for the other man to cover him while Nick went after Hayes.

Knight nodded.

Nick held up his hand, silently counting to three.

Hayes came out shooting as soon as Nick broke cover, heading for the front door before Nick could prevent it. The only thing that would stop the man would be a bullet.

Knight kept up his fire, but none of his shots hit the mark.

Hayes had almost made it to the door when Nick winged him.

Cursing, Hayes turned and fired, his shot going wide as one of Knight's rounds hit him in the leg. Hayes stumbled, and Nick shot him, double tap to the chest, then a head shot.

He crumpled. Nick reached him, kicking the gun away, and knelt down to feel for a pulse, though he knew the man was dead. Hayes's eyes were open, sightless and staring.

Breathing heavily, Nick waited for the adrenaline rush to subside. "Hayes is dead, Knight. You can come out."

No answer. Maybe the cop had passed out from loss of blood. Or maybe Hayes had hit him again and killed him this time.

"Here I thought you needed the cavalry, but it looks to me like you've handled it." Travis stood in the front doorway, smiling at him. His smile faded. He crossed the room quickly. "How bad are you hit?"

"It's a scratch." At Travis's skepticism, he added, "Look if you don't believe me." Which to Nick's annoyance, Travis did.

Satisfied Nick hadn't been lying, Travis handed him a dish towel from the bar and recommended he apply pressure. "You'll live, but it's bleeding like shit."

"Knight's hurt or dead. He's over there," Nick said, jerking his head in the direction he'd last seen the man.

"You took out both of them?" Travis asked.

"Not exactly. Knight switched sides at the last." Though it irritated him to say it, he had to give the man his due. "I wouldn't be standing here if he hadn't thrown in with me."

Travis and Nick found Knight, passed out on the floor behind the bar. Travis felt for a pulse, but Knight knocked his hand away. "Leave me the hell alone. I'm not dead yet."

Nick stepped behind the bar to find another towel. He handed it to Travis, who knelt down beside the injured man and applied pressure.

"I thought Knight was in on it, along with the chief?" Travis said to Nick.

Knight had closed his eyes again, whether from pain, loss

of blood, or because he didn't want to deal with anyone, Nick didn't know.

"He was in on it with the chief. Until today." Knight would need a damn good lawyer, but the fact that he'd come clean in the end and helped take down the chief, as well as recover the stolen goods, would help him a lot. "Are Della, Allie, and Mary Lou still outside? Are they all right?"

"They're all out there. Nine-one-one is on its way."

"Is Allie okay? Hayes used her as a hostage." Nick didn't think she was hurt, but he wanted to make sure.

"The kid's fine. Now that she's safe, she's feeling pretty proud of herself. But your lady's a little banged up—"

Nick didn't hear any more. He was out the door the minute he heard Della was hurt.

NICK BURST OUT the door, his heart in his throat. "Della, what happened? Were you shot? Are you hurt?"

"I wasn't shot. I'm okay," Della said as he scooped her into his arms and sat on the step with her.

"You're sure? Travis said you were banged up." He kissed her, fast and hard. "God, don't scare me like that. I had visions of you bleeding out from a gunshot wound."

Della flushed. "I'm fine, Nick. I just had a little accident." She scowled at the dog, lying beside her, panting cheerfully. "You can put me down."

He ignored her, continuing to hold her.

"You're the one who's bleeding." She touched his side where the blood had soaked his shirt. "I knew it when we heard all that gunfire. You've been shot."

"It's a scratch. Don't worry about it."

"Don't worry? You were shot again. Let me see." He scowled, but lifted up his shirt so she could see the bullet had only grazed him.

"It looks nasty," Della said.

"Looks worse than it is," Nick told her.

"Mom broke her ankle," Allie announced. "When she tripped over Sophia."

That explained the killer looks Della had been aiming at the dog.

Allie crooned to Sophia, "But you're a good girl not to run away. She was out here all alone, but she didn't run off."

Della rolled her eyes but didn't say anything.

Nick looked at her leg. Her ankle was swollen, her knee scraped. "Wow, you really did do a number on it. Your ankle is already swelling. We'll have the EMTs look at it when they get here."

"It's just a sprain."

"Maybe. But you wince every time you move. You're getting it checked out."

"What happened to Hayes?" Della asked.

He glanced at Allie, who was crooning to the dog still. "Dead. He won't be taking anyone hostage again."

She put her hand on his arm and squeezed. "Thank you."

Her hand was trembling. He patted it, took it to his mouth and kissed it.

"Allie was the heroine. And you."

"Me? I didn't do anything but stand there uselessly."

"You're the reason Allie knew what to do. That self-defense class you all took was a lifesaver. Literally."

Mary Lou finally spoke. She hadn't said a word since he'd come outside. "What about King? Is he—is he dead too?"

"No, he's alive," Nick said, exchanging glances with Della

again. He shook his head. "He's been shot. I don't know how bad it is. Travis is with him."

"I need to see him." She wiped her eyes, squared her shoulders, and walked back inside.

"Put me down," Della told Nick again. "I want to go inside with her. And don't try to tell me it's a private moment. It won't be with Detective Taylor there."

Nick wondered if she'd ever call Travis by his first name. "You're not walking on that ankle," he said as she tried again to get up.

"I'm going in there, Nick. Mary Lou needs me."

"Fine." Nick got up with her in his arms and carried her in, setting her down on one of the barstools.

Travis knelt at Knight's side, holding pressure on his wound. He looked up when they all came inside. "Any sign of the EMTs? He's lost a lot of blood."

"Not yet," Nick said. "They should be here any minute now."

Ignoring Travis, Mary Lou sat on the floor on Knight's other side. "I don't know what to say to you," she told him. "I keep asking myself why I didn't see that you were just using me."

Knight had opened his eyes when Mary Lou started speaking. "I . . . wasn't. I fell . . . for you."

Mary Lou gave him a sardonic look. "Forgive me if I'm having a hard time believing anything you say."

"I love you, Mary Lou," he said, speaking slowly, and in obvious pain.

"Apparently you love money more."

"I wanted both. I wanted you to come with me." With his uninjured arm, he reached for her hand but she kept hers in her lap.

"Did you really think I'd condone what you've done? Did you think you could explain it all away? Did you believe I'd go away with you once I knew the truth?"

"No. By then I was in too deep. Hayes would have killed me." He laughed briefly. "Might have anyway."

"Cheer up," Travis said. "You'll live."

"Will you come see me?" Knight asked Mary Lou, ignoring Travis. "Later? We could . . . talk."

"The only thing I have left to say is good-bye, King." Mary Lou rose and without a backward glance, walked out of the Last Shot.

A few minutes later, the EMTs arrived.

CHAPTER THIRTY-ONE

THE EMTS HAD their hands full trying to stabilize Knight before taking him to the hospital. At Della's and Travis' insistence, Nick let them slap a bandage on his side. They looked at Della's ankle and agreed someone could drive her to the hospital later. They also checked out Allie, over her protests. She was physically unharmed and appeared to be handling being held at gunpoint as well as could be expected. Della wanted to take her to the hospital when she went, and have someone professional talk to her.

"Are you hanging around?" Nick asked Travis.

"No." He patted his briefcase where he'd put the jewels. "After CSI gets through with the scene, I'm taking these babies to Houston." He glanced at the EMTs loading Knight's gurney into the ambulance. "The Sweeney PD is helping out," he said, naming the closest town with a police department. "With Hayes dead and Knight out of commission—maybe permanently—they'll need it."

"There are only two others on the force here," Nick said.

"From what I could tell, neither of them had a clue what was going on."

"So, this case will be wrapped up soon," Travis said. "Got any plans yet?"

"Not yet." Although he was sure he didn't want to go back to Dallas. Exactly what he did depended on Della. "I remembered what happened. What really happened with . . . the case." He didn't have to specify which case since Travis knew what he was referring to.

"Yeah? When did that happen?"

"A few days ago."

"That's good, isn't it?"

"Beats the hell out of me. I guess it means I'm not whacked anymore." Not completely, anyway. "I haven't talked to the Captain or to Brad yet. I can't see calling them up and telling them. Besides, if I'm gonna resign, I need to do it in person."

"You really want to resign?"

"Yeah. It's time for a change."

"That wouldn't have anything to do with Della, would it?"

"Partly. Not totally. I've thought about investigating cold cases part-time."

Travis smiled. "Freedom doesn't have a police chief anymore."

"True enough. That's a possibility," Nick admitted. "Like I said, though, some of it depends on Della."

"Do you think you'll like it? A police chief in a small town is a far cry from a Dallas detective."

"Jewel thieves and murder. Doesn't sound so different to me."

Travis laughed. "You have a point. Still, I doubt that's the norm around here."

"Probably not."

"So you're staying here?"

Nick looked at Della, Allie, and Mary Lou, who had come back inside once Knight was gone. "Yeah. For a while, anyway."

They shook hands. "Thanks, Travis. It was good to work with you again."

"Same here," Travis said. "It's not every day you bring in a million dollar bracelet and keep the Blasters from making off with the entire haul. Of course, this could have all been wrapped up weeks ago if it hadn't been for two crooked cops."

"More Hayes than Knight. At least Knight did the right thing in the end." Nick would never like Knight, or trust him. But he had to give him credit. "If Knight hadn't switched sides . . ." He didn't even want to think about it. "It could have been bad. Really bad."

Travis shrugged. "He could still go to prison. Even if he doesn't, he won't keep his badge."

"True. His days as a cop are over."

Travis glanced over at the women. "What about the pretty little blonde? Think she'll take him back?"

"Mary Lou? I don't know her that well. Della says her ex was bad news. She might be soured on all men by now."

"That would be a crime." Travis sent another appreciative look in Mary Lou's direction. "She's way too young to give up on men."

"Good luck with that," Nick said, wondering if Travis would ever change.

Travis gave him a dirty look. "Give me some credit. All I meant was it's too bad to see a nice woman taken in by a jerk like that."

Maybe his friend was capable of change, but Nick didn't

plan to hold his breath. He changed the subject. "I want you to do something for me when you get back."

"Sure. What?"

Nick handed him a piece of paper with the names of the two men who had raped Della printed on it. "These two men were Houston cops about thirteen years ago. Will you see what you can find out about them and let me know?"

"No problem." Travis looked at the names and frowned. "One of them is familiar but I don't remember . . ." He shook his head. "It'll come to me. Do I need to know why you're looking for them?"

"No. I can handle it once I know where they are."

"All right. But tell me if you change your mind."

"Don't worry, I will. Now I need to get Della and Allie to the hospital." Nick stuck out his hand. "I owe you, Travis. Give me a call if you need anything."

Travis shook hands with a grin. "Don't think I won't take you up on that."

Nick walked over to Della, who had her ankle propped up on a chair with an ice bag on it, with Allie, Sophia and Mary Lou beside her. "Are you two ready to go to the hospital?"

"Just dying to," Della grumbled. "I can't wait to go sit in the ER for hours."

"What about Sophia? Can she go to the hospital too?" Allie asked.

"I'll take her home," Mary Lou said. "Bring her to the car, Allie."

Allie said she'd meet Nick and Della outside and followed Mary Lou out.

"How are they doing?" Nick asked, picking up Della over her protests. "Stop arguing. It's going to hurt like hell if you put weight on your ankle."

She subsided grumpily. Nick carried her to the car and helped her in.

"Allie seems okay," Della said after she was settled. "She's still shaken up, but she's resilient. I want her to see a psychiatrist or counselor." She sighed. "Which she'll probably need after I come clean about my past."

He hadn't realized she'd made the decision to tell Allie the truth. "Are you sure you're ready to talk to her?"

"No. But I'll have to at some point. I might not tell her everything, but she needs to know more than she does now."

He squeezed her hand. "I think that's wise."

"I don't know about wise, but it's necessary. I'm going to tell Mary Lou, too. Once she's not so broken up."

"What do you think Mary Lou will do?"

"I don't know. Too bad there's no cure for a broken heart, or I'd make her go to the hospital too. She really loved the bastard."

"It sucks to fall in love with the wrong person. When you find out almost everything about them was a lie."

Della lifted an eyebrow. "Voice of experience?"

He laughed. "Yeah, you could say that. I was thinking about the first woman I fell for, just after I graduated the Academy." He shook his head. "She put the bad into bad news."

"Is she the reason you're still a bachelor?"

"She didn't help." Looking at Della, he added, "But I never met anyone I could imagine being with all the time. Until you."

They left shortly after that for the hospital. Which was just as well, Nick thought. Della had that "oh, my, God, I don't know what to say" look on her face.

IT WAS LATE THAT evening before everything was taken care of and Della and Allie were able to go home. Della's ankle was badly sprained, though not broken. She was given a pair of crutches, which she hated. *It will be a miracle if I don't bust my ass*, she thought as she hobbled up the steps and into the house.

Nick and Allie had both been checked out too. The doctor changed Nick's dressing and agreed he shouldn't have any problems from a minor wound. Allie was fine physically, but shaky mentally, to no one's surprise. Della was worried about her, but she thought Allie was coping as well as could be expected after a crooked cop had put a gun to her head. The doc had recommended counseling for Allie as well as Della. Della agreed, more for Allie's sake than her own. She couldn't see opening up about her past to a total stranger. She was going to have a hard enough time telling Mary Lou.

Della wasn't sure what was going to happen with Mary Lou. She'd really loved Knight. Still did, Della thought. She was a strong woman, but even the toughest woman had a breaking point. Mary Lou hadn't come out of her room since she, Allie, and Nick had come home from the hospital. Della had knocked on her door and stuck her head in, but Mary Lou had either been asleep or pretending to be asleep, so she clearly wanted to be left alone. Allie too, had gone to bed, or rather, passed out from exhaustion.

Which left Della and Nick. He'd driven them home, put Allie to bed, and then seen to Della. Fetching her ice bags, water, pillows to prop up her foot, and aspirin. Fluffing the pillows behind her back, for God's sake. Driving her crazy until she finally said, "Stop being Holly Homemaker. It's unnerving."

He laughed and sat on the bed beside her. "I'm just trying to get you comfortable before I go back to the Last Shot."

She held out her hand. He looked surprised but he took it, and just looked at her with that smile that always got to her. "Do you have to go? Can't you stay here?"

"If you want me to. I can sleep on the couch."

"No. I want you in here with me."

"What about Allie?"

"After today, she knows how it is between us. As long as I don't have a revolving door of men coming through my house, I think she can deal with you and me."

He looked at her more soberly. "How is it between you and me, Della?"

"You're going to make me say it, aren't you?"

"Say what?"

The words weren't hard to say. She said them to Allie every day. But she'd never said them to a man. Until Nick, she hadn't thought she ever would. Even before today, she'd known she wanted Nick in her and her daughter's lives. Not just for now, but for a long time. Maybe even forever. Everything that had happened today had brought home what she really wanted. Suddenly, it wasn't hard at all.

"I love you, Nick."

He didn't smile. In fact, he looked skeptical. "Are you sure this isn't misplaced gratitude?"

Della stared at him. "Because you saved my daughter's life?"

He shrugged. "Not long ago you were positive you didn't love me. Now suddenly you do? What's changed besides that?"

It hadn't occurred to her that he wouldn't believe her. "Are you kidding me? You believe I told you I love you because I'm grateful to you?"

"I don't know. Did you?"

"No, you big jerk. I said it because I meant it."

He still didn't look like he was buying it. "Why now?"

"Because I was scared before. I wasn't sure I could have a normal relationship. I mean, for all I knew, it was just sex between us." She tugged on his hand, pulling him closer. Put her hands on his cheeks and kissed him. Long, deep, and sweet. "Don't get me wrong. I love the sex, but I've known for a while that I love *you*. It doesn't have a damn thing to do with gratitude." He looked a little bit less skeptical. "I mean it, Nick. Knowing I could lose you scared the hell out of me, and it made me realize what you mean to me. You know me. You know my history. Do you really think I'd tell you I loved you if I wasn't absolutely sure?"

Finally, he grinned. "You love me."

"Yes, damn it. Don't sound so smug. That doesn't mean I'm not annoyed as hell at you right now."

Nick put his arms around her and kissed her. Strong, hard, heating up immediately. Della moved, trying to get closer, and yelped when she jarred her injured foot. "I forgot about my foot."

"Do you want me to get another ice pack?"

"No. I want you to make me forget about the pain."

"Hmm. Now how are we going to accomplish that?"

"You're pretty inventive," Della said. "I'm sure you'll figure something out."

"Bet on it," Nick said, and kissed her.

The End

ACKNOWLEDGMENTS

Huge thanks go to Emily McMahon for her willingness to share with me her knowledge about the running of a bar/restaurant. I'd have been lost without you! Any mistakes regarding restaurants/bars and their workings are mine alone.

For all my buddies: Lenora Worth, Julia Justiss, Katherine Garbera, Denise Daniels, Justine Davis, Donnell Ann Bell, the Romex gang, and the many people I've no doubt forgotten. I can't thank you enough for the plotting, thinking, listening (I'm sure endlessly at times), suggesting, critiquing, and being my friends. You are the best!

Many thanks to my editor, Pat Van Wie.

ABOUT THE AUTHOR

Eve Gaddy is the award winning, national bestselling author of forty novels. Her books have sold over a million copies and been published in many countries and several languages. She writes contemporary romance, romantic suspense, romantic mystery, and a bit of paranormal romance as well.

Eve's books have won and been nominated for awards from Romantic Times, Golden Quill, Bookseller's Best, Holt Medallion, Daphne Du Maurier and many more. Eve was awarded the 2008 Romantic Times Career Achievement award for Series Storyteller of the year, and was nominated for a Romantic Times Career Achievement Award for Innovative Series romance.

Eve loves her family, books, electronics, the mountains, and East Texas in the spring and fall. She also loves a happy ending. That's why she writes romance.

Want to hear more about upcoming releases, special deals and other fun stuff? Subscribe to my newsletter .

Find Eve on the Web:

www.evegaddy.net
eve@evegaddy.net

If you enjoyed Last Shot and would like to hear more about my new releases and special deals, sign up for my newsletter and receive a FREE BOOK! Free exclusively for my newsletter readers!

Casey Fontaine and Nick Devlin

Can this rooted-to-the-land beauty dare gamble her heart on a man who has never called just one place home?

Reviews

"Casey's Gamble delivers everything I love in a romance novel; passion, suspense and the kind of sweet romance that is addictive. Can't wait to read more titles by Eve Gaddy." Katherine Garbera, USA Today Bestselling Author

"Bayou atmosphere so thick you can almost smell the magnolias! You'll be rooting for Nick and Casey to find a love as sweet as the sugar cane she grows--if she survives the threat to her beloved Bellefontaine." Justine Davis, 5 Time RITA Award winner

http://newsletter.evegaddy.com/subscribe

BOOKS BY EVE GADDY

A Marriage Made In Texas (Book 2)

Somewhere In Texas (Book 3)

That Night In Texas (Book 4)

Remember Texas (Book 5)

A Christmas Baby in Texas (Book 6)

Baby Be Mine in Texas (Book 7)

Redfish Chronicles (Books 1-4)

Redfish Chronicles (Books 5-7)

THE GALLAGHERS OF MONTANA

Sing Me Back Home (Book 1)

Love Me, Cowgirl (Book 2)

The Doctor's Christmas Proposal (Book 3)

The Cowboy and the Doctor (Book 4)

Return of the Cowgirl (Book 5)

THE BROTHERS OF WHISKEY RIVER

Texas Heirs by Eve Gaddy and Katherine Garbera (Book 1)

Texas Cowboy by Eve Gaddy (Book 2)

Texas Tycoon by Katherine Garbera (Book 3)

Texas Rebel by Eve Gaddy (Book 4)

Texas Lover by Katherine Garbera (Book 5)

Texas Bachelor by Eve Gaddy & Katherine Garbera (Book 6)

WHISKEY RIVER CHRISTMAS

A Texas Christmas Past by Julia Justiss

A Texas Christmas Reunion by Eve Gaddy

A Texas Christmas Homecoming by Nancy Robards Thompson

Once Upon a Texas Christmas by Katherine Garbera

FREE WITH NEWSLETTER SIGN UP
Casey's Gamble

Romantic Suspense
Last Shot
Cry Love

LONE STAR NIGHTS
Fully Engaged
Cowboy Come Home
Just One Night
Amazing Grace
Midnight Remedy
Too Close For Comfort
On Thin Ice

Multi Author Series
THE AMALFI NIGHT BILLIONAIRES
The Billionaire's Pleasure by Katherine Garbera (Book 1)
The Billionaire's Touch by Mimi Wells (Book 2)
The Billionaire's Bride by Nancy Robards Thompson (Book 3)
The Billionaire's Heart by Kathleen O'Brien (Book 4)
The Billionaire's Lover by Eve Gaddy (Book 5)

RETURN TO CADDO LAKE
Uncertain Past by Ken Casper (Book 1)
Uncertain Fate by Roz Denny Fox (Book 2)
Uncertain Future by Eve Gaddy (Book 3)

Made in the USA
Middletown, DE
28 September 2022

11457329R00196